HUNTER'S WORLD

HUNTER'S WORLD

Fred Lichtenberg 6/25/11

FRED LICHTENBERG

FIVE STAR
A part of Gale, Cengage Learning

GALE
CENGAGE Learning

Detroit • New York • San Francisco • New Haven, Conn • Waterville, Maine • London

GALE
CENGAGE Learning

LIBRARY OF CONGRESS CATALOGING-IN-PUBLICATION DATA

Lichtenberg, Fred.
   Hunter's world / Fred Lichtenberg. — 1st ed.
     p. cm.
   ISBN-13: 978-1-59414-960-3
   ISBN-10: 1-59414-960-7
    1. Police chiefs—Fiction. 2. Man-woman relationships—Fiction. 3. Murder—Investigation—Fiction. 4. Suicide—Fiction. 5. Long Island (N.Y.)—Fiction. I. Title.
   PS3612.I2465H85 2011
   813'.6—dc22   2011004265

First Edition. First Printing: May 2011.
Published in 2011 in conjunction with Tekno Books and Ed Gorman.

Printed in the United States of America
1 2 3 4 5 6 7 15 14 13 12 11

To my mother, Iris,
the beautiful butterfly,
whose faith in me never wavered,
and who watches over me from above.

ACKNOWLEDGMENTS

Next to completing my first novel, nothing gives me more satisfaction than to thank all those involved. If not for my family, friends, and professional acquaintances, I would not be writing this.

This book exists thanks to the efforts of Roz Greenberg at Tekno Books, who validated my writing and presented it to Five Star Books. And as for Tracey Matthews and the gang at Five Star for putting it all together, and of course, my copy editor, Gretchen Gordon, a big thanks.

My deepest appreciation to Mike Vogel, a great friend and mentor, who persistently reminded me that less is best. A special thanks to Nelson DeMille for his generosity in reading part of the manuscript. He guided me away from the landmines. Another big thank you to my editor, Alice Duncan, for identifying errors and cleaning up my work. Thanks to my friends at MWA, for their support and encouragement. Thanks also to my budding writer friends at the Writer's Group of Abacoa, particularly Judy Lucas, our commander in chief.

During the first draft, Anne Barnett helped with her critical eye. Thanks, sister. And for the final cleanup, thanks to Marla Berger.

For their technical support, I'd like to thank the folks at the Suffolk County Medical Examiner's Office. Thanks to Keith Hernandez and Richard Dimarino, from DHQ Solutions, who gave my website a fantastic look. A special thanks to Charles

Johnson who constantly saved my work from crashing.

I could have never come this far if it were not for my wife, Sonia, my muse, researcher, and toughest (affectionate) critic. Many times, she kept my frustration in check. Thanks, honey, now on to the next book. And thanks to my son, Mark, whose love and support kept me going, and whose psychology background kept the book authentic.

I'm sure I missed a few folks, and I apologize in advance. You know who you are. Thank you all.

And finally, thanks to Paul Lichtenberg, where it all began.

1

Double parking is prohibited in downtown Eastpoint. Not that anyone actually could double park on the narrow three-block Main Street, but it's on the books. It's also against the law to steal farm animals or purposely drive into haystacks. Oh, and cow tipping. That's a no-no. In my five years as Eastpoint's police chief we haven't had one violation, though I'm not certain about cow tipping, since none of our farmers or their livestock have come forward with a complaint.

I mention this to demonstrate that Eastpoint is pretty much crime free. This might have something to do with its location and values. Eastpoint lies about seventy miles east of New York City on a small patch of rich earth that most farmers would die for. And with a population of about four hundred, not counting the livestock or weekend city folks, people tend to respect each other and their property.

That's why I'm surprised on this Saturday night when my dispatcher, June Winters, a woman in her sixties who gave up farming after her husband died, alerts me about an altercation at Salty's Bar and Grill. She sounds excited. Who wouldn't be? Like I said, we don't have much crime in this town.

I wildly increase my speed to about forty in a thirty-mile-an-hour zone and pull up to Salty's in five minutes, where I find Paddy Murphy, the owner, alone and leaning against the wall of his bar smoking a cigarette, his usual equanimity showing through. He sees me, takes a hard pull on his cancer stick, flicks it in the street, and produces a wide Irish smile. That's a misdemeanor—not the smile, the littering—but I'll let Paddy slide tonight.

I emerge from the car, glance around, then shrug. "Say, Paddy, I got a call, something about an altercation. What's up?"

He spreads his hands. "Already taken care of, Hank. A misunderstanding, is all," he says in his usual pleasant singsong brogue. "Two college kids from the city were fighting over a local. It was nothing. A patron must have called it in."

I nod. "A woman?"

"One of Broderick Hall's daughters. The one who attends Columbia. I guess she wanted to show off the town to a couple of classmates. Only the gents had a few too many shots and started fighting over her."

I grin. "Typical kids. Who won?"

Paddy winks. "She did, of course. Don't women always?" He shoots a look inside the bar window. "Anyway," he says, turning back to me, "she got pissed off over their childish behavior and left."

"That's it?" I ask, disappointed.

"What can I say, Hank? I broke it up and put them in a cab." Paddy checks his watch. "They should be on the ten-twenty-two to Manhattan as we speak. I was just taking a break. It's pretty hectic tonight."

"You want to join the force?" I ask, my crooked front teeth showing through. "You won't be subjected to that karaoke noise." I laugh, pointing to the bar with my chin.

Paddy shakes his head. "Not for me, Hank. Too boring. I'm happy serving drinks. And as for the karaoke, I tune it out."

"I hear you. Sometimes I wonder if I made the right decision to leave the county," I say almost to myself, then shrug. "Anyway, if there's nothing else going on, I'll get back to my rounds."

"Hey, it's your town, Hank."

I'm about to ask Paddy about his wife, Sheryl, when June's voice beckons me from inside the squad car.

"Looks like you're a busy guy tonight," Paddy says, removing a pack of smokes from his corduroy shirt pocket.

I hop inside the Crown Victoria. "Just a misunderstanding," I assure June. "You can call off your gossip posse tonight," I say, smiling into the phone.

"We have another situation, Hank."

I roll my eyes. "June, we don't have that many bars in town. Where to now?"

She hesitates. "It involves a friend of yours. John Hunter."

I let that sink in a moment, then ask cautiously, "What kind of situation?"

"A woman just called, said she was walking by Hunter's house and saw the lights on in his living room. Not that it's unusual. After all, it's dark outside."

"And?" I interrupt, trying to keep her focused.

"Right. The woman noticed that Hunter was lying back on his sofa in a weird sort of way, like he wasn't asleep. She said there was a mess around him, vomit or something." June pauses. "The woman thinks he might be . . . dead."

"Dead," I repeat. "Come on, June, I just saw the guy yesterday. He looked healthy to me. Hunter probably just had one too many."

"It's not my theory, boss. I'm just passing along the information."

I watch a few young patrons heading toward the parking lot. "So who's this mystery woman who just *happened* to be strolling around Hunter's neighborhood?" I ask with interest. "Some local walking her dog?"

"Here's the strange thing, Hank. She wouldn't leave her name."

"Doesn't sound like a local to me."

"And she insisted that I call the paramedics before it was too late."

I start the car engine. "Doesn't sound like a disinterested party, either. You get the number she was calling from?"

"A blocked call. Anyway, you might want to have a look."

I nod into the phone. "Call the county."

"I already did. They're on their way."

"I'll call in later," I say, glancing back at the bar. Paddy must have already headed inside. I flip on the overhead light bar, make a quick U-turn, then gun the engine, hoping my drinking buddy is only fast asleep.

2

I'm relieved to find a Suffolk County Fire-Rescue and Emergency Services vehicle parked in Hunter's driveway, but as my eyes shift to an unmarked car parked across the street, I get a knot in my stomach. Inside, I find a couple of jock-types snapping pictures, collecting evidence and joking like they're at a frat party. Upon seeing me in uniform they give me a polite hello.

"Say, Hank."

I turn, and after recognizing the short, balding detective with a Dunkin' Donuts gut, offer a thin smile. "Earl, it's been a while."

He smiles back. "Too long. Never thought I'd see you on your turf. Not on business, anyway."

"Me neither," I agree uncomfortably. "What's going on?" I motion to Hunter, who is deadpan on the sofa, his head facing the ceiling, his right hand hanging motionlessly. My drinking buddy, a handsome *GQ* guy, is wearing a white t-shirt, which is dotted with vomit, and a pair of jeans stained from who knows what.

Earl approaches, extends his hand. "First, let me apologize for jumping the gun before you got here. The front door was open when we arrived."

I shoot a look at the door, then back to Earl.

"We were hanging around when the call came in. It sounded like someone died." He pauses. "Guess they were right."

I shake his hand quickly as my eyes study Hunter, whose once-animated dark brown eyes are now dead like the rest of him.

"You would have called us anyway," he says, his tone friendly.

My eyes remain on my friend. "Looks that way, doesn't it?"

"So technically, you're in the middle of a crime scene."

I regard his remark and turn back to him.

"That's the way we found him," Earl adds. "Normally, with all that shit around him, it would appear that he just choked on his own vomit."

We exchange looks. "I'm not sure I follow. It wasn't an accident?"

He motions me away from the others. "Your neighbor here killed himself." He waits for my reaction. In spite of my homicide days, I'm struggling to accumulate enough brain-power to let Hunter's apparent suicide sink in.

"You sure?" I finally ask.

He offers me a pair of elastic gloves, and when I snap them on, hands me a single sheet of copier paper.

Two thoughts strike me as I begin reading Hunter's last message to the world: *I know John Hunter isn't suicidal; he's too egotistic. And vain. But if he were suicidal, his would be Eastpoint's first. I know this because I was born here. People don't kill themselves in Eastpoint!*

"As you can see, he didn't have much to say," Earl says with a shrug. I nod after reading it for the second time. "It's his signature," I tell Earl, glancing around for a computer. Earl must sense my interest and tells me it's in the study.

"Interesting," I say, handing back the note.

"What's that?"

"The note. It's short and to the point, nothing like his flowery romance columns."

"No way! He's that Hunter?" Earl blurts out. "Shit, I read

14

the guy all the time. He's good."

"Was," I correct.

"Right."

"He was a good friend," I add with a touch of sadness. "I just saw him yesterday."

"Never hinted about doing himself in?"

I shake my head. "He was always upbeat."

"Sounds like he was good at hiding whatever was troubling him." Then Earl adds, like one of Hunter's columns, "If it was about a woman, he didn't heed to his own advice. No one is worth killing themselves for."

"Guess not, but I knew him pretty well. It wasn't about a woman."

Earl smiles. "Maybe that was the problem."

3

I need to find solace, and I tell Earl I want to search the premises.

"Sure, Hank," he says. "It's your crime scene."

My crime scene. I remove my hat, wipe my brow, then step out of the room and find the stairs leading to the second floor. Hunter's suicide has baffled me because it's inconsistent with his philosophy on life, which he wrote about with passion and humor in his syndicated romance columns. Hunter was seemingly happy and successful without the romance. Looking back, I realize that the subject never entered our conversation; he never talked shop or relationships, and I never brought up my own less-than-ideal marriage.

Reaching the landing, I glance around, still unsettled. With morbid curiosity, I open the door closest to the landing and begin my quest, searching for Hunter's demons. I flip on the light and find what appears to be an art studio, though there aren't any paintings or signs of acrylic paint, only a metal folding chair facing an easel and a few clean brushes sticking out of a kid's beach pail.

I cross the room and gaze out the window. It's dark, but the waxing moon guides my eyes toward a densely wooded area lined with oak trees. I shrug. Maybe Hunter was into nature, though quite frankly, he never mentioned he had an interest in art.

I turn to leave and glance up at the ceiling. My eyes fix on white rope hanging innocently from a trap door that leads to an attic. I study the rope a moment, then slide the metal chair under it, step up and steady myself. I give the rope a gentle tug, the ceiling opening just a crack. I hop off the chair and yank the rope toward me.

A ladder attached to the back of a hatch leads me to a black hole. I remove a flashlight from my belt and search for a light switch. When I find one, a room emerges, stretching the entire length of the house; one big room divided by a king-size bed, a night table and lamp, and a ceiling mirror positioned strategically above the bed.

I scratch my head and wonder: what in the world is this place? The bed is neatly made with a red comforter and matching pillows. I snicker to myself, stepping over an Oriental rug and work my way to the other side of the room, where I find a door, open it, and switch on another light.

Unlike the room below, this one is filled with canvases scattered about in different stages like an assembly line. At first glance, the wavy textures and rich colors appear to be nothing more than oils of copulating couples, Hunter indulging himself in every scene. I grin to myself. *No wonder you didn't date, my friend. You were too busy getting off here.*

I remove a finished canvas and study it, my expression suddenly turning cold. I blink hard, testing my vision, but there is no doubt what's going on here. I pick up another painting, then another. Then, as though a light bulb goes on in my head, I clumsily rifle through Hunter's private collection. My chest tightens. Hot, stale breath ricochets off the back of my hands as I race through his sordid works.

I stop and give my eyes a good rub, relieved that my worst nightmare is not a part of Hunter's repertoire. I poke my head outside into the *room* and get this chilling feeling that Hunter's sordid passion for art somehow had something to do with his demise.

I need to get back downstairs before Earl and his boys decide to check up on me. The last thing I need is for Hunter's suicide to turn into a public display of his artwork.

I approach the door and discover another painting leaning casually against an easel, only this one had been sloppily X'd out, as though the artist was in a rage. I instinctively touch it, a black residue staying on my finger. I point my flashlight into a space between the lines of the X, struggling to identify the couple. The guy is Hunter, all right, the telltale sign a tattoo he'd gotten on a dare during his college days. The head of a slithering green boa is needled to his upper right arm. He's sitting at the foot of his king-size bed like a preacher, face cocked, eyes closed, head tilted upward toward the sky, his hands outstretched. I shift the light from my flashlight to get a better look at his lover, her head tilted slightly toward the artist, toward me. Those dark eyes and long black ponytail. Hunter's lover is kneeling seductively between his legs, her accentuated crimson mouth devouring the remains of her lover.

I raise my flashlight then catch myself. *You bastard!* I want to smash the painting into pieces and burn it along with the rest of Hunter's artwork, only Earl is shouting my name.

I turn to leave, but I know I'm not finished here.

4

Later that night, I'm driving west on Harbor Drive, my boot pushing the accelerator as my cloudy brain tries to make sense of Hunter's artwork, including the one of him and my wife. Were those paintings just a part of Hunter's twisted imagination? Or was he Eastpoint's celebrity *stud*, preying on the minds and bodies of small-town women?

I reach Locust Road, ease up on the gas pedal, and take a hard right, shutting off my headlights in the process. There are three houses on Hunter's dead-end street. His is a two-story colonial that sits at the end on two acres of land. I hang a left into his driveway and turn off the engine. As I emerge, the cool October air smacks me in the face, which I find refreshing under the circumstances. I jiggle the doorknob open, then fold my six-foot frame under the crime scene tape and let myself in, locking the door behind me before flicking on my flashlight.

I own the place now that Earl and his investigators are gone, which, according to my watch, is about four hours after finding Hunter's body.

I retrace my steps and enter Hunter's sex chamber, my breathing erratic. It's not from the climb, but the thought of removing *that* painting. The room is technically part of the crime scene and off limits, though in my capacity, I wouldn't be challenged unless Earl found me burning the stuff in Hunter's backyard. But since there isn't a soul around and the investigators never discovered Hunter's treasure trove, I'm not about to reveal my little secret.

At some point the public might feast its eyes on Hunter's artwork, minus the one I'm after. I can't risk destroying all of the paintings. It's my own moral dilemma.

Inside Hunter's upstairs studio, I aim my flashlight on the easel and keep it there for a few uncomfortable moments before bouncing the light wildly around the room.

"Where the hell is it?" I hear myself shouting as I drop to the floor and start crawling around on my hands and knees, knocking over a few copulating couples. Who knew about *this* room? "Who?" I demand, upset with myself for not being able to destroy the painting earlier.

Then, as though Hunter's spirit had been set free, I hear the sound of rapid movement coming from downstairs. Within seconds the back screen door slams against the house.

I spring for the ladder and charge downstairs, listening for a car engine to turn over, but the only sound is coming from my breathing. I race out the back door waving my flashlight at the trees, but it's too dense to see anything.

The metal sound of a car door echoes through the trees, followed by a roaring engine. I sprint for my patrol car and grit my teeth. The keys are missing!

I pop open the hood and retrieve a spare key, then peel out, spitting up dirt.

Arriving home I block the driveway and dash inside, stopping at the kitchen table to catch my breath. I casually enter the living room, where I find my wife, Susan, sitting comfortably on the sofa reading a Patricia Cornwell paperback. She glances up and smiles faintly.

I give her a quick hi and ask, "Been reading long?"

"Ah-huh. Almost finished. I know who did it."

I'm wondering if she's referring to the painting. "The butler?"

She smiles. "Not in Cornwell's books."

Our eyes stay on each other for a few moments before Susan returns to her reading. I gaze at my wife of fifteen years, who is as beautiful as the day we met, her black silky hair draping over her shoulders, not bound in her usual ponytail. Susan's soft, pallid skin shows few signs of aging. When my eyes stop at her lightly painted crimson lips, the knot in my stomach returns and I trudge off to the kitchen.

"Your stomach again?" Susan asks.

I don't turn, but sense her standing at the door. I nod and pop a few antacids into my mouth, chewing with a vengeance.

Susan approaches quietly, her warm breath hitting my neck. The scent from her favorite Zinfandel fills my nostrils. It's a little too close, but I can't move. She gives my rear a quick squeeze. "Not bad for an old guy, Hank."

I turn abruptly. "Like John Hunter?"

She recoils, throws me a confused look. "Hunter?"

"Yeah, him. Only he's dead."

"How?" she asks, her voice lacking emotion.

"Overdose. Evidently, he swallowed too many pills with his booze," I say straightforwardly.

"What a horrible way to go," she says, shaking her head.

I search my wife's face for signs of infidelity or guilt, but Susan is good. She can be cold and withholding, especially when it comes to sex, which is one of the issues that has been dragging our marriage down for the past few years.

"Did he leave a note?" she asks, suddenly interested in my dead friend.

"Yes, why do you ask?"

She shrugs. "Just curious. What did it say?"

I'm debating whether to tell her, but since the suicide is cut and dry, I say, "Only that he couldn't live with himself anymore."

Susan remains deadpan, so if she's relieved that the note didn't mention her, she doesn't let on.

"Guess he was in a rush to go," I add sarcastically.

Susan scowls. "That's not funny, Hank. The poor guy was obviously in a lot of pain."

I finally drew some emotion out of my wife.

"Ironic, don't you think?"

"What?"

"John was an advice columnist—"

"John?" I interrupt.

"That was his name, wasn't it?"

"He went by Hunter."

"Whatever." Susan's eyes gaze past me. "A shame he couldn't help himself," she says thoughtfully, then sighs. "Oh, well, I guess I'll get back to my book. I was just getting into a love scene when you walked in." She smiles wistfully.

"I gotta go out for a while," I say before Susan has an opportunity to invite me to join her and her book. Outside, I lean against Susan's black Honda Civic, contemplating my next move. I now realize how Hunter's suicide and betrayal has clouded my instincts. Something so simple, so elementary. I touch the hood of Susan's car.

It's warm.

5

I've been staring into darkness for hours when my cell phone vibrates through my pants pocket. I dig inside and flip open the cell phone and am greeted by a woman whose hurried voice conveys a sense of urgency. The matter in question has to do with John Hunter, and she needs to see me *now*.

"Oh, and Hank, sorry for the late night call."

Right. The apologetic woman is Gloria Wollinsky, a single, thirty-five-year-old, chain-smoking pathologist who works for the Suffolk County Medical Examiner's Office in Hauppauge. I've known Gloria since she was a skinny kid. Her eyes were the bluest in the neighborhood, and she had brown hair that always needed combing. Back then when most girls her age enjoyed dressing Barbie dolls, Gloria already knew her calling. She twisted and removed Barbie and Ken's body parts, then analyzed them. Maybe it had something to do with her father's business. Marshall Wollinsky is Eastpoint's only undertaker. Gloria worked for him, but she got bored for lack of business and eventually went to work for Suffolk County.

Though Eastpoint is part of the county, it's an incorporated village, meaning jurisdiction on running the community stays with us. But when it comes to unusual occurrences like murders and suicides, I call on the county folks for assistance.

I arrive at the ME's parking lot forty minutes later and find Gloria standing outside the building dressed in jeans, a white blouse, and sensible navy shoes. She has a cigarette dangling from her mouth and a Styrofoam coffee cup glued to her hand, and when she sees me, she smiles and waves with exuberance, obviously juiced up on caffeine. Then, with precision, she flicks her cigarette into a butt receptacle and gives me a quick hug.

Gloria apologizes again for the wakeup call, then removes an official-looking document from her jeans back pocket and waves it at me. "Guess what?"

I glance at her, then the paper, then shrug. "Kind of late to be playing twenty questions, Gloria."

She takes note of my drawn face and stops waving. "Sorry, Hank. I forgot you're a late morning person. How about we talk in my office?"

I follow Gloria through the double glass doors, past a young night receptionist whose flaming red hair belies the dark, dreary environment. She manages a weak smile as I pass. We enter Gloria's office, which is devoid of windows: a small firetrap with piles of folders scattered throughout her workplace. Her walls are adorned with at least a half-dozen calendars of dogs, cats, and other domestic animals.

I tiptoe over a few files and collapse into a hard wooden chair across from Gloria's desk, then push aside an ashtray filled with dead butts and rest my elbows on her desk. "Talk to me."

Gloria takes a seat, then shifts a wall of paper aside to see me better.

"Hank," she says, her tone neutral. "I wouldn't have gotten you out of bed at this hour, but I need a positive ID on Hunter." She pauses, offers a thin smile, then says, "and since I couldn't find a next of kin, I figured you wouldn't mind. For the record."

I drop back in my chair and frown. "Christ, Gloria, this couldn't have waited till morning? I mean, what's the big deal?"

She checks the inside of her coffee cup, swigs down the contents, and tosses the cup into an already full wastepaper basket. "Let's take a walk."

I lift my girth out of the chair with great effort and follow her to the refrigeration room, where John Hunter and a few other johns are laid out. The chill envelops us like a meat locker and I button my collar, watching Gloria open Hunter's slab. "Don't mind the mess."

I gather Gloria is referring to Hunter's body, which has been slit down the middle and filleted. My eyes narrow with anger as I view his remains, and it's not because he left without saying goodbye. I turn to Gloria and nod. "That's him."

"Good." She pushes Hunter back into the vault, his body disappearing before us. "You okay, Hank?" she says, nudging me out of the room.

"He was a friend," I force out.

"I know. That was one of the reasons I asked you to stop by. Like I said, I couldn't find a next of kin."

I nod. "Hunter's parents died years ago, and he didn't have any siblings. Or a wife." I stop; meet Gloria's eyes. "What do you mean it was *one* of the reasons you called me down here? What's going on?"

Gloria remains silent until we reach her office. "Look, Hank, I wouldn't have called you at this ungodly hour just for an ID." She motions to the chair.

I slouch back and glance up at the wall, my eyes setting on Ms. October, a Vietnamese potbellied pig standing on its hind legs.

"When things change, time is an element."

My eyes leave Miss Piggy and meet Gloria's. "An element? Things change. For Chrissake, Gloria, what could have changed with John Hunter?"

Gloria's blue eyes stay on me. "Hank, we have a pretty good group of investigators. These guys can sniff out stuff that others would have overlooked. But even they wouldn't have realized it out at the crime scene."

I throw my hands up. "Realize what? Get to the point!"

"John Hunter was murdered."

6

My face must have drained its color like Hunter's inside. I remain silent, watching Gloria light up a cigarette, take a hard drag, and blow the smoke toward the ceiling.

I blink hard. "I thought smoking was off-limits in public places."

"Christ, Hank, do you see anyone around? It's a perk for working the night shift, for chrissake." She winks. "You're not gonna turn me in, are you?"

My eyes follow the trail of smoke. "It's just that I gave it up six months ago and it's distracting."

"Damn convert!" she complains, then takes one more pull and kills it.

I watch the smoke dissipate and turn to Gloria. "You sure someone killed him?"

She nods. "Oh, yeah."

"But your people didn't find anything suspicious at the crime scene," I protest.

"That's what I've been trying to tell you. The investigators wouldn't have known. We just assumed it was suicide because of the note and the sleeping pills. He apparently OD'd on pills, so we opened him up and checked his stomach. That's when I noticed it."

"It?"

"An odor. More than what you'd expect from alcohol, which we also found. I think they said he was drinking bourbon at the

27

time. What we found was more bitter, like quinine. So we took a few tests."

I shift in my seat.

"That's when we discovered traces of strychnine in his blood-stream."

"Rat poison?"

"It doesn't take much to kill a person, and Hunter had enough in his system to kill him more than once." She stops. "The guys found an empty vial of Halcion at the crime scene. At least we suspect Halcion. Someone wrote the name on one of those white address labels. I assume it was Hunter."

"No store label?"

Gloria shakes her head. "He must have been taking it for insomnia. We don't know how many tranquilizers he consumed before he died and didn't find any traces of it in his stomach, only in his blood stream, so I figured whatever he took, it had to be laced with the poison." Gloria pauses, her eyes searching mine. When I don't reply, she says, "You with me so far, Hank?"

"I get the picture." I nod.

"But then I'm thinking," she continues. "Maybe we ought to check the bourbon." Gloria stops. "Technically, Jack Daniel's isn't bourbon. It's Tennessee whiskey, but everyone calls it bourbon."

I roll my eyes.

So we tested the contents," she continues. "And guess what?"

"It was laced with the poison," I volunteer.

"Bingo. Whoever spiked Hunter's bourbon obviously knew what he was doing, because the combination cuts the poison's bitterness. Pretty smart, don't you think? I mean, if we hadn't done an autopsy . . ." Gloria stops. "We always do autopsies in suicide cases." She reaches for another cigarette, then stops and mumbles something unintelligible.

"But Hunter could have taken the poison himself, right?" I

ask, not happy about where this is leading.

Gloria squeezes her eyes. "Gee, Hank, anything's possible. Sure, he could have killed himself. But then all he needed were the sedatives. Why would he spike the bourbon with strychnine, no less?"

I can't offer an explanation.

Gloria smiles as though she's about to hit me with an epiphany. "I had the crime boys probe further for trace evidence and guess what they found?"

"Gloria, it's almost two o'clock in the morning!"

"Don't get so grouchy, Hank," she says, gesturing me with her hands to relax. "I'm just trying to make the story more dramatic. You and Susan have a fight or something?"

That settles me down. "Go ahead."

"They found rug fibers in his chin."

"Fibers?"

"As in living room carpet. They also discovered small bruises under Hunter's armpits, as though someone had dragged him around like a fucking untrained dog after he convulsed from the poison. His face wasn't bruised, so whoever did it broke Hunter's fall, then dragged him over to the sofa where you guys found him neatly packaged."

I'm about to suggest that Hunter might have broken his own fall, but realize how absurd it would sound. I settle for, "Damn."

"In case you didn't know, convulsions from strychnine are generally violent. Each one can last up to several minutes, but between each attack, the victim can breathe and appears relaxed. Hunter probably died within an hour of swallowing the stuff." Gloria gives me a moment to absorb her theory. "The murderer watched, of course. Probably enjoyed the show while Hunter fought for his life. Great entertainment, huh, Hank?"

I press my temples. "I'm sure."

"You like my scenario so far?"

My head bobs about like I'm giving it some thought. "Gee, Gloria, it sounds plausible," I finally admit, then throw in, "You're positive about this?" hoping Gloria has a less-menacing theory.

"Well, not completely. I wasn't there." She offers an impish smile, displaying stained teeth. "Know anyone who was?"

I return a thin smile and wish I hadn't given up smoking. "It's just that we never had a murder in Eastpoint before," I say, ignoring her question.

"Sorry, Hank. There's always a first time. I'll admit that strychnine is difficult to administer as a homicidal agent, but weighing the mixture with bourbon to mask the bitterness and the newly discovered fibers and bruises, I'd be looking for Hunter's killer."

"Killer," I repeat almost to myself.

Her eyes weigh on mine. "Look Hank, I'm not telling you how to run your shop, but I think you ought to take our team back out to the crime scene and sniff around one more time."

The crime scene! For sure, Hunter's paintings will find their way to the public. Maybe even on the Internet! Except for the one of Hunter and my wife, and I can only guess who lifted it. I just pray it finds its way out of Eastpoint and gets buried somewhere. "Sounds like a plan, Gloria."

Gloria escorts me outside the building, she lighting up another smoke and me trudging back to my car. It's one thing if my wife slept with Hunter. It's another if she killed him.

7

"What are you up to this evening, Wayne?" I ask my deputy entering the stationhouse. His head snaps to attention.

"Hank, you're up late tonight!"

He's obviously up to no good. Wayne Andrews is my second in command, which sounds impressive but when you consider that Eastpoint has only six deputies and Wayne has been around longer than anyone else, including me, *second* doesn't have the same ring to it.

Evidently overcoming boredom from the night shift, and not a man of literature, Wayne attempts to slide *Hustler* under his desk blotter.

"I've seen them before," I say, offering a weary smile.

He pulls the magazine back out, then tosses it casually into his outbox.

I frown. "Kate might not appreciate you leaving that smut in there. Not that she's a prude."

"Right." He retrieves the magazine, steals a quick peek inside, then drops it in his desk drawer.

"Anything come in on Hunter?" I ask.

Wayne points toward my office. "Inside on your desk. It's from the ME's office."

I nod.

"I didn't open it, Hank."

I nose the drawer. "It's no wonder."

"It was addressed to you, anyway."

"Just kidding."

"I didn't think it was pressing enough to get you out of bed, considering how he died."

Unlike Gloria's discovery. "I appreciate it."

Then he asks, "Hank, if you don't mind me asking, what are you doing here at this hour? It's almost three o'clock in the morning."

My eyes rise to the wall clock. "Couldn't sleep."

" 'Cause of Hunter?"

I ponder his question, then nod.

"Too bad about him. He was a friendly guy."

"Very."

Wayne threads his hands and leans back in the chair. "Anything special you want me to do, boss?"

I shake my head. "Do whatever it was you were doing," I say, heading toward my office, then I catch myself. I turn back to Wayne, who flashes a quick smile.

I shake my head and open the door to my office. At this hour, there isn't a hell of a lot going on in Eastpoint, so I suspect Wayne will gravitate back to the drawer once my door is closed.

I glance around my small but adequate office. At least it's clean. Not like Gloria's. I glance across the room, stopping at my office window. Nothing but darkness. During the day, the window allows me to survey downtown Main Street, a whopping three blocks long. I could spy on my citizens if I wanted to. Not that I need to spy on anyone, though on occasion, I might remove my spyglasses from the draw and see what's happening in front of the Eastpoint Bar and Grill, a popular haunt with the old-timers. Quite honestly, nothing ever happens at the bar or in this town. Until now.

I cross the room to my desk and pick up the crime-scene analysis report, then gaze out the window again. Local shopkeepers won't be crawling out of bed for at least another hour. Then, in typical fashion, they'll converge with smiles, waving to each other and setting the tone for another day of business and sociability.

And apparently, this town is very sociable. Ask Hunter.

Outside of my home, my office is where I seek tranquility and introspection. And lately, even before Hunter's demise, I've been spending more time here.

I tear open the official-looking report, stamped "Preliminary—Pending Final Pronouncement," and begin to read. After perusing a few pages, I realize this report won't contain the same language Gloria used during our meeting. It's a courtesy copy that under most circumstances mirrors the final report, suggesting that Hunter died from an overdose of the tranquilizer Halcion, washed down with Jack Daniel's. Not a bad call, considering there wasn't much else found at the scene.

My thoughts are interrupted by a knock on the door.

"Hank, you okay in there?"

Of course, I'm not okay, and I'm not looking for company, but I invite Wayne in out of courtesy.

He stands at the door with a mug of coffee and says, "You look like you can use some."

I motion Wayne in and watch him negotiate the coffee, setting it in the center of my desk. He takes my invitation as a sign to chat, so he slides into an old brown leather chair opposite me.

Though I feel vulnerable right now, Wayne is not the person I would confide in. Don't get me wrong. I like Wayne and consider him a friend. But his mouth has been known to be used as a receptacle for gossip: collecting and dispensing. At five-seven, my deputy weighs in at about two-twenty. Fortunately, Wayne hasn't had to run after anything faster than a wayward calf. His eyes are brown, matching his closely cropped hair. Wayne isn't an unattractive fellow, just unkempt.

I suspect my deputy's ulterior motive for serving me coffee is the report, because his eyes haven't left it since he arrived. I drop it on my desk, his eyes following. I provide him a few moments until he senses me staring at him. We exchange looks, then he asks, "Hunter ever mentioned he was . . . considering it?"

Like placing an ad in *Newsday*? "I had no idea," I tell him.

"Me neither." He pauses. "What makes a person do something like that?" he asks innocently.

Wayne has been insulated from the real world too long to understand human weakness. I'm too tired to go into Psychology 101 with him, so I offer him a shrug.

"What does the report say?"

"Not much," I tell him and wait for Wayne's response.

"Come on, Hank." he says, his eyes begging. "There's gotta be something."

I'm such a tease. I lean back in my chair and open the cover. "The house was undisturbed, devoid of anything of a suspicious nature." I stop. "In other words, the place wasn't tampered with," I explain as though reading to a layperson.

He nods.

Then I paraphrase, discuss the booze and sleeping pills, then glimpse over at Wayne, whose elbows are resting on my desk like an attentive schoolboy. "As for fingerprints, a few were obtained and will be analyzed. It appears that Hunter penned his own suicide note. That is, he signed it. As for the body, there were no obvious bruises or lacerations. In the words of the investigators, there was no foul play." My eyes remain on the last line and for one fleeting moment, I'm relieved. Death brought on by a mixture of alcohol and tranquilizers. Suicide.

"Cut and dry," he says.

I close the report. "Looks that way."

"He was a nice guy," Wayne says, his eyes softening.

"Sad," I force out.

"He seemed to get along with everybody."

"Just about." I swallow hard.

Wayne works his frame out of the chair. "I guess I better get back to work."

I nod mechanically, then ask, "Whaddaya know about him? Hunter?"

Wayne thinks a moment then shrugs, "Only that he wrote a syndicated sex column in the newspaper."

"A romance column," I correct.

"Right. But for a guy who wasn't married, he sure knew a lot about married life. And sex, too," he emphasizes.

"You don't have to be married to know about that stuff, Wayne. All you need is a partner," I say, choking on my words.

"I suppose. Wasn't he a psychologist?"

"Trained in the field, but he hadn't practiced since moving out here."

"Guess that's where he got his experience to write that stuff. From all those city folks with sex problems." He chuckles with amusement.

My stomach feels like a medicine ball smacked into it. "Unlike where you get your answers from." I smile thinly.

Wayne laughs. "Hey, I'd rather read Hunter's columns. He's good."

"Was," I correct. "I didn't realize you followed his column. You're not married, and unless you found yourself someone recently, you haven't been with a woman in years."

Wayne's round face deflates. "It's not like I haven't tried," he defends. "There just aren't any available women in this town."

Hunter thought so, but I nod in sympathy. "Sorry. I guess I'm not myself right now."

"At least you have a good wife, Hank," he tries. "I mean, you and Susan probably have one of the best marriages in Eastpoint. You probably don't even have to read Hunter's columns."

I want to scream. "Appreciate it, Wayne."

Then Wayne throws a curve ball. "Hey, maybe Hunter was gay."

Wayne must have seen my expression change.

"Could be why he killed himself," he says, seemingly satisfied with his theory.

I shake my head. "How'd you arrive at that conclusion, Wayne?"

He makes a sweeping motion for emphasis. "Think about it, Hank. You ever see him with a woman? Maybe his columns were just a front to hide his true feelings."

I wave dismissively. "Get real. I knew the guy, for chrissake."

Wayne smiles with a degree of satisfaction. "Is there something you wanna confess, boss?"

I point to the door. "You got something to do?"

"Just a theory," he mumbles, heading out.

When Wayne closes my door, I return to the report, thumbing back a few pages and stopping when it discusses the Jack Daniel's found at the scene.

I lean back in my chair, ease my tired legs on the desk and close my eyes. Years ago, when Susan and I were feeling amorous, she would remove a beer mug from the freezer, then slowly pour in a bottle of Samuel Adams, all the while watching my face. Her seductive expression told me I was in for more than beer.

I rub my eyes. Had Susan done the same for Hunter? Poured his last drink? Did she offer him a seductive smile while thinking about rat poison? And since Susan doesn't drink bourbon, she wouldn't have participated. That might explain why only one glass was found on the coffee table.

I give my eyes a good rub. Right now, I can't buy into that morbid scenario. Not so much that Susan could have been responsible, though that's very troubling. What doesn't make sense is that the report mentioned an open bottle of Jack Daniel's found at the scene. I knew Hunter. He didn't drink the stuff.

8

With great effort I lift my head off the desk, where it must have landed during the wee hours of the morning, and glance across the room, my eyes fixing on an early American pastoral wall print. My thoughts remain too consumed on Hunter to appreciate the isolated log cabin and a barn standing at the foothills of the Grand Tetons. Or the gentle morning sun reflecting off the snowcapped mountains.

I stay on the poster a few moments longer before shifting to the ME's report on Hunter's suicide, which is now old news.

I brush the inside of my mouth with my tongue and realize that outside of a few Tums, I haven't eaten since yesterday morning.

The outer office is stirring, so I suspect the gang has already polished off a pot of coffee. Good morning to you all.

I stand and stretch my aching muscles, then step over to the window and peer out. The townspeople's mood appears to reflect the weather: sunny. Lucky them. I'm debating whether to call home when my office door opens.

"Morning, boss."

It's Wayne.

"You looked like you needed some sleep so I didn't disturb you, although your snoring kept me awake," he says with a chuckle.

I rub my temples. " 'Preciate it."

"I'm punching out," Wayne tells me. "What about you? You off or on?"

I check my watch. "Both."

He chuckles again. "Doing a double shift?"

"If I can stay awake."

"Well, there's nothing doing around here now that the case is closed."

The case isn't closed, of course.

"Why don't you go home and get some real sleep?" Wayne insists. "Charlie will call if he needs to you."

Wayne is playing big brother. He means well, but he should only know I'd rather be here. "Maybe I will," I tell him.

He closes the door behind him, leaving me alone in my thoughts again. I glance at the phone but decide I'm not ready for a confrontation. Right now, I'm only interested in checking out my dead drinking buddy's house.

Hunter's front door is still adorned in yellow and black police ribbon. As I emerge from the car, my eyes shoot upward to the window leading to the *room,* my brain inviting unhealthy visions. As painful as this place has become, it seduces me like a carnal magnet, and I continue my masochistic journey inside.

Hunter's master bedroom is located on the first floor. It's an average-size room with a window, white metal blinds rolled up to the top of the pane, allowing in the soft morning sun. Below the window sits a brass queen-size bed. But unlike his *boudoir* upstairs, this room doesn't have a mirror plastered on its ceiling. It does have a dark, antique-looking dresser, which centers one side of the room, a small flat-panel TV resting on top. They face a wall-to-wall mahogany bookcase that is filled with more books than our local library.

I snap on a pair of latex gloves and approach the bookcase with curiosity. Hunter was an eclectic reader, or at least a collector of books; mysteries are ensconced between classics, poetry, and biographies. His rich collection of literature and authors leaves me chagrined at my own lack of appreciation for the written word.

I remove *Bleak House* from one of the shelves and thumb through the pages. Perhaps it's the title that grabs my interest. Or my mood. I slip it back in its slot, then slide my fingers slowly across one of the shelves, passing the likes of Shakespeare, Chaucer, and Scott Fitzgerald. My attention is captured by a thin orange ribbon dangling from a book ensconced between Henry Miller's *Tropic of Cancer* and his *Tropic of Capricorn*. I remove the leather-bound book and sit at the edge of Hunter's bed. The title, *Hunter's World,* is engraved in gold lettering.

I wiggle the bookmark and open to a page that was handwritten in ink, a diary perhaps. My guess is that it belonged to Hunter, given that the writer used the same wavy motion that penned the suicide note. I suspect the title and contents were the imagination of Hunter himself. He kept referring to himself as a satyr. Like one of those Greek mythical characters, part human, part horse or goat, with an insatiable sexual appetite. I shake my head as I continue reading, thumbing forward a few pages and then stopping at an entry apparently written not long before his murder.

"You're gonna die, you bastard!" Hunter wrote. "The voice resonated through the phone line, carrying a slight but distinct lilt in spite of its rancor. It was a foreign voice. Only it wasn't foreign to me."

I ponder Hunter's words, which were written in a quick, almost nervous scribble. This is obviously a threat. I think of my wife. Susan has a nasal intonation but is certainly not foreign sounding. I ease myself back on the bed. Hunter *knew* he was in trouble. And apparently knew his killer. Why hadn't he told me about the threat?

Someone he knew. A foreign voice.

The front door opens, and I instinctively reach for my revolver.

"Hank?"

I slip it back into my holster. "In here," I call out, wondering what my deputy is doing here.

Wayne pops his head in, surveys the room. "I saw your car in the driveway."

"I thought I'd have a look around," I tell him.

Wayne has a puzzled expression on his face. "How come?"

I hesitate. "There's been a development."

Wayne removes his felt hat and scratches his head. "A development?"

Wayne likes to repeat things. I bring him up to date on my meeting with Gloria Wollinsky.

He shoots me a look. "Murder?"

" 'Fraid so."

I watch Wayne search the room, not that he will find anything. His eyes meet mine. "Who do you think?"

I shrug. "That's what we need to find out."

Wayne is quick to point out that Eastpoint has never had a murder before.

"I know that, too, Wayne."

He nods. "You suspect anyone?"

My wife and a half-dozen other women in town.

"No," I reply.

His eyes search the room again like maybe he missed something the first time. "So whaddaya gonna do?"

I shrug again. "We gotta investigate."

"Just us?" he wonders.

"For now, yes."

"But the county, they oughta be involved."

That's not a good idea, of course, and I remind Wayne that

my past life as a county homicide detective should be sufficient. But to satisfy any concerns he might have, I assure my deputy that if something develops, I'll be the first to contact the county for help.

"Or doesn't," Wayne chimes.

"If we don't have any luck within a few days, I'll bring them in."

Wayne seems satisfied with my plan and asks how he can help move this investigation forward. Right!

"Run along, Wayne. You're off duty," I say, my tone probably a little too dismissive. "I'll call you later."

Wayne nods dejectedly, then asks about the book in my hand. I raise it. "It's just a book."

He turns to leave. "See you, Hank," he mumbles.

I'm about to return to the book when I say, "Say, Wayne, what brought you out this way, anyway?"

He stops, turns back to me, and shrugs. "Like I said, I saw your car outside."

I nod. "Yeah, but you live on the other side of town."

Wayne searches the floor, tells me he had nothing better to do.

Of course, I know why Wayne showed up: he was curious, and I tell him so.

Wayne holds back a grin. "Maybe a little."

I wave him out the door, then thumb forward a few entries, hoping to find clues. Instead, I get a completely different scenario. It reads more like Hunter's paintings. Evidently, my murdered drinking buddy kept a diary on everything he did or imagined with these women. Everything!

Repelled, I close the journal and stare out the window. One thing is certain. Hunter's killer's identity lies somewhere between the pages of *Hunter's World*.

9

John Hunter was Eastpoint's most famous celebrity, though some might use *infamous* to describe him, particularly our more conservative folks. "Never read his trash," they would tell me, though you'd never know by the sold-out copies of *Newsday* from Dwight's Candy Store. Which only goes to show you that curiosity has a strong hold on people, especially when it comes to sex.

Most of Eastpoint's residents, though, found John Hunter a novelty item and watched him with interest, especially the women, who would giggle as he passed them on the street. As much as Hunter wanted to blend in to the small-town landscape, he could never hide his big-city persona. As he strolled down Main Street with a spirited gait, straight shoulders, narrow hips, and wearing designer clothes, Hunter was anything but a local.

Hunter and I would meet at Salty's on Friday nights. Our conversations never centered on his advice columns. I never brought up the subject, since I didn't have much of a sex life and wasn't interested in sharing my misery with him. I did read his columns regularly and found them occasionally aggressive, at times bordering on angry. But generally, Hunter wrote with a less strident tone, often adding humor. I remember one column addressing a timid couple struggling with their mundane love-making. "Try new positions," he would encourage. "In every room any time of the day. Just watch your back. And remember, if it's doable, it's normal."

Looking back, and in light of Earl's comment, it's evident that Hunter had not heeded his own advice. Only Earl thought Hunter's troubles stemmed from a lack of companionship, the absence of a woman. Quite the opposite. Apparently, Hunter had as many local women as he wanted. What he suffered from was lack of intimacy. In fact, he was dispassionate about everything but lust.

At least that's my interpretation from Hunter's seedy journal. He was graphic about his likes and dislikes. And John Hunter had plenty of dislikes.

I'm sitting at my usual corner table inside Salty's, tucked away from the seventies music and barroom chatter. From my vantage point, I can take in a view of the spectacular Hidden Island, a residential enclave where only a few affluent locals can afford to reside. The majority of the homes belong to wealthy Manhattanites, who prefer Eastpoint's serenity to the more glitzy Hamptons.

There is a mystique about the island. I often tease myself with the "what if" question, when I think of those secluded mansions surrounded by old oak trees, which have grown so high they appear to kiss the clouds, and of the private beach, where sea gulls and other wildlife frolic without fear of extinction. Sometimes I try to imagine what it would be like to live there. Only I wasn't thinking about that today.

My waitress approaches with my usual: tuna on rye toast, with a sour pickle and coleslaw, then she follows up by refueling my cup with strong Colombian coffee. I peer up from my reading and smile. "Thanks, Sheryl."

Sheryl Murphy is Paddy's wife. At twenty-nine, she has the type of angelic face men easily fall in love with. With short blond hair, deep blue eyes, and a breezy smile, Sheryl almost always radiates beauty without needing to wear makeup.

Not today, though. Right now, Sheryl has a weary, almost

resigned expression on her face, which seems streaked with pain. Her eyes are red, lacking the sparkle I am accustomed to seeing, and her voice is strained as she asks, "How's it going, Hank?"

I catch her staring at Hunter's journal, and I quickly close it. "Guess you heard about John Hunter?" I say, searching her eyes.

She nods absently. "Sad."

Unlike Susan, Sheryl doesn't ask questions about Hunter, and my sense is this has nothing to do with lack of interest, so I provide her with as much information as is professionally appropriate, including the ME's theory. I watch her face pale, and after a few moments I add, "Eastpoint has never had a murder before on my watch."

She steadies herself on the table, then forces a smile. "You've only been our police chief about five years, Hank."

"True, but I don't remember a murder ever occurring in Eastpoint. And I was born here."

"Murder," she breathes.

I survey the room, realizing the "M" word isn't on the street yet. I don't need a panic on my hands.

Sheryl sighs. "The town's got faith in you, Hank. You'll get him." Then, like a ghost, she disappears to another table.

I gaze at the empty chair facing me where Hunter used to sit. We met about two years ago, soon after he arrived in Eastpoint. I recognized him immediately from the black and white column photo. Not that I'm into those prurient indulgences. I'm not a prude, mind you. Apparently, neither is my wife.

Hunter recognized me from my picture in the *Eastpoint Times*. As police chief, I'm a bit of a celebrity myself. Only I don't paint as well as he did. We hit it off immediately and began meeting on a regular basis. He generally wore a disarming smile, which I believe helped mask a deep emotional pain. I discovered this one night after Hunter, consuming one too many beers, became philosophical. He filled me in on why he began writing his column. He said he wanted to climb inside peoples' heads and transform mundane lovemaking into an art. For Hunter, though, it wasn't entirely altruistic; it was more a cleansing. Living through his readers' foibles excited him.

It was soon after his fortieth birthday that Hunter turned his back on a lucrative psychotherapy practice, which he attributed to classic burnout. After regrouping, he started writing an advice column, but the sterile city environment stifled his writing, so he sold the contents of his Upper West Side apartment and moved east.

After replaying some of Hunter's history in my head, I go back to his journal, reading with as much enthusiasm as I have for my sandwich, then I wash down my food with coffee without missing a word. His writing is tame at first, describing Eastpoint as a sleepy town, a golden nugget far away from the saturated metropolis. I like that. He was also very flattering about the townsfolk. I like that, too.

About a year ago, I notice as I continue to read, Hunter's writings had begun to reveal a man growing increasingly restless with himself and jaded with his advice column. He needed a diversion, and he seems to have found it in some of Eastpoint's women. That's when his entries turned dark, perverse. But I find myself getting caught up in *his* moment, sick though compelling. Hunter really knew how to write pornography.

I ease up, catching my breath between entries. After reading a few more pages, I close the book and set it aside. Porno can exhaust a person.

As my eyes drift toward Hidden Island, I realize I hadn't known John Hunter at all.

"More coffee, Hank?"

I glance up at Sheryl. A little color had returned to her face. "Sure."

Watching her pour, I ask, "How well did you know John Hunter?"

I detect a slight jerk in her hand. She stops, shoots a look toward the bar, then back to me. "Hunter? He was a regular. Seen him with you occasionally."

"Ever have a conversation with him?" I press.

"Only to take a meal order. Am I a suspect, Hank?" Sheryl tries to make light of her words, but my question clearly rattles her.

"Hell, we all are," I say. "Until I catch the guy. The person."

She takes a moment. "I didn't really know him that well, Hank, I swear."

I lightly touch her hand. "Easy, Sheryl. I'm just trying to find out as much as I can about the guy."

She recovers, realizes she overreacted. "Oh, why didn't you say so?"

I thought I had. I pat her hand and smile. "Just trying to solve the first murder in Eastpoint."

She nods, closes her eyes as though going into a trance, then says, "Sorry, Hank. I can't help you unless you want to know what he ordered."

I remove a pen from my shirt pocket. "That's a good start."

"You're kidding!"

"No, really," I tell her, pressing down on the head of the cap.

She sets down the coffeepot and mulls over my question. "Cheeseburger, rare, and fries. He never ordered desert."

"What did he drink?" I ask, jotting a few notes on a paper napkin.

Sheryl doesn't bother to think about the question. "Jack Daniel's on the rocks—" She stops, catches herself. "No, he ordered Sam Adams, like you. I really have to get back to work, Hank."

I finish writing down her responses, crossing out Jack Daniel's on the rocks, then peer up and smile. "You did great, Sheryl. Appreciate it."

When Sheryl leaves, I ponder my notes, then take my pen and underline the crossed out Jack Daniel's. Sheryl knew Hunter's drinking preference, all right. Her first quick response wouldn't have meant anything to me if we hadn't found an open bottle of Jack Daniel's at the crime scene. I rub my chin a few times. Maybe Sheryl knew more about John Hunter than just cheeseburgers and beer.

10

I'm about to shovel a spoonful of peach cobbler in my mouth when my cell phone vibrates on the table. I scowl, polish off the contents of the spoon, then reach for the phone.

It's Kate, my secretary. "I'm not interrupting your lunch, am I, boss?"

"I'm finishing my dessert," I say, choking on a piece of peach.

"I thought you were on a diet, Hank," she admonishes. "Let's see, you're at Salty's and in the middle of a peach cobbler."

No one can hide in this town. Almost. I clear my throat. "Good call."

"Sorry to bother you, but there's been a development over at Hunter's house."

I lift an eyebrow. "What kind of development?"

"Nothing to be alarmed about, but Charlie was doing his rounds and found a woman inside the house. She claims to be Hunter's sister."

I shoot a glance out the window. "I didn't know he had one."

"Evidently, he did."

I nod. "Okay, tell Charlie I'm on my way."

"Before you finish the cobbler, Hank."

I smile into the phone. "Right."

"Oh, I almost forgot. Gloria Wollinsky called. She said the revised report on Hunter is on its way. What's that all about?"

"I'll discuss it with you later."

I hang up, study my dessert for a few moments, then slap

down a ten for lunch. I say goodbye to Sheryl, who offers me a thin smile, and head for the door.

The afternoon is unusually warm for this time of year, so I lower the driver's side window and take in some fresh Long Island air. I pass the local farm stand and wave to Greta Lewis, who is too busy selling pumpkins to notice me. The Lewis farm is overrun with parents and schoolchildren searching for the perfect jack o'lantern. Judging by the number of customers, I'd say Greta is having a healthy season.

I turn down Hunter's street and wonder about the sister. Why hadn't he mentioned her? Then again, he never told me he was doing my wife either.

I find Charlie Slater, my only African-American deputy, chatting with a woman in Hunter's kitchen over coffee like they were old friends. Charlie, whose lean body hasn't changed much since he played running back at UM eight years ago, is a gentle soul and very religious. He also has the gift of gab, so I suspect Charlie has been doing most of the talking. He introduces me to a twenty-something woman who goes by the name of Carol Hunter. She is petite with short red hair, appropriately dressed for the occasion in a fashionable black suit and white blouse. Ms. Hunter is quite attractive, although when she extends her hand and smiles, she wears a wistful, almost resigned expression.

The presence of these two in Hunter's house suddenly makes me uneasy. I should have updated the staff on the ME's murder theory. This crime scene shouldn't be used for a coffee klatch.

I extend my condolences to Hunter's sister and explain in a cordial way that she should have checked in with us before crossing the yellow tape outside her brother's house.

"I apologize, Sheriff, but the door was open and—"

"Open?"

Carol points to the back door.

It dawns on me that I was the culprit, forgetting to lock up after chasing the painting snatcher. "Oh."

"I was going to stop by the stationhouse before seeing John," she says. Her eyes search the floor. "I'm really not looking forward to that."

"No, of course not," I sympathize.

"I found out about it in the paper. Can you imagine?"

Hunter's photograph had been plastered all over the newspapers. Bold headlines like "Popular Advice Columnist Takes Own Life" sell papers. With Hunter gone, the papers lost one of their meal tickets. His advice column was about to be buried with him.

"Sheriff?"

I blink. "Sorry. I was thinking about your brother."

Carol smiles warmly, then begins to discuss Hunter at length, as though they'd been inseparable. Charlie and I encourage her with our smiles.

She then shifts course, her expression turning sullen. "The truth is we had a falling out. I haven't seen my brother in a few years." Carol Hunter takes a tissue from her purse and wipes away the tears from her past. When she recovers, she says, "I was hoping John left behind a memento. You know, a gesture of the good times we had together."

There are about a dozen paintings in the attic, but I don't believe she had that in mind.

"I'm in therapy," she admits, kneading her hands. "My past."

I nod sagely. "It's always about the past." I should be puffing on a pipe. Who am I, Sigmund Freud?

"I'm a change-of-life baby," she continues. "When I was about five, John took off for college. He didn't come home very often, and I guess I felt rejected."

I offer a sympathetic nod this time. "Too bad he couldn't have helped you, being a shrink and all."

51

She shakes her head. "It was too close an issue for John to be objective."

Charlie interrupts, "Carol—I mean Ms. Hunter, would like to look around. I told her it was probably okay but we needed your approval first, Hank."

I turn to Charlie then Ms. Hunter. "There's been a change in the way we believe your brother died." I pause. "We think he was murdered. I'm sorry."

Her body stiffens. "Murdered!" She searches my face, as does Charlie.

"Hank, I don't understand. When did things change?"

I exaggerate a bit. "The ME just called. I was going to set up a meeting with everyone."

"What happened?" Charlie presses.

"He was poisoned."

"Oh my God!" This comes from Hunter's sister.

" 'Fraid so. Unless he gave himself a lethal cocktail," I add as a hopeful afterthought.

"No way," Carol protests. "John would never have killed himself."

Images of my wife and Sheryl Murphy flash in front of me. "We'll do everything we can to catch the person responsible."

She rubs her eyes lightly, gazes out the window.

I glance over at Charlie, who still has a puzzled look on his face. "Ms. Hunter, I'm not supposed to release anything in the house because it's a crime scene. But if you find something that could help you in therapy, point it out. I'll see what I can do to have it released to you."

She turns, brushes my hand. "Thanks, Sheriff. Please call me Carol."

I let a few awkward moments pass before asking, "You guys ever try to patch up your differences?"

She sighs. "John tried a few times. I'm afraid it was me. I was older by then and more obstinate."

"Too bad."

She laughs softly. "I guess I was angry with the company he kept." Her eyes turn cold. "They probably poisoned him!"

I blink hard. "Who?"

She points with her chin toward the window. "Those women he hung out with. Losers, whores and motorcycle chicks. Can you imagine a psychologist dating women like that? He would tell me about his sex life like I was one of his drinking buddies."

I glance over at Charlie, who appears mesmerized by Ms. Hunter's story.

"It was sick!" She pauses, settles down a bit. "I'm sorry, I'm rambling. It's just that the wounds are still pretty deep."

"I understand," I assure her.

She shakes her head in sadness. "John should have settled down a long time ago. Only something inside wouldn't let him. He used to tell me that no *one* woman could ever satisfy him. He reminded me of those ancient mythical Greek characters—."

"Satyrs," I blurt out.

She gives me a look. "That's it," she nods. "Then you know what I mean. John probably hadn't changed."

Losers and whores. What a way to describe my wife. "Ms. Hunter, I knew your brother fairly well, and as far as I know, John wasn't into that sort of thing."

Her eyes brighten. "Really? Maybe he did change."

"He did," I say offering a comforting look. Till the day he died.

11

My overwhelming obsession to confront Susan has finally peaked. The time has arrived. I pull into the driveway and gaze out at our modest white Cape Cod house with its blue slate shutters and rhododendrons lining the front. It's been our home since we got married. I love this house, and until a few years ago, Susan and I had been relatively happy here. Like most couples, we have had differences but Susan's sudden distance and moodiness in recent months created a barrier between us. I never know what to expect from her. And while antidepressants had become a way of life for my wife, a temporary reprieve from her pain, hell might be waiting just around the corner.

I step out of the car and enter the house through the kitchen door, expecting to find Susan preparing dinner, though probably only for one today. Instead, the house is alive with deep guttural sounds coming from the upstairs bathroom. I take the stairs two steps at a time and place my ear against the door like a stranger. I tap softly. "Hey, you okay in there?"

Susan doesn't answer so I knock harder.

"Susan?"

"Nice of you to come home," she says in a gruff voice.

I pull my ear away from the door but remain silent.

"Where the hell have you been?" she demands.

I place my hand on the doorknob then stop. "Looking for Hunter's killer. Can I come in?"

Susan opens the door barely enough for me to glimpse her

struggling to the commode. She drops the seat cover, sits, then stares at the floor, pasty-faced, her mouth stained with whatever she had for breakfast or lunch. "Murder? I thought you said he killed himself."

I slowly open the door wider and search her eyes. "That was before I found out he was poisoned," I say. "You got any strychnine in the house?"

Susan narrows a look on me. "What the hell is that supposed to mean?"

I shrug. "You tell me."

She presses her stomach. "Is that what this is about? Hunter?"

I don't answer.

Susan jabs a finger in the air. "What's going on inside that head of yours, Hank?"

My eyes are burning, my heart pounding. "Did you sleep with him?" I finally demand, my body slackening.

Susan scowls. "You're sick, Hank. You know that? What the hell's gotten into you?"

I sneer. "I have proof, Susan. Visual proof."

Susan flashes a cynical grin. "This ought to be good. Show me."

I can't, of course, since Susan is probably hiding the painting somewhere out of my reach. I have to backpedal, and tell her I can't at the moment.

"Why not?" She attempts to get up, thinks twice.

" 'Cause it's evidence," I say, explaining that she is not privy to my investigation findings even if she is the police chief's wife.

Susan shakes her head. "That's bullshit, Hank. If you're accusing me of infidelity, you better show me some proof. And as for your dead friend, the poor guy can't even defend himself."

I snicker. "Defend himself. That bastard was screwing half the women in this town."

Susan rolls her eyes. "Right, a town this size, and nobody

knew about it. Give me a break."

I manage an impish grin. "Obviously, you were discreet about it. I'll give you that much."

"Well discretion is everything, isn't it?"

"That's not an answer," I charge. I then lean against the wall and proceed to tell Susan about finding Hunter's *love room,* as though it were some important archeological discovery.

My wife leaps off the commode and storms past me into the bedroom. I follow her, stopping at our bed, where I find her sitting and gazing into the dresser mirror, her hands raking her hair.

"How could you do this to me? To us?" I ask, my tone defeated.

She stops, watches me through the mirror. "Hank, it's not a good time for *this* type of conversation." She pauses, closes her eyes a moment then says, "I will tell you that I've never slept with Hunter or anyone else since we've been married. And I don't care what evidence you have."

She's good, my wife. I finally show my hand and let on about the painting.

She rubs her stomach lightly. "What painting?"

"The one of you and Hunter in a compromising position. I don't have to tell you what position."

Susan chuckles with amusement. "Come on, Hank. It doesn't take too much imagination to paint someone." She turns to me. "Okay, let me see this *compromising* painting."

I snort. "I was going to ask you the same thing. Is it just a co-incidence that your car engine happened to be warm the night of the murder, soon after that compromising painting went missing? Let me guess. You were out buying a loaf of bread."

Susan throws up her hands. "I ran out of wine, okay? Go ahead, check Rusty's, they'll vouch for me." She shakes her head. "First, you accuse me of infidelity. What's next, Hank, murder?"

I don't answer.

"Oh, for God's sake, this is crazy! Is that why you didn't come home last night? You think I killed Hunter?"

I lick my dry mouth. "I can't stay here right now, Susan. Not until this matter is settled."

My wife closes her eyes for a moment and starts breathing deeply. "Hank, let's be rational about this. You were Hunter's drinking buddy. Don't you think it would have slipped out that he was having an affair with at least one of the women you're accusing him of? Give me another name."

I search the floor, then meet her eyes. "Sheryl Murphy."

Her jaw drops. "Sheryl? Can't be."

I nod. "I have proof."

"She's married."

"So are you!" I point. "Or have you forgotten?"

"You're disgusting, Hank."

"Me? I'm not the one screwing around."

"You're not well in the head."

"Maybe, but tell me, Susan, did you kill Hunter because of Sheryl, or did she kill him when she found out about you?"

"Get out of my sight!" she screams. "Of all times."

I bolt for the door, then stop. "What's that supposed to mean?" I say turning back to Susan. Her hands tremble in anger.

"Stay away from me until you get your act together." Susan gasps, tries to hold back her tears.

I approach her tentatively. "What does that mean, 'of all times'?"

"You bastard. I'm pregnant!"

12

After shooting blanks for years, I should be ecstatic that my wife is going to present me with a child. Hell, I ought to be thinking about handing out cigars!

As I'm pushing seventy on Carriage Drive leading to Rocky Beach, the full weight of the situation hits me. Susan is suddenly pregnant and John Hunter is dead.

I ease up on the accelerator and pass the town beach shack, the "Residents Only" sign hanging precariously from it. I stop at the last parking space facing the water.

Long Island Sound is remarkably quiet, not a boat in sight. I get out of the car and scoop up a handful of flat stones, scaling a few into the water.

At the water's edge, I breathe in some fresh air. Suppose Hunter was responsible for Susan's pregnancy. Would she have told him? Maybe, but she certainly wouldn't hold him financially responsible. That's where I'd come in. John Hunter might have charmed the pants off my wife, but I was going to pay for their indiscretion.

Walking along the beach, I pick up a few more scalers and toss one about. Would Hunter threaten to tell me if Susan refused to an abortion? That might silence her. Or him.

I toss the remaining stones in the water and pass a few sea gulls fighting over trash. We all fight over something. Me, I need to take back my dignity.

Then there's Sheryl. Hunter's journal detailed just how

rattled he was over her emotional dependence. Sheryl was clearly hooked on him. "She wants to leave her husband," he wrote. "Not good. I NEED TO FIND A SOLUTION! FAST!"

What if Sheryl found out about Susan's pregnancy, confronted Hunter, and threatened to expose both of them if he didn't force Susan to have an abortion? What would an enraged woman in love do? X out a painting of her nemesis and kill the beast?

I stop in front of a boulder jutting out of the water ten feet from shore. I remember the day I swam out to that rock and carved *our* initials on it. The next day, I invited Susan to the beach for a picnic. Before we sipped champagne and fed each other imported cheese, I handed her my binoculars and aimed her in the direction of the rock. She cried, we laughed, but most of all, we were very much in love. That was sixteen summers ago.

I first met Susan Ward when I stopped by the Eastpoint Diner for a cold drink. It was a sweltering August day and my car air conditioner had stopped running. I would have walked past her if Mrs. Lange hadn't dropped her cane near Susan's table. I quickly bent down to retrieve it, and as I slipped the neck over her wrist, my eyes caught Susan's. In that one frame, she smiled and my heart fluttered.

I have never forgotten the way Susan looked that day, her black, shoulder-length hair slightly frizzy from the humidity. She wore a rose-colored summer dress, and her shoulders were lean and bronze. One of the straps had slipped slightly, revealing her true silky skin. But there was sadness in Susan's eyes. I wanted to scoop her in my arms and tell her everything would be okay.

Susan admitted that she was vacationing in Eastpoint to get away from the city heat, but by the end of the summer, I knew the real reason for Susan's sojourn out east. She had gone through an emotional nightmare watching her mother succumb to Lou Gehrig's disease two months earlier. Her father had passed away a few years before that, and because she was an only child, the only person Susan could turn to was her boyfriend. But in untimely fashion, he let her down, leaving Susan for another woman. Forlorn and alone, Susan needed to break away from life's madness, if only for a while. She reached the shores of Eastpoint and never looked back.

Susan's sadness eventually shifted into a loving, enriched life for the both of us. The only thing missing in our lives was a child. We both wanted one, she especially. As it turned out, I was the culprit—low sperm count. At one point, I laughingly suggested we'd find a surrogate if my sperm wouldn't multiply and sail into her uterus. I hadn't meant it literally.

Our emotional disappointment continued for a while, until one day we just stopped trying. I was satisfied with just the two of us, but Susan needed more. Perhaps what I couldn't provide my wife, Hunter could. And no one, not even Hunter, was going to force her to give up that precious cargo.

13

John Hunter's casket sits next to a maple tree in the middle of Calverton's Cemetery. A few city types, probably from Hunter's New York office, are among the crowd paying their respects.

I'm standing by myself observing the mourners, searching their faces. Not surprisingly, most are women. From Hunter's paintings alone, at least four of them are present. The missing must have had other plans today.

Sheryl holds a handkerchief under her dark sunglasses, catching a steady stream of tears. My wife, standing next to her, remains stoic in her own classical way. She and Sheryl have been best friends for years. Still, it's strange to see them together under the circumstances.

Susan catches my glance and is about to acknowledge me. Instead, she turns back to the casket. I shake my head. The whole town must know something's up between us. We're always standing together at weddings and funerals. Sheryl must sense something. She gazes over and smiles sadly through her tears. I smile back.

I turn my attention to our parish priest, Father O'Brady, who is gesticulating and offering final prayers. Next to him is a woman I have never seen before. She is dressed in black and her expression, though sullen, radiates above her apparent bereavement. She is definitely not from Eastpoint. My eyes hold on her until she glances my way and smiles softly. I nod.

"Pretty big turnout, huh, Hank?"

"Say, Charlie. Looks that way, doesn't it?" I say, my eyes staring straight ahead at the casket. "Hunter was a popular guy."

My deputy lets a few minutes pass before telling me about his experience with Hunter's sister. "She's a real piece of work, that one. You should have seen the way she acted after you left yesterday."

I turn my head slightly. "What do you mean?"

"She got pretty worked up about a memento she was looking for and didn't like the idea of me following her around. She finally demanded that I wait in the kitchen. Said she needed closure."

"You didn't—"

"Of course not," he says shaking his head rapidly. "I told her it was a sensitive matter and still a crime scene. She got real hostile, started raising her voice and swearing."

I tug on Charlie's sleeve, pull him aside. "Seriously?"

"Yeah, but I told her I don't put up with that kind of talk. Don't care who died in her family."

I nod. "Did you force her to leave?"

"I was about to, but she calmed down, got control of herself as though nothing had happened."

"Strange behavior. Did she find anything?"

"No, and she wasn't too happy about that either. She had a real interest in Hunter's bedroom, though."

"His bedroom?" I say, hoping Charlie hadn't meant the lust room.

"You know, next to the living room. Brass bed, dresser, night stand—"

"I know what a bedroom is!"

"She kept sniffing around his bookcase, staring at the books like she was looking for something in particular. She wanted to pull a few out, but I stopped her. That's when she got all bent out of shape. You think maybe that's why she's not here today,

Hank? She's too upset?"

My eyes dart about. "Christ!"

"What?"

"I gotta go, Charlie."

"But the service . . ."

I point my chin toward the woman standing next to Father O'Brady. "Find out who that woman is and make sure she doesn't leave town until I get back," I demand.

Charlie glances over at the woman in black. "Sure, Hank," Charlie says. "But I don't think she's going anywhere. That's Hunter's ex-wife."

14

My drinking buddy was full of surprises. God only knows how many other secrets Hunter kept from me!

There is no sign of life on Hunter's block, including his driveway where I nose my car in, stopping a few inches from the garage door. I pan the immediate area and suddenly feel derelict for not posting a deputy out front and treating this investigation with professional indifference.

Knowing the front door is locked, I head around the side, taking in the woods where the paint snatcher escaped. I stop short as I approach the back door, realizing someone has already been here. I draw my weapon, turn the knob, and push the door in gently with my gun.

"Police," I call out.

Not surprisingly, no one answers, so I step tentatively over the broken glass and work my way past the dark living room, which hasn't been touched, to the master bedroom. Evidently, the intruder wasn't particularly fond of Hunter's classics, because the contents of his wall-to-wall bookcase are now strewn about. And there doesn't appear to be anyone around I can discuss the matter with.

Not bothering to check the other rooms on this floor, I take the stairs two at a time and enter Hunter's lower art studio on the second floor. Not good. The hatch is open, the ladder extending downward. I take a quick look around, then climb slowly, the dark hole widening with each step. I flip the light switch several times without luck, then step into the room, feeling around and wishing I had changed the batteries in my now-dead flashlight. It's too dark to continue, so I turn to reverse my steps. That's when I hear the sound of wind whirling from behind me that stops with a thump to my head.

My brain registers a voice in the distance. "Up here," I grunt, touching my head and swearing to myself. "Up here," I cry out, then I crawl over to the opening and look down. Charlie's gun is aimed at my head, along with a beam from his flashlight.

He stops. "Hank, are you okay?"

I blink hard. "Think so," I force out.

"What the heck happened? And what's up there?"

I have no intention of answering the second question, so I give him a brief answer to the first.

Charlie climbs a few more steps, then shines his light past me and enters Hunter's cave. "Damn, what kind of place is this?"

I get to my feet and shrug. "Beats me, it was dark. My flashlight ran out of batteries."

We exchange looks then he says, "It was her, wasn't it?"

"Hunter's sister? I don't know. Like I said, it was dark. She—Whoever it was hit me from behind."

Charlie slips his revolver back in the holster. "I told you she was nuts. Think she took anything?"

"Only part of my scalp, I hope."

"Hunter's bedroom is a mess."

"I know. I saw it."

I follow Charlie toward Hunter's sex bed, hoping his curiosity ends there. Instead, his light bounces off a few walls and stops at the studio door. "What's in there?" he says, almost to himself.

"Maybe we oughta come back when we have more light," I advise.

But Charlie continues anyway, opens the door carefully, and then he shines his light inside. "What the fuck?"

Charlie doesn't usually swear.

"What?"

"Friggin' paintings of people friggin'. And . . . and this!" he says, snatching a painting off the floor. "Looks like Hunter and Jackie Hopkins."

That's one.

"There's more. Shit, that rich woman from the island."

I'm about to offer a name, but stop. "Who?"

"Can't remember her name. The one married to that New York banker."

"That would be Olivia Patterson." I was getting good at this.

"Her. Damn, Hunter is—"

"Be careful. That stuff is evidence, and your fingerprints are all over it."

Charlie drops the loving couple on the floor and wipes his hands on his pants. "Sorry." He steps past me and aims his flashlight at the bed. "What the heck was Hunter doing up here?"

"Apparently not meditating," I suggest.

"Think it might have anything to do with his murder?"

That's my deputy, always thinking. "It's possible." I press hard on my temples. "I gotta get something for my head," I say, and I struggle back to the hole.

When I reach my patrol car, I grab a few Tylenol from the glove compartment, pop them in my mouth, struggling to swallow, and then get on the car radio.

"You sound a little out of it, Hank," Kate says. "What's going on?"

I give her the abridged version.

"Sweet Jesus, are you okay?"

"I will be after the painkillers kick in. Anyone with you?" I ask.

"Just Wayne."

"I need him to bring out a couple of pairs of latex gloves. ASAP."

"Don't tell me you found another body!"

"No, and don't go spreading that around, either. It's something else."

"You're not going to elaborate?"

"Paintings," I offer.

"What the heck kind of evidence is that?"

I ignore the question. "I need to speak to Hunter's ex-wife. She was at the funeral."

"She's staying at the Royalty Inn."

The woman has class. There's a reason it's called the Royalty Inn.

"She told Charlie she'd probably stick around as long as you needed her. And Wayne thinks she's hot."

"This time I agree with him. She's . . . sexy."

Kate tells me she hasn't heard me use that word in a long time.

"Maybe not in front of you." I laugh.

"Funny," Kate chimes.

I check my watch. "I want you to find out if Norman picked up any passengers going to or from Hunter's house within the past couple of hours. Or anywhere near his house."

"Looking for someone in particular?"

"I'm thinking maybe Hunter's sister. I don't remember her having a car yesterday."

"Her description, boss."

"White, early twenties, red hair."

"Sexy?"

"Crazy."

"I'm on it."

"Thanks, sexy."

"Don't patronize me." She laughs and hangs up.

By the time I return to Hunter's sex shop, the attic light is on. "I see you found a light bulb, Charlie."

"It was there all along. Whoever got in here earlier unscrewed it just enough so it wouldn't go on."

I raise an eyebrow. "Figures."

Charlie is examining the paintings as though he were an art dealer. "This doesn't look too good, does it, Hank?"

I shake my head. " 'Fraid not, Charlie."

Charlie remains silent a few moments, looking around nervously as though we might be expecting a reporter to show up and ask questions. "So whaddaya think, Hank?"

"About the paintings? Probably Hunter's imagination."

"I mean, do we have to . . . show them?"

"I don't know, Charlie. Probably."

"And the women. You gonna interrogate them?"

I shrug. "What choice do I have?"

He makes a sweeping motion. "But Hank, they're our neighbors!"

"What am I supposed to do, Charlie?"

He nods anxiously.

I touch his shoulder lightly. "I'll be as discreet as possible."

He nods, but I can see from his expression he's not reassured. "Anyone home?"

Charlie and I exchange glances. "Up here, Wayne."

Wayne makes his way up the ladder and joins us in the studio. "You bring the gloves?" I ask.

Wayne's eyes are zoned in on the paintings like radar. "What the hell?"

"I'll discuss it later. Did you bring the gloves?"

Wayne slides them out of his back pocket and extends his arm.

"I want you guys to start carting this stuff out to my car. I'm gonna have another look around."

They nod in unison and slip on the gloves.

I clap my hands. "Let's go."

As I watch my deputies nervously lift the paintings off the floor, their silence and glum expressions tell me that the proverbial shit is about to hit the fan.

15

The Royalty Inn is a small but elegant lodge located just outside town near the Grand Inlet. Each guest is treated to a private terrace overlooking the breathtaking Little Peconic Bay. In the summer, lilacs and the sweet fragrance of jasmine line the walkway leading to the grounds along the length of the property. The place has a reputation for pampering New York's royalty, including ex-mayors and city councilmen, and has been in the Williams family for over fifty years.

I approach the front desk and tip my hat to Janet Williams, the daughter-in-law. She offers me a pleasant smile, which widens an already rotund face. Her eyes are brown or black. I can never get close enough to tell.

"Morning, Hank."

"Say, Janet. When did you start working behind the desk?"

"I'm filling in for Mom. She and Dad took off for a few days."

The "Mom and Dad" belong to her husband, Douglas Williams. Janet's the bookkeeper. A good one, I'm told.

"I'm here to see Mrs. Hunter. At least I think she goes by that name."

Janet motions me closer and whispers, "Is this about her ex?"

"Good detective work." I wink but decide not to go into the particulars. Janet has a big mouth, both figuratively and literally.

"She's registered under Margaret Hunter, room one-oh-five," Janet informs me. "I saw her step out to the patio a few minutes ago."

"Thanks." I turn to leave, when Janet asks, "Is it true what they say about Hunter?"

She could have heard anything so I ask, "Like what?"

"Don't be coy, Hank. You know. The paintings?"

Like I said, news travels fast in this town. "How did you find out?"

She winks. "I'm a good detective, remember?"

I have to schedule a meeting with my staff concerning their lack of discretion. "We found a few paintings."

"Am I in any of them?" she asks encouragingly.

Janet could have taken up the entire canvas. "Sorry, you were spared." We were all spared!

"Darn."

I smile. "I think I'll join Ms. Hunter."

"She's very nice, Hank."

Unlike Hunter's sister, I hope.

The ex–Mrs. Hunter is sitting comfortably in a lawn chair near the pool, her white slender neck easing back, swan-like. Her delicate-looking face is basking in the sun, lips pursed. She is clearly enjoying the mild autumn day as I watch her with interest.

"I've been waiting for you, Sheriff," she says, sensing her surroundings. Margaret Hunter opens her eyes, shifts in her chair slightly, and greets me with a breezy smile.

"I'm not a sheriff," I say, approaching her. "I'm the police chief. And please call me Hank."

She extends her hand and shakes mine with exuberance. "Sorry, Hank. I just assumed any top-ranking police officer outside a big city is a sheriff."

"Counties have sheriffs," I inform her. "We're just a small town."

"And beautiful," she emphasizes, spreading her arms. "You don't find these views in Manhattan."

Margaret Hunter is in her late thirties, with almond-shaped eyes, porcelain-like skin, and a silver-blue clip in her shoulder-length black hair.

She senses my stare and says, "Is there something wrong?"

I blink. "Sorry. I just can't imagine Hunter leaving such a beautiful woman."

Her smile fades. "What makes you sure he left *me?*"

I place my hands up defensively. "Sorry, that's not what I meant."

Margaret Hunter forces a smile. "The truth is, I left him."

I pull up a white wooden Adirondack chair across from her, shielding the sun from her face.

"Does that surprise you?" she probes.

I remain silent. Nothing surprises me about Hunter anymore, especially when it comes to women.

"Did you know John personally?"

I nod. "We were friends, yes."

With a wistful smile, she asks, "Did he ever mention me?"

I regard her rather odd question, then say, "Actually, Hunter told me he was a confirmed bachelor."

She gazes beyond me toward the bay. "That would be John." Her eyes drift back to me. "Since you are investigating his murder, I might as well tell you that John cheated on me. That's why I left him."

Of course he did. I nod sympathetically.

"I guess I didn't pay enough attention to his needs," she answers, her tone cynical.

I wait for more dirt, but when she doesn't offer any, I ask, "His sexual needs?"

Her eyes sweep the lawn. "Let's just say that John was oversexed." She stops, meets my eyes and covers her mouth, then giggles like a schoolgirl. "Oh, God, I can't believe I'm telling you this."

"It's okay," I encourage. "It might help in the investigation."

Margaret Hunter softens her gaze on mine. "It's just that I haven't been able to talk about it very much since I left John." Her hand floats toward me and rests on mine. I resist the urge to move it. It feels warm, safe.

"I'll try to make this as quick and painless as possible so you can get back home," I say, managing a smile.

Margaret leans back in her chair, her hand sliding off mine. "I'm here as long as you need me, Hank."

I nod. "Thanks. May I call you Margaret?"

"No." She watches my expression, then produces an alluring smile. "My friends call me Maggie. Please call me that."

I return the smile. "Okay, Maggie."

Her face turns serious. "One of your deputies told me how it happened. How John was killed."

I nod. "I never thought anything like that could happen here."

Maggie leans forward and in a low voice asks, "Who would do such a thing?"

"I really don't know, but I promise you we'll find out."

She shakes her head repeatedly. "Do you have any suspects?"

I avoid her eyes. "At first we thought it was a suicide, so this recent development hasn't produced much yet." I pause. "But we're encouraged."

She nods. "Of course. Look, if there is anything I can do." She stops, laughs softly. "Sorry, typical cliché."

I smile warmly. "No, really, I appreciate the thought." I let a few moments pass, then mention the open prescription vial of tranquilizers at the scene. "Do you know if John took sleeping pills?"

Maggie shifts in her seat. "Never when we were married."

"Not even after he suffered from job burnout?"

Maggie shoots me a puzzled look. "John told you that? That he got burnt out?"

I nod. "He said it was the reason he left his practice."

Maggie chuckles cynically. "John was a good liar. The truth is, he lost his license." She pauses. "But I guess he wanted to keep that a secret."

Now it was my turn to express confusion. "How?"

"The reason I left him." She stops, gives me an opportunity to come to my own conclusion.

"He was sleeping with a patient?"

Maggie lowers her eyes and nods.

Damn. That Hunter couldn't keep his pants on.

"Apparently, John was under the impression that his patient could handle a little fun. In truth, she became obsessed with him and threatened to go to the authorities if he didn't leave me." She lets a few moments pass. "Of course, he wasn't about to do that. So I stood by him and played the loyal wife, listened to his lies, went through his review and appeal. When it was over, he lost his practice and me in that order."

Her hurt eyes rested on mine. "But during that whole period, Hank, he never used tranquilizers."

I take in this revelation, then ask, "Couldn't the patient have lied? I mean, it was his word against hers." I can't believe I'm defending the bastard.

"It was until I watched them on video. That was her revenge." Maggie stops, catches her breath as though the incident had just occurred. "I guess John never expected her to tape them at her place and send the video to me gift-wrapped." She pauses, collects more air. "Sorry. Outside of my shrink, I haven't been able to discuss this with anyone." She closes her eyes a moment, then says, "Actually, I find talking about it rather liberating."

I smile. "I'll do what I can to keep it confidential."

Maggie nods, places her hand on mine again. "You're easy to talk to, Hank. Have you ever thought of changing your profession? You'd make a great psychologist."

"Thanks, but I like what I'm doing."

"Are you married?" she asks casually.

I let Maggie's question sink in. Here I am, sitting with Hunter's ex-wife and wondering about mine, whom I'm certain slept with Hunter and is probably carrying his child.

She pats my hand. "Come on, Hank, I thought it was an easy question."

"We're having problems," I confess, pulling my hand away slowly.

"Sorry. I shouldn't have pried."

I produce a quick smile. "That's okay."

Maggie's reassuring smile tells me to trust her, but I need to stay focused. I ask her if she and Hunter stayed in touch after the divorce.

Her eyes become wistful. "Once, about a year later. By then, John had already started his advice column. I called and wished him luck. He invited me to dinner, and I accepted. That was the last time I saw him." Maggie closes her eyes a moment. "He did call me out of the blue soon after he settled in Eastpoint. I guess that was about two years ago. He sounded edgy, unsettled. I was a little surprised that he had moved out of New York. He said he needed to get away from his past. From her."

I lean closer to Maggie. "It hadn't ended?"

She shakes her head gravely. "For John it had, but she wouldn't let go. She continued calling him, leaving messages on his machine. She must have sent him reams of love letters. After that, she began stalking him." Maggie stops. "I guess he messed around with the wrong woman."

I remove my hat, gently rub my bruised pate, then return the hat to my head. "Do you know if the woman ever found out where Hunter moved to?"

Maggie thought a moment. "At the time of the call, she

hadn't. John said she tried unsuccessfully to track him down through his employer, *City News,* but outside of his boss and a few close friends, nobody knew his whereabouts. And John gave them strict orders to keep it that way."

"Scary," I say.

"He even went so far as to threaten her with the police after she trashed his apartment."

I shoot her a disapproving look. "He let her in?"

"God, no! The doorman did after she persuaded him that she was Mrs. Hunter and had forgotten her key." She stops, her expression changes to sympathy. "The poor guy was new. And gullible. He wound up losing his job. Anyway, I guess after that John became rattled and moved out."

I tilt my head slightly. "Why here?"

Maggie shrugs. "I don't really know. But John was familiar with Eastpoint. I remember him telling me he'd been out this way a long time ago on vacation. That was before we were married. He said the people were nice. And that it was quiet." She stops, dread registering in her face. "You don't suppose . . . ?"

My same sentiments. "It's possible, but that incident happened over two years ago. I would have known if he was threatened recently. Like I said, we were friends."

"I suppose," she says, not reassured.

I remove a pad and pen from my shirt pocket. "I'd like to talk to this woman. Do you know if Hunter kept a file on her?"

Maggie thinks a moment. "He did keep a file on all his patients. At one point, they were stored in some warehouse in Queens." She stops. "I believe deep down inside, John was hoping the problem would blow over and he'd eventually get his license reinstated."

Trying to contain my excitement, I ask, "Do you think I can get my hands on those files?"

"I don't know the name of the place." She shrugs. "But it

might be in his checkbook or files."

I smile.

"What?"

"Ever think of becoming a detective?"

She laughs breezily. "If I were that good, I would have found out about Carol Warner sooner."

16

By the time Maggie and I arrive at Hunter's place, the county investigators had completed a sweep of the area for the second time, including returning Hunter's books to their shelves. Maggie surveys the room, probably trying to make sense of what Hunter's life was like out here, so I leave her to her thoughts.

I recall that Hunter had a small, dark brown desk in his bedroom. That's where I am, kneeling on the floor, rummaging through a manila folder that reads "To Be Paid." I'm thumbing through a pile of bills, but my thoughts are on Maggie.

"Thanks for letting me see the place, Hank."

I recoil, suddenly feeling guilty.

"Sorry, you must have been in deep thought."

If she only knew.

"Don't you just hate it when people do that? Interrupt your thoughts? Hope it wasn't too exciting."

I smile to myself.

Maggie is standing at the doorway and gives the room a quick once over. "Looks like John led a pretty simple life out here."

She should only know about the king-size bed above us.

"Anyway, you're busy. I'll be outside," she says and disappears. A few minutes later the screen door slams. I continue searching and eventually come across a bill from City Storage Company, buried under Hunter's unpaid bills. I take out my cell phone and punch in the number. When the party on the other end picks up, I identify myself, explain the situation, and ask the guy for his help. After a slight pause, I get a polite but firm "I can only do it if you provide a death certificate and power of attorney or a subpoena." I tell him that shouldn't be a problem.

"Stop by around eight tonight and ask for George. Hold on a second."

When the guy returns, he informs me that Hunter's November bill is due soon. I'm about to tell him not to hold his breath, but instead I say, "I'll see what I can do."

I stand up and stretch my legs, then walk over to the window and gaze out at Maggie, who is sitting on a rope swing, which is hanging from a long elm tree branch. She looks like a carefree schoolgirl, her legs pumping in the air, her hair flying about. She's wearing a tight pair of blue jeans and a loose powder-blue sweatshirt. Maggie catches me staring and waves. I wave back, the warehouse bill fluttering in the air.

"I found the warehouse," I call out.

She places a hand to her ear and continues swinging.

I open the window. "The warehouse is in Long Island City."

She stops, runs over to me, slightly out of breath. "Great. Do you mind if I join you?"

I hesitate.

"I might be able to help. Besides, you'll be doing me a favor."

My eyes light up. "I will?"

"In a big way. Not that I mind taking the railroad, but it took over two hours to get here." She shrugs and smiles. "What can I say? I'm one of those New Yorkers who don't drive."

"Won't you be cutting your stay kind of short?" I say, trying not to be disappointed.

"Unfortunately, yes, but I should be getting back." She smiles thoughtfully, wipes her lips with her tongue. "I'm a little thirsty."

I motion to the rear door. "C'mon inside."

I shut the window and meet Maggie in the kitchen. Outside

of some green-looking food, the refrigerator is empty. "Sorry, all we have is water."

"Water's fine." She's about to reach for a glass. "Should I be touching this?"

"It's okay," I assure her. "Everything has already been checked and collected."

Maggie pours herself a glass. "Want some?"

"No, thanks," I say, then watch her take a long gulp.

"Nothing beats city water, but this isn't too bad," she jokes, wiping her mouth.

I let a few moments pass, then ask, "Maggie, do you know of anyone who might have wanted to harm Hunter? Outside of maybe Carol Warner?"

She thinks a moment. "Not really. But you have to understand that John was a celebrity. There are a lot of nutcases out there, Hank. Some psychopathic deviant might have taken issue with one of his columns. John's advice could be brutal at times."

I nod in agreement. "I'm going to contact the *City News*, find out if there were any threats made against him lately."

Maggie says, "Outside of the *News* people, I don't know of anyone you could ask. He had no family."

"You mean outside of his sister," I correct.

Maggie gives me a puzzled look. "What sister?"

"John's younger sister, Carol. She was here yesterday. A bit weird if you ask me."

Maggie puts up a hand. "John was an only child, Hank. He didn't have a sister."

I stare heavily past her, my mind racing.

"Don't you think I would have known if John had any siblings?" she says pointedly.

I blink hard. "But—"

"Hank, someone's been playing games with you. This woman

who claimed to be John's sister, you said she went by the name of Carol?"

"Right." I describe her.

Maggie bites her lower lip. "Hank, that sounds like—"

The piercing sound of Hunter's phone interrupts us. We exchange looks, then I race to retrieve it, but not before the answering machine kicks in, with Hunter's baritone voice coming alive, back from the dead. I press the stop button and pick up the phone.

"That's eerie," my secretary says.

"How come you called on this line?" I ask, confused.

"Hello to you, too, Hank."

"Sorry, Kate. I just wasn't expecting you. Or anybody for that matter. Is everything okay?"

"I've been trying to reach you on your cell phone. Don't you pick up for me anymore?" she asks, laughing lightly.

I remove my phone from its case, shake my head, then turn it back on.

"You turned if off again, didn't you?"

"I must be losing it."

"Anyway, you told me you were going to Hunter's place."

"Oh, right."

"Norman called and apologized for not getting back sooner, but he was in Riverhead and just picked up his messages. He said he remembered having one rider fitting Carol Hunter's description, only he didn't pick her up at Hunter's house. She wanted him to pick her up on the corner of Sound and Tulip and then drop her off at the Saint James railroad station."

I scratch my neck. "Strange place to be picked up. And dropped off. Did she say why?"

"Only that she was meeting a friend at the train station."

"You'd think her friend would have picked her up in Eastpoint. It's closer." I stop. "Of course, she probably wanted to stay as far away from Eastpoint as possible," I correct myself. "Did she tell Norman where she was heading after that?"

"No, and he was glad to get rid of her. He said she kept babbling to herself."

"Sounds like Charlie's experience with her." I glance over at Maggie, who appears to be engaged in Hunter's book collection. I whisper into the phone, "Did he mention anything about her carrying something with her?"

Kate snorts. "You mean like a painting?"

"Maybe."

"Can you just imagine?"

"In her mental state, nothing would surprise me."

"Testy, aren't we, boss? Must be that love tap she gave you. Anyway, I asked Norman the same question. He said she wasn't carrying anything other than a handbag."

"What time did he pick her up?"

"Around one."

I nod into the phone. "That sounds about right. Give Mick Reynolds from the hundred and ninth precinct in Queens a call and ask him to check out a Carol Warner in his database. All boroughs and the surrounding areas. Tell him I owe him one."

"Gotcha. You coming back soon?"

"In a while, why?"

"Peter Hopkins has been looking for you."

"Peter? Did he say what he wanted?"

"No, but he's very upset."

I sigh. "Okay, I'll be back in an hour."

I hang up and am about to remove the tape from the machine, but instead, I rewind it and press the play button, then wait for the one and only message to end.

Maggie and I exchange looks. "Who was that?" she asks.

I shrug. "Not sure. I'll take it back to the station and see if anyone recognizes the voice."

"She sounded desperate," Maggie says. "Scary desperate."

I nod, but let it go.

Hunter's living room suddenly becomes uncomfortably quiet. "I better get back to the office," I tell Maggie.

She nods and starts for the door. I follow Maggie outside, my lungs filling up with fresh Long Island air.

Somehow, with all of my problems, Eastpoint's brisk autumn weather never felt so good.

17

Inside the stationhouse, I find Kate alone, sitting at her desk painting her fingernails. She glances up, fans a hand at me, and says, "You like?"

I steady her hand to get a better look. I'm in a better place now that my recent discovery at Hunter's house might bring me closer to his killer. Or maybe my good mood is from being around Maggie. I pay Kate a rare compliment, tell her she looks great in any color. Then I quickly add, "Why the new shade?"

"I got tired of pink," she says, pulling her hand back. "You know me, always trying something new. It's called fire-engine red."

"Let me guess. You have a date with one of our volunteer firemen."

"Actually, I might have had a date if he hadn't died," she says, working on another nail. She glances up and gives me a wily look. "Or should I say, been murdered."

I frown. "I think you've been sniffing too much of that polish."

While Kate is finishing her pinky, she points out that her torso is missing from Hunter's collection.

I grab her wrist lightly. "Wayne was supposed to lock them up in my closet."

She motions to my office. "They're in there, all right. You don't think the Gestapo would give me a peek, do you?"

"Then?" I ask, taking the bait. "How did you find out?"

Kate's wolfish grin is followed by an admission. "Wayne likes the way I make coffee. He said I was spared." She then turns serious. "It doesn't look good, does it? I mean, this town wasn't meant to have another scandal."

The biggest scandal to hit Eastpoint before Hunter was when Kate's ex ran off with a young woman from a nearby town.

"We'll get through it," I say encouragingly. But Kate is right. If I don't find Hunter's killer, and soon, a number of husbands are going to be lining up to piss on Hunter's grave.

She nods, but her expression belies my confidence. "You think the paintings are connected to the murder, don't you?"

I shrug. "I'd rather not speculate."

"That means yes. How many women are we talking about?"

I hold up six fingers.

"That's half the town," she says, trying to make light of the situation.

"Of course, I'm hoping Hunter's killer was an outsider."

Kate motions to my head. "You mean like Hunter's sister?"

"Yeah, only Hunter didn't have a sister."

Kate leans back in her black swivel task chair. "You want to help me here, boss."

I give Kate a stern look. "Okay, but don't spread this around. The woman we met at Hunter's house was an impostor. Her real name is Carol Warner. And according to Hunter's ex, he was an only child."

Kate raises a brow.

I leave my secretary pondering that revelation. At least that will take her mind off her new fire-engine-red nail polish.

A large envelope from the medical examiner's office is waiting for me on top of my desk. I pick it up, hold it in my hands as though weighing it. I'm about to tear open one end and read the revised autopsy report when a faint knock on my door causes me to stop.

"It's open," I call out.

Peter Hopkins opens the door, peers at me with anxious eyes. He doesn't bother to enter.

Peter, one of Eastpoint's elder statesmen and a good family friend, is wearing a haggard expression. I suspect the reason for his visit has to do with one of Hunter's paintings. I feel his pain, but play innocent and beckon him in. "Peter, what brings you out of the store at this hour?"

He struggles toward me without answering.

Peter Hopkins is not only a good friend; he is also Eastpoint's druggist, who has kept Susan's antidepressant medication a secret, so I owe him. Only I was hoping my friendly druggist wasn't looking for payback today.

Peter's breathing is labored. "Hank," he says in a tone more formal than usual. He stops at my desk, his hands leaning on it for support. His sullen expression begs to be relieved of his burden.

"What can I do for you?" I ask, as though Peter is about to ask me to fix a parking ticket.

He clears his throat. "There's talk."

"What kind of talk?" I ask, throwing the burden back on him.

He clears his throat again, swallows hard. "Come on, Hank, don't make this any harder on me. It's all over town."

I sigh. "If you're referring to the evidence we found at Hunter's place," I say, my head tilting toward my closet. "I locked them up."

He points a gnarled finger at me. "Is that what you call that crap, Hank? Evidence?"

This is not going to be a friendly visit.

Peter slips his arthritic hand in his pocket. "How much?"

I watch Hopkins pull out a wad of bills. "Come on, Peter, let's not go there."

He gazes at the bribe money, then shoves it back in his

pocket. He averts his eyes. "For chrissake, Hank, my marriage is already destroyed." He stops, faces me tentatively. "Please don't humiliate me."

I drop the report on my desk, walk around it, and place a friendly arm on his shoulder. "Peter, I understand your concern. I'll try—"

"You don't know what it's like," he snaps, shaking my arm off with effort. "She's a slut!"

I wince, cross the room, and shut the door. "Don't you think I want those paintings destroyed?" I say, returning to him. "I can't do that right now."

Hopkins glares. "You owe me, Hank."

I lower my eyes a moment. "I know, Peter, and I appreciate your friendship."

"The town is not happy about this," he threatens.

I throw my hands up. "Jesus, Peter, we just found them."

He snorts. "Don't be so foolish, Hank. You know we're all connected. Nothing gets past us." He pauses. "Except deep secrets between friends."

I squeeze my eyelids. Personal fear overrides everything. And this town has been insulated from fear; it is foreign to us. I explain my position to Peter, reminding him that he and the others townspeople elected me to uphold the law.

"We're all victims, goddammit! That bastard was an *auslander*."

"I realize that, Peter, but the law requires an investigation. The killer could be one of us."

He waves a hand. "Who cares? He's dead. Let it be suicide."

"We're not dead, Peter," I say, attempting to tap into his moral compass.

He shakes his head in disgust. "What do those fucking paintings have to do with anything?"

"I don't know," I say honestly. "But I have to follow through on all the *participants*." I pause. "Look, Peter, I don't like this any more than you do. Those women are friends of mine, too."

Peter finally broaches the real reason for his visit. "So you think Jackie might have killed him?"

I've been waiting for the question, and I admit that every woman Hunter painted is a suspect at this point until I get alibis.

"You're crazy, Hank. You know that? We'll be laughed out of this town." He points a finger at my chest. "You wouldn't be doing this if Susan's tits were gonna be displayed in public."

I attempt to assuage Peter, tell him that *when* I find Hunter's killer, those paintings will be history.

He shakes his head. "Why don't I believe you, Hank?"

I'm getting nowhere with Peter, and so I change the subject, become more the interrogator. "Did Hunter come to you for Halcion?"

Peter evidently doesn't care for my line of questioning and gazes out the window without saying a word.

I ask again. "Did Hunter ever ask you to fill a prescription for sedatives?"

His gaze returns indoors, searches the floor. "I don't remember, why?"

Peter might be old and frail, but he still possesses a great mind. He's evading my question, testing me, and with good reason.

I press. "Come on, Peter, Hunter got sleeping pills from somewhere. And you own the only pharmacy in town."

Peter has had time to mull over my question. He must know I'm only speculating. He finally says, "He could have gotten the prescription anywhere. Did you check the store label?"

He knows I must have looked, and therefore knows I wouldn't be asking him if there was a label on the vial. I take another, more sensitive approach. "What about Jackie? Maybe she—"

"Sleeping pills didn't kill the bastard!" he roars, his tired, aging jaw jutting aggressively.

Christ, the autopsy report must have been published in *Newsday*. I backpedal slightly, not wanting to admit that Hunter most likely died from poisoned bourbon. Instead, I tell him that the sleeping pills might have been tainted.

Peter shrugs. "What can I say, Hank? I can't help you."

I try another angle. "What about you, Peter? Do you have an alibi?"

He sneers. "Jackie and I were together all night. Ask her."

"I will."

Peter looks as though he's about to have a coronary. "Whatever makes you happy, Hank. If you're not going to arrest me, I'm leaving."

I don't need to give him permission, so Peter turns, trudges toward the door. When his hand reaches for the doorknob, he stops. "I thought we were friends," he says with resignation, not looking back, and then disappears.

I grab the phone and dial Jackie, hoping she's sober.

"Hello?" Her voice is faint, but at least she's home.

"Jackie," I say casually. "It's Hank."

"Oh, hi. Looking for Peter?" she slurs.

I turn toward the window. "No. I need to ask you a few questions."

There's an uncomfortable silence.

"Where did Hunter get Halcion?"

More silence.

"Jackie?"

"What's that, Hank?"

I watch Peter walking back to his store. "Sleeping pills. Did you provide him with any?"

Silence.

"Jackie?"

"Gee, Hank, Peter's not here."

"I'm asking *you*, goddammit! Did you supply Hunter with pills?"

I imagine Jackie staring at a wall or the tube, but she's not with me. "I don't understand why you're asking me that, Hank."

"We found the paintings, Jackie."

She manages to say, "Do I need a lawyer, Hank?"

"You need to tell me what happened. Look, I know you and Hunter were lovers."

She whispers something unintelligible into the phone.

"Six months ago?" I say, grasping her meaning. "Where were you the night he was killed?"

"Hank, I don't feel so good. I gotta go."

"Stay with me, Jackie . . ."

The phone goes dead.

18

There is a refreshing charm in the air as Maggie and I drive through the heart of Long Island City, its streets lined with cobblestones. We pass a row of prewar buildings, fire escapes attached to the front, and mom-and-pop stores, which seem to thrive despite the Walmarts of this world. Long Island City is an urban community where kids can still play stickball in the street.

Long Island City also has the advantage of sitting across from Manhattan, divided from it only by the East River. The million-dollar view is relatively cheap and the rewards plentiful. Though there are a number of factories and smokestacks scattered unevenly about, the City's beauty lies within. Long Island City became the first town in Queens leading out of Manhattan, a place where early-twentieth-century immigrants lived and worked and where their children and grandchildren still reside.

Maggie has been sharing history with me, and I'm captivated by her presence, though I am completely out of my element. I haven't been this close to the Big Apple since Susan and I celebrated our fifth wedding anniversary. Great weekend; too many people.

But here I am, feeling comfortable and away from my troubles, if only for a few hours. The air is crisp. Manhattan's skyline glistens and is within reach. Sitting next to a beautiful woman doesn't hurt either.

We arrive at the City Storage Company warehouse, its perimeter wrapped in barbed wire, and are met by a guard at the front gate, who studies my shield and asks a few questions. I hand him the legal documents he requests, which he compares to some computer-generated printout. Satisfied, he directs me to the main building.

Inside the drab, quiet facility, a red arrow sitting on top of a pole directs us to a hallway, which Maggie and I follow until we reach a guy sitting back in a chair, his face stuffed inside the *Post*. "Prompt," he says, not bothering to look up.

Maggie and I exchange glances.

He lifts his eyes over the paper, studies me, then Maggie, staying a little longer on Maggie.

"Evening," I wave.

When the guy drops the paper, I notice he's wearing a nametag on a dark green plaid shirt that reads, "Hi, I'm George Garis."

He catches me studying his tag and motions us to follow him.

"Friendly guy," I whisper to Maggie.

She giggles.

Garis, who is walking with a slight limp, stops in front of a door on the far side of the warehouse. He shoves a hand in his pocket and removes a key. "That's it." He motions with his nose and drops the key in my hand. "I'll take it on the way out."

"Hey," I call as he leaves. "Don't you wanna see some ID?"

He waves me off without turning. "The guard already told me you were coming." Then he disappears.

"Must be the evening shift."

Maggie giggles again, but this time I sense a slight apprehension in her laugh.

Hunter's storage area is no bigger than a large walk-in closet. I locate the light switch and flip it on, look around. Except for a small metal chair squeezed between two metal cabinets, the room is bare. Then again, it wasn't meant to be lived in.

Maggie stays outside. "Maybe you oughta do this alone, Hank."

I nod in agreement.

"I'll be over by friendly George."

I watch Maggie leave, then open the cabinet closest to the door. Inside the top drawer, I find an alphabetical listing of Hunter's patients. Judging by the number he had on the list, I'd say he had a pretty impressive practice. Carol Warner's name appears at the bottom of the fourth page. I smile to myself, then search a few drawers, thumbing through beige manila folders before arriving at the Ws. Her file should be sandwiched between Paul Verity and Joanne Williams, but it's missing. I guess that shouldn't surprise me. Hunter probably destroyed it like *she* destroyed him.

Disappointed, I return to the first drawer and thumb through a few patient files. Hunter was meticulous and consistent in his format. Each file contained a detailed history of his client, which is how he refers to them, starting with their prognosis. Straightforward, yet interesting stuff: phobias, neurosis, compulsive behaviors, sprinkled with strange dreams and weird fantasies.

John Hunter explored the inner world, the psyche most people don't understand. And he was apparently good at it. At least the progress on his analysis sheets suggested as much. I'm looking for a pattern, but also a connection, something in his writing that might reveal Hunter's own psyche. And, of course, a possible link to his murder.

I exhaust the first cabinet with little more than a sense of the profession. Other than proving that mental illness exists, I find nothing unusual about Hunter, the man or psychologist. Nor do the files offer me any leads to a suspect.

I drum the top of the second cabinet with my fingers a few moments before opening the next drawer. After flipping through a few more patients' files, I come across an untitled folder. I remove it and slide myself into the hard metal chair. As I begin to read, I get a picture of a more intriguing and colorful character. Apparently, John Hunter liked writing journals.

The professional life of John Hunter began shortly after he received his PhD in psychology. He took a much-needed vacation to San Juan, Puerto Rico, staying at a local hotel, then returning to New York City two weeks later. He worked six stories above Madison Avenue and Thirty-first Street with a group of psychologists.

At the time, Hunter's diary consisted of dates with brief notations. His mind was clear; an idealist at heart, he had high aspirations of becoming a worthy therapist. I scan through the pages and decide that Hunter was in control of his life back then.

The next journal picks up a few years into his practice. Hunter's expectations had begun to diminish: dollars per session, number of clients per week, less on ideology, more on the American way. By then, he and Maggie had married, she moving into his Manhattan apartment. He wrote about their love and devotion toward each other. I suddenly feel like a voyeur and glance over to the door.

I skim through the journal and stop somewhere in the middle. Hunter's once tender and passionate voice gets lost as though another author had taken over. He writes about his sudden insatiable sexual appetite. His once brief and tender comments are now graphic, similar to his columns. Words describing their acts are no longer dictionary friendly and are commonplace. His bedroom becomes a sexual gutter; he and Maggie explored every inch of their apartment, Maggie reluctantly becoming a willing participant. "Maggie's sexual repression has been lifted; she is finally liberated," Hunter writes like a conquering warrior.

My heart pounds from a mixture of excitement and jealousy, yet I feel guilty for entering their most intimate life.

"I got bored."

My head snaps up. "Hi."

"Sorry. I have a habit of doing that. How's the reading coming along?"

My hand attempts to cover the page. "Okay."

"I've been chatting with our friend out front. He tells me the last time John checked in was the day before he was killed."

I ease out of my chair. "Really? He was here?"

She nods. "But before that, he hadn't been here in over a year."

I smile. "Remind me to pin a detective's badge on you later."

She returns the smile. "Maybe over dinner."

I check my watch. "I'm sorry, Maggie. I hadn't realized how late it was."

I start returning a few files when Maggie says, "Our friend told me about a woman they found snooping around outside trying to get access to John's storage room."

I turn. "When was this?"

"The day before John was here. The guard wouldn't let her in because she wasn't listed as an authorized person." Maggie pauses. "She claimed to be John's wife."

"Carol Warner?"

She nods repeatedly. "Has to be, according to the guy's description of her. Remember, she was stalking him."

I thumb back to the cabinet. "Her patient file is missing."

"I'm not surprised, Hank. It was a very painful time for John. He probably destroyed it."

Maggie's sullen expression is obviously a painful reminder of the past.

"You hungry?" I say, changing the subject.

She smiles tentatively. "Famished."

95

"Give me a few minutes to wrap up, okay?"

Her eyes stray to the open file cabinet. "Sure."

I close Hunter's journal and place it on top of the cabinet before thumbing through the rest of the file, when my eyes catch a folder titled "Miscellaneous." As I remove it, several photographs drop to the floor and scatter about. I glance down, then over at Maggie, whose eyes are glued to the glossies. Before I have a chance to retrieve them, she scoops a few up.

Evidently, Hunter had an interest in photography and was adept at using a self-timer; one photo showed Carol Warner lying on her back smiling for the camera while Hunter's hard dick was about to enter her. I can only imagine what Maggie was looking at.

"You shouldn't be looking—"

She waves me off. "It's okay," she snaps.

But it's not okay, and I can't help her. I give her time to let loose whatever emotion she needs to release and thumb through the last of the files, checking the likes of a legal document that closed down Hunter's passion for therapy and a copy of his restraining order against Warner.

I close Hunter's past, scoop up the files I'm interested in, take Maggie by the arm, and lead her out the door.

"Sorry you had to see these," I say, removing the photos from her clenched hand.

She shakes her head. "Just another reminder."

I return the key back to "Hi, I'm Mr. Personable," who must be a slow reader because he's still nosing through the sports section. "You need a release for these?"

Without glancing up, he says, "Just send a check by next week."

Right.

Maggie and I cross the Fifty-ninth Street bridge in silence, the city now feeling dirty, drab.

"Still hungry?" I ask, turning to her.

She shakes her head slowly. "If you don't mind, I'll take a rain check."

"I understand. I really should be getting back anyway."

"I appreciate the lift," she says, touching my shoulder softly.

"Hey, I really enjoyed the company," I tell her, my voice giving way to disappointment.

I pull up in front of Maggie's apartment, shove the car in park, and start fidgeting with the wheel. I'm afraid to turn to her. Afraid she might see disappointment on my face.

"Would you like to come up for a while, Hank?"

My eyes turn to meet hers. My marriage is in the garbage can, and I'm vulnerable right now. Maggie's hand is inching toward mine, which is still holding on to the steering wheel for support. When she touches me, the familiar warmth returns, relaxing my hand. She smiles. I can't tell if the smile is friendly or seductive. I'm trying to resist the temptation, trying hard to stay focused. This could get complicated, Hank. The investigation is a priority. Or is it?

I turn to Maggie's hand, her fingers sliding playfully up and down, causing my heart to pump faster. I focus on her nails and for a split second I'm thinking *fire-engine red*.

A quick blast of radio static fills the car, killing whatever decision was in my head.

I scowl and pick up the receiver. "What's up?"

"It's Peter Hopkins," Wayne answers in a rush.

"What about him?"

"He's dead, Hank."

"Hold on, Wayne." I place the receiver on mute and glance back at Maggie; her hand is no longer on mine. "I better go."

She nods slowly, her lips pressing against each other, then reaches for her overnight bag from the back seat and opens the door. She offers a thin smile. "See you, Hank."

The fragrance of Maggie's perfume stays with me, and I take a deep breath to keep my day with Maggie alive. I watch her walk slowly, her eyes settling on the ground. I press the talk button. "How?"

"He killed himself."

"Oh, Peter."

"There's more, Hank. We found a suicide note near his body. Peter confessed to killing Hunter."

19

Peter Hopkins' young widow, Jackie, hasn't responded to any of my questions; she barely recognizes my presence. Her glazed eyes have settled on the tube, where a talk show host was sitting between two women who had undergone sex change operations. The significance of this segment was the similarity of their faces. They're identical twins, separated at birth, who later discovered each other after their sex changes. It's enough to make me want to join Jackie with whatever she's on.

"Did you see Peter take the pills?" I ask, tapping Jackie's shoulder for the third time.

Her eyes remain on the tube, but she manages to shake her head slowly. I gather that's a no, but it's an improvement nonetheless.

I've been standing in Jackie's living room for the last fifteen minutes, five of which were trying to wake her up. She's wearing wrinkled jeans and an equally wrinkled t-shirt that reads, "Smile If You're Horny."

"Wayne told me you called the stationhouse around eight. Is that when you found Peter slumped over on his desk?"

She blinks several times, sniffles.

"I gather you didn't see him write the suicide note?"

A few tears form. "He killed 'im, Hank."

"I know, I read the note. Did Peter tell you he came to see me yesterday?"

She turns, looks through me.

"It had to do with Hunter," I tell her.

Jackie blinks a few times. "Peter thought you were gonna arrest me."

"He took the rap for you, Jackie. We both know you killed Hunter—"

Jackie shakes her head violently. "That's not true!"

"Settle down, Jackie. I needed to ask for the record."

She begins to weep softly.

"Peter found out about your affair and killed Hunter, then killed himself. Does that about sum up the story, Jackie?"

I give her time to wipe her eyes before continuing. "The investigators found a prescription near Peter's body, Celebrex, for his arthritis. We don't know yet how many he took or if it killed him, but the lab didn't find poison in the remaining pills." I pause. "And since Peter didn't have convulsions like Hunter did, we know he didn't taint the pills with rat poison. That would make sense since Peter didn't need rat poison to die." I stop. "Unlike Hunter."

Jackie sheds a few more tears, only this time I'm not sure which deceased she's crying over.

I rub my temples. "You have to help me here, Jackie. Why would Peter kill Hunter *now?* I mean, you told me yesterday your affair ended six months ago."

Jackie's silence tells me otherwise.

"For Chrissake, were you still sleeping with Hunter?"

Her limp arms flap in the air. "A few times, Hank. Please don't hate me."

Fucking Hunter had a revolving door to his stud farm. "Even though he was screwing half the town?"

"He said he needed me."

"Oh, he needed you, all right," I say. "You were his delivery girl."

"That's not true!"

"Think about it, Jackie. Hunter didn't need a prescription. He had you. And sex was your reward."

Jackie starts to protest, then stops.

"Face it, Jackie, Hunter used you."

She wipes her pasty mouth. "He needed them. Needed me."

"Right. And Peter found out."

Jackie pulls at her hair. "It was Peter's fault," she cries. "He surprised me at the store so I had to lie, tell him I needed something to help me sleep."

"This happened the night of Hunter's murder," I say, completing the picture.

She nods. "He gave me that look, like he knew I was up to something and told me to come back later."

"And?"

She shrugs. "When I returned, he handed them to me."

"How many pills?"

She thinks a moment. "Just two. He said it was plenty for the time being."

Peter wasn't kidding, especially if they were loaded with rat poison. But if only the bourbon was laced with strychnine as Gloria suggested, Hunter probably wouldn't have died on two pills. And Peter's suicide note never revealed how he killed Hunter. He kept it open-ended, simple, like Hunter had done— or, that is to say, the suicide scribe did. I can only guess that Peter wasn't specific because he didn't kill Hunter. If his note described the crime, and he was wrong, then Peter's suicide would have been executed needlessly. I sigh. Peter's admission to Hunter's murder was his final gift to Jackie and the town he loved, to spare them further humiliation. He knew I couldn't stop the investigation without finding the killer and so he decided to take the fall.

I smile sadly. I knew better, of course. While I know Peter to be an honorable person, his suicide was actually his last gift to himself. He was dying. Only a few intimate friends, including me, knew that he had a brain tumor. He hadn't even told Jackie. So suicide wasn't a leap for Peter. It was a blessing in the long run.

Nevertheless, I ask Jackie, "How did Peter convince you to take a bottle of Jack Daniel's over to Hunter's place that night?"

"Bourbon?"

I nod. "We found an opened bottle in Hunter's living room laced with poison."

"Poison in the bottle?"

"Yup."

She blinks hard, but my comment doesn't register.

"Peter must have wanted you to watch your lover die a slow, painful death. Some kind of morbid penance for your sins." I pause. "What about you, Jackie? Do you drink bourbon?"

My meaning finally hits her. She glares. "That's not funny, Hank."

"No, but if Peter killed Hunter, how did he manage to get the bourbon over to his place if *you* didn't bring it?"

"Hank, I swear, it wasn't me."

"Damn it, Jackie, you delivered the pills!"

"John couldn't sleep."

"He can now, honey!"

Jackie holds her head in her hands, mumbling something about her professed love for Hunter. I roll my eyes. Sick puppy.

"Are you gonna arrest me, Hank?" she asks, peering up at me.

Jackie's histrionic skills appeared to have worked for the moment. "Not if you're telling me the truth," I tell her. But to put the fear of God in her, I warn Jackie that I won't tolerate lying, that jail time is one lie away.

"What about the painting?" she asks innocently.

I wave a hand. "If I don't need it, it's yours. Hang it up on your wall for all I care!"

"And the others?"

"I'll carve them up into little pieces."

"Including Susan's?"

I freeze.

"I've seen them all, Hank."

I remain silent, calculating.

"It was his last," Jackie says, her voice turning cold.

Maybe the fear of God is working. Jackie claims she found it by accident the night of the murder.

"After you delivered the pills and had sex?" I say disapprovingly.

"We didn't make love that night," she insists. "I was upset and left after seeing the painting." She looks at me sympathetically. "I didn't wanna have to tell you, Hank."

I give my forehead a good wipe with my hand. I ask Jackie what condition the painting was in.

Her expression changes, shows confusion. "Like the others. Why?"

"Susan's painting wasn't . . . tampered with?"

Jackie shakes her head. "Susan was on her knees—"

I put a hand up in protest. "Please, spare me the details." My mouth is dry but I force out, "Did you ever see them together?"

Jackie shakes her head slowly. "That's why I was upset. I didn't know. I figured he was still with *her.*"

"Sheryl?"

Jackie waves a hand. "He was bored with her."

Jackie notices my confusion. "Because of the painting, Hank. Every time John took a new lover he'd do a portrait of her."

I bow my head, stare at the dark parquet floor. Suddenly I feel Jackie's warm breath on me, her hands stroking my hair. "I know how you feel, Hank."

I don't answer her.

"Whaddaya gonna do?"

"I really don't know," I answer truthfully.

"You can always stay here."

My instinct tells me Jackie is just being neighborly, but I don't need another scandal on my hands. "Thanks, but I'm gonna stay with Wayne a while."

"Oh. That's nice."

Nice is a Nissan 370Z. Staying with Wayne isn't what I'd consider nice. "I appreciate your offer anyway."

We remain silent for a moment. "I gotta pee, Hank." Jackie excuses herself, giving me time to clear my head. When she returns, her eyes are more focused.

I study her for a moment. "Any idea on how Peter wrote Hunter's suicide note?"

She shrugs. "I really don't know, Hank."

"And you didn't see anyone snooping around Hunter's place that night?"

She shakes her head. "It was just me and John."

"Just you and John."

20

As I approach Rusty's Spirits, the Miller Lite neon sign is lit up inside the window. Rusty's son is dusting off a few wine bottles and looking bored. When I open the door, he glances over and offers me an uneven smile. "Say, Hank, it's a little early to be buying beer."

I smile back, glance around. "Morning, Junior. Your father around?"

He points to the window. "Dad stopped off at Breyerharts for coffee. He should be back in a minute."

"That's okay. Maybe you can help me. I was wondering how much bourbon you sell?"

Junior fixes his eyes on the ceiling. "Bourbon?"

"Jack Daniel's, to be exact."

Junior fidgets, rubs his chin, then glances over at me. "Hold on a second, I'll check." He walks down the aisle where the hard stuff is shelved, shifts a few bottles around, then turns and gives me a shrug. "We're stocked, Hank. Not much of a market for it these days. Vodka is our big seller."

I nod. "I'm thinking over the past week, month maybe. Any takers?"

He takes a moment, then says, "I personally haven't sold any, but you might wanna check with Dad. He locks up at night."

I nose toward the back. "Your dad keep any records on what he sells?"

Junior shrugs nervously. "Gee, Hank, I'm not sure."

"That's okay, Junior. Maybe I will wait for your dad to come back."

"Can I offer you something, Hank?" he asks with a slight stutter. Junior knows I don't drink on duty.

"Thanks anyway, son. I'll just hang out if you don't mind."

He points to a cardboard carton sitting on the floor. "I better get back to work."

"You go ahead."

Junior peers outside, then excuses himself and goes back to dusting.

I watch him remove a few bottles of Grey Goose from the carton, blow off a few particles of dust, then place them neatly on the shelf.

I drift over to him and ask, "Holds twelve, right?"

He nods, continues stocking without glancing up.

I let him stock the rest of the bottles before asking, "What's the gossip like these days?"

"Talk?"

"You know, about Hunter?"

He stands up, wipes his hands on his jeans, then shrugs. "Not much as I can tell. I mind my own business."

"How about me and the investigation?" I probe.

Junior shoves his hands in his pockets, averts his eyes. "I hear a little. Some people are upset."

"With me?"

He digs deeper. "Gee, Hank, I think you're just doing your job. A man gets murdered and you're looking for the guy who did it."

Right. The guy. "They think I should be putting the investigation to bed."

He remains silent.

"That's okay, son. I don't want to make you feel uncomfortable."

Junior fixes his eyes on the neon light. "It's just that they're scared on account of . . . the paintings."

I smile warmly. "Your father has nothing to worry about, Junior."

He blinks, then lets out enough air in his chest to fill up a room. "Really?"

"Your mom's a nice lady."

"Gee, Hank, thanks."

Junior's mother can shoulder a half-dozen cases of beer and walk through a field of cow dung without blinking. Definitely not Hunter's type. "I gotta do my job, son. Ask sensitive questions, stuff like that."

"I know that, Hank."

"The town's gotta trust my judgment on this. I'm not out to hurt anyone."

"It's not me, Hank. I know you wouldn't do that to nobody."

I pat him on his crown. "You're a good kid, Junior."

The front door opens, and a man in his mid-forties with thinning gray hair enters. He stiffens as he catches Junior and me huddling together. I'm beginning to think I'm the Grim Reaper.

"Hank."

"Say, Rusty."

He turns to Junior. "Son, why don't you take a break and go in the back for a while."

"That's okay, Rusty. I was just telling Junior you have nothing to worry about. You know, 'bout Hunter."

Tension eases off Rusty's body, and he mumbles something like *thank God*.

"But I have to ask you a few questions anyway."

"What about?" he asks guardedly.

"I need to know if you sold any Jack Daniel's over the past few weeks."

His hesitates, then says, "I'm not sure. Why?"

"It might help the investigation," I say, trying to keep it simple.

"How come?"

It's never simple. "We found poison inside the bourbon that killed Hunter."

"I didn't do it, Hank! I swear."

I put up my palms to calm him. "Easy, Rusty. I'm not accusing you of anything. I'm looking for your customer."

He thinks a moment, then says, "Gee, Hank, I thought you already had the case solved. You know, the note." He doesn't mention Peter Hopkins by name.

"I know what the note says, Rusty. But I have to follow through on some loose ends just the same."

His eyes stay on me a moment before asking, "So you think whoever bought the bourbon killed Hunter?"

"It's possible."

He cocks his head. "Jesus, Hank, you're really screwing around with people's lives. If *he* claimed he did it, let it be. Why do you want to hurt more innocent people?"

I grit my teeth, edge closer to Rusty. "As much as everyone would like to accept Peter's statement, I don't think he did it." I pause, keeping his stare. "Wouldn't you rather I find the real killer than falsely convict *our* friend?"

He stops, but only for a moment. "The town isn't happy about this, Hank. There's talk."

There's always talk.

"Look, you've been a great sheriff, always taking care of things. Of us. Why can't you just take care of this? Make it go away."

They call me "sheriff" out of affection, so I believe Rusty is still my friend, especially now that his wife hasn't been included in Hunter's repertoire. "I am taking care of it, Rusty. What if it was one of *us* who were killed? Wouldn't you want me to investigate every angle?"

"It's not the same," he snaps. "That . . . evidence doesn't belong here. We're good people. We don't deserve this."

I nod. "And the women in the paintings, they live here. They're good people, too, but one of them might have killed Hunter. Or one of their husbands. We already assumed Peter did it."

Rusty studies me, realizes he's not winning.

"I'm not going to show those paintings to anyone if I don't have to. I told Peter that."

Rusty wipes his mouth. "What if I told you Peter bought the bourbon the day of the murder? Would you accept that, burn the stuff, and stop the investigation?"

I turn to Junior, whose eyes are anxiously fixed on his father. I ask him to go in the back, away from the lies.

"Go ahead, son," Rusty tells him.

I turn back to Rusty. "Peter was your friend, for God's sake! Can you live with that? Blaming an innocent man for murder—a friend—knowing that someone else might have killed Hunter?" I stop, jab a finger at his chest. "Or is that what you and the others want me to do if I want to keep my job?"

Rusty kneads his hands and waits a moment, then he says in a conciliatory tone, "Peter's dead, Hank. We can't bring him back. Why not let him save us?"

The disapproving expression on my face doesn't change. I tell Rusty I have to sleep nights.

"Don't you see what's gonna happen?" he explodes, anointing me with his spit. "This town will be front-page news. It'll be like a circus. People driving all over Eastpoint staring at us like freaks. Is that what *you* want, Hank? More Hunters moving into town looking for free pussy!"

"Are you going to tell me if you sold any Jack Daniel's?" I

demand. "Or are you trying to impede my investigation?"

Rusty locks his eyes on mine. "Can't remember."

"Fine." I storm out the door.

"People are going to remember this at election time!" he calls after me.

I pick up my pace and find myself heading toward the center of town. People are throwing darts at me with their eyes. Fuck them all!

"Hank."

I stop short. Junior is standing in an alley between the deli and bakery.

He makes a few furtive glances around, then motions to me. "I shouldn't be telling you this, but Dad keeps a log on everything we sell. We haven't sold that brand of bourbon you asked about in about a month." He stops, glances around nervously.

"Go on, Junior."

"So I checked the log over the past year," he says hurriedly.

"And?

"It was Hunter. He generally purchased a bottle once a month."

"Jack Daniel's?"

He nods.

I wipe my brow. "So he was due to make another purchase this month but hadn't yet," I say, almost to myself.

Junior shrugs. "Apparently."

"And you're sure no one else bought any within the past month?"

"Well, except for Salty's. They usually buy a case at a time."

I raise a brow. "When was the last time they bought a case?"

"I checked. It was the day Hunter was killed. Only . . ."

"Tell me, Junior."

"They didn't want a case this time, just a bottle. Said they'd pick it up later that day."

My eyes light up. "You took the call?"

"I wanted to tell you before, but Dad told me I shouldn't get involved. It just isn't right, though."

I smile warmly at the kid. "You did the right thing, son. What time did Sheryl call?"

"Not Sheryl. Paddy."

21

Adrenaline pumps through my body as the patrol car barrels down Christmas Lane.

"You're gonna die, you bastard," Hunter wrote in his journal. "It was a foreign voice, only it wasn't foreign to me." Why hadn't I picked up on Paddy's brogue before?

When I reach Salty's, Sheryl is waiting on a customer. I hold off until she takes his order. She's about to head toward the kitchen when she catches me waving at the entrance like I'm attempting to stop an oncoming car.

Sheryl approaches. "Say, Hank," she says, an apprehensive look on her face.

"I know about you and Hunter," I snap out quickly.

Sheryl's shoulders slacken. "Can we talk about this later?" she says, stealing a furtive glance inside the restaurant.

"Sheryl . . ."

"C'mon, Hank," she begs, turning back to me. "We can't talk out here. You know I'm not going anywhere."

Unlike Jackie, I can trust Sheryl. Only I can't afford to wait until she creates a solid alibi. "Just a few," I insist. "Then we'll meet after you get off."

She screws up her mouth. "Okay." Then she adds, "For the record, Paddy doesn't know."

The spouse is always the last to know. When I discovered the paintings in Hunter's attic, I came across one of Sheryl and Hunter. Yet I couldn't account for it when I brought the collection back to the station. So I mention it without being accusatory.

"Missing?"

"You didn't remove it, I gather?"

"Of course not," she stutters. "I was devastated when I heard you found them." She stops, narrows her eyes on me. "Then how do you know it's missing?"

I inform Sheryl about my discovery and how I hadn't wanted the other investigators to see my treasure trove, so I returned later that night. "Yours was missing," I tell her. I leave out the part that hers wasn't the only painting taken, though perhaps Sheryl was well aware of that, too. "I find it a little too coincidental," I continue, "that your painting went missing the same night Hunter was killed."

"Well, it wasn't me," she defends.

I nod unconvincingly. "Then maybe Paddy knows more about you and the paintings than you think, Sheryl. Maybe it's Paddy I need to speak to."

Sheryl tugs at my sleeve, pulls me outside. "Hank, please don't." When she realizes I'm not giving in, she says, "Besides, people are saying Peter Hopkins did it, that he confessed."

I assure Sheryl that Peter is posthumously innocent. "Where was Paddy the night of the murder?"

She shrugs. "At the bar, I guess. Look Hank—"

"Till closing?" I interrupt.

"I don't know. I wasn't here."

"Because you were with Hunter." I pause, let it sink in. "It's not a question, Sheryl."

Sheryl gazes into the distance. "Hank, I get off at five. Meet me at Rocky Beach on the far end around six." She pauses. "I don't want anyone knowing about our meeting. You understand?"

"I'll be there."

Then she says in a rush, "There are a few things at John's house you might want to find before anyone else does."

My eyes catch a shadow coming toward us. It's Paddy. Sheryl registers my concern and stops.

The door opens, and Paddy emerges. He stares heavily at us. "I was wondering what happened to you, Sheryl."

Sheryl glances over her shoulder and smiles thinly at Paddy. "A few customers ran out of coffee."

She nods rapidly. "Catch you around, Hank. Send Susan my regards."

Paddy keeps the door open for his wife, but he remains standing there and studies me for a moment. "Say, Hank, what brings you around this hour of the day?"

I shrug. "I thought I'd stop by for a Jack Daniel's on the rocks."

He offers a wide, mischievous grin. "I thought you were a beer guy. How about a Samuel Adams?" he says, motioning his head inside.

I take a step toward Paddy. "I need to ask you a few questions about John Hunter's murder."

Paddy recoils, his expression turning cold.

"When did you find out?" I ask pointedly.

He rubs his chin, softens his look on me. "About the murder? Let me see, I read it in the newspaper." He shakes his head. "Sad."

I shake my own head disapprovingly. "Are we gonna play the *questions game,* or should I spell it out for you?"

Paddy hunches his shoulders, his hazel eyes narrowing in on me. "A couple of weeks ago, okay?"

"And you threatened Hunter."

"Threatened him!" he says, his brogue punctuating the air. "That bastard was sleeping with my wife!" Paddy stops, composes himself. "What would you do, Hank?" he says, flashing a quick smile. "That Hunter was some stud, huh, Hank?"

"I'll ask the questions, goddammit."

Paddy motions me to the side, smiles at a few patrons entering the restaurant. "Okay, I had a few words with him," he says calmly. "I was pissed off. But if you're accusing me of murder, forget it."

"So if I asked whether you stopped by his house that night and offered him a swig of bourbon, you'd deny it?"

He snorts. "Right, like he'd open the door and let me pour him a drink. Get real, Hank. Besides, as far as I know, he was a beer drinker." He offers a quick, nervous smile. "Why? Were my fingerprints on the bottle?"

I resist the urge to tell Paddy that only Hunter's prints were found on the bottle. Instead, my silence throws him off guard.

Paddy searches the floor, tugs on his tight ponytail, then says calmly, "I thought you had your man."

"We both know Peter didn't do it."

Paddy nods a few times like he's about to broach something important, then savors a smile and spreads his arms like a cormorant. "Hell, Hank, I couldn't have killed him. Don't you remember? You stopped by that night on account of the altercation." He stops for emphasis. "As I recall, it was just before the ten-twenty-two train took off for the city."

It dawns on me that Paddy has the perfect alibi. Me. Staged? Perhaps. But the bar was jumping. Paddy could have easily slipped out the back for a quick murder. That is, if Hunter was cooperative and let him in for a drink.

Paddy is gloating, watching me trying to piece together his moves. He waits patiently, knowing he has me by the balls. But before I attempt to chip away at his rock-solid alibi, he says, "And as for Sheryl, she was here until closing, too."

22

It's not exactly a beach night. A light mist, which had been off and on for most of the afternoon, has turned into fog and heavy rain. Not that I'm concerned. I can find my way to Rocky Beach with my eyes closed. My mother taught me how to drive on that road after my father, who had little patience for such things, deferred to her; he had been arguing that a sixteen-year-old should pick up driving naturally. Easy for him to say. My father learned to drive on my grandfather's potato farm and rarely contended with more than a few slow-moving farm animals.

I glance at the patrol car's digital clock as I pass the beach shack. I doubt if Sheryl has arrived yet. In her state of mind, she'd be concerned that someone would spot her and wonder what she was doing there alone on a dark, rainy night in October. "Waiting for the chief of police, of course. Hmm!"

As planned, my car is sitting on the west side of the beach, where even during the summer folks don't bother to go: too many rocks. Hopefully, no one will decide to take a walk on the beach tonight. Paranoia!

I lower my window to draw in just enough air, without inviting the rain, and I lean back in my seat, my head snuggling against the headrest. I close my eyes.

Since the beginning, I've been handling Hunter's murder investigation on my own. Perhaps my pride and past experience as a Suffolk County homicide detective has interfered with my judgment about seeking help from outside my jurisdiction. I didn't want outsiders charging into my town telling me how to run things. As far as I was concerned, Hunter's murder was an internal matter.

To make matters worse, I've alienated my staff. Subtle remarks from my deputies lately suggest I've created a wedge between us. Aside from asking them to assist with a few phone calls, I haven't used them in the investigation.

In addition to my hubris, the real reason for the delay in calling in outside help has been to avoid the inevitable: discovering that Hunter's killer was a neighbor, a friend, or my wife.

Maybe Rusty was right. Why continue the investigation and ruin more lives? The town wanted to believe Peter Hopkins was guilty. He was their martyr. No. Peter Hopkins was their scapegoat.

My lungs stretch for air. As I release the tension, I feel oddly relaxed and begin to think about Maggie Hunter for the umpteenth time since we met.

She appears like an apparition in front of large, ominous clouds that are looming and vibrating and throwing off bolts of lightning. Then, as Maggie spreads her arms, the clouds disappear, replaced with a deep blue sky. Like an angel, she floats past me in a white, cotton summer dress, her hair tied in a red bow and barefooted.

Maggie turns, waves blithely, and calls out to me. Effortlessly, my body drifts upward and follows her past the beach perimeter toward the stilted houses high above the bluffs. My heart dances with excitement. The townspeople are cheering me on. "Go for it, Hank! Catch her." Even Peter Hopkins.

I sail past Susan, who gives me a thumbs up. When I catch up with Maggie, she is sitting on the sand next to a large rock, her arms outstretched. She draws me in like a magnet and whispers, "You're the one I want, Sheriff."

"Hank."

I smile to myself. "Maggie."

I hear a thump and stumble out of my slumber, my eyes staring into the rain beating against my windshield.

"Hank!"

I blink hard and turn toward the window. Instinctively I reach for my gun, but the rain is falling so hard, I can't make out the face. Then the shadow disappears as though the muddy road swallowed it up. I carefully open the door and find Sheryl lying face up, eyes closed, her gray raincoat opened at the bottom. She must have fallen and hit her head on the ground. The pelting rain bounces off her face. I remove my raincoat and shield her from the rain. "Sheryl!"

I attempt to lift her off the ground, but I lose my footing and slip, landing beside her.

"Sheryl!" I call out again, jumping to my feet and opening the back door. I scoop her up and gently slide her on the seat. The dome light is on, and I can see Sheryl's pale, clammy face. I dry my hands on the back of the seat, then unbutton her raincoat. That's when I notice that Sheryl's white Salty's t-shirt is drenched in blood.

It takes the ambulance less than fifteen minutes to reach us, but it wouldn't have mattered when they arrived. Sheryl's only conversation would be with her creator.

"Hank, what happened?"

Wayne is holding an umbrella over my head, his flashlight pointing at the wet, sandy ground that is mixed with Sheryl's blood.

I shake my head. "I don't know. Sheryl was supposed to meet me here."

"Out here? Why?"

I hesitate, then say, "She had information on Hunter's murder, only she never got a chance to tell me."

"What could she have known?" he probes.

I shrug. "I don't know, Wayne. Like I said, we never got the chance to speak."

Wayne's voice cracks. "Why her, Hank?"

My eyes tighten. "I don't know, but we're gonna need help unless I figure out who did this and soon."

Wayne and I stand in silence, engaged in our own thoughts. I watch the ambulance take off, its red flashing lights fighting the night. The fog has lifted enough for me to notice Sheryl's car parked a good hundred yards from us near the restrooms, the driver's-side door opened.

"What was she doing over there?" I ask, almost to myself.

Wayne catches my stare. "You just said she was supposed to meet you."

"Yeah, but we were supposed to meet here, not near the restrooms."

Wayne pulls on his ear. "Maybe she had to pee."

I shake my head and start for Sheryl's car, my boots sloshing through puddles. "The bathrooms are closed this time of year. Sheryl would have known that."

"She could have stopped to use the phone," he suggests, trying to keep up with me. "It works year round."

"I doubt it," I say dismissively. "Besides, Sheryl must have had a cell phone."

When we reach the car, Wayne flashes a beam from his flashlight inside the driver's-side door. "Nothing out of the ordinary," he says. "The keys are still in the ignition."

I nod, then caution Wayne not to touch anything without gloves. He steps back and aims the light at the public phone, which is resting in its cradle. "Could be whoever did it followed Sheryl and cut her off here."

"Or was her passenger," I say, adding to Wayne's theory.

"That would mean—"

"Sheryl knew her killer," I finish.

Wayne tugs on my wet jacket. "Hank, I wanna help with this."

I turn to my deputy. Wayne's pained expression suggests I need to consent to his plea. "Stay here and wait for the county." I point to the phone. "Ask them to check for fingerprints."

Wayne's eyes light up.

"Then check with the phone company. See if any calls were made from it tonight."

"Thanks, Hank."

I fix my eyes on Sheryl's car. "I'd better inform Paddy."

I'm about to leave when Wayne asks, "You staying over tonight, Hank?"

"Is there a problem?" I ask innocently.

He shrugs. "I was just wondering, that's all."

Wayne never just wonders.

"It's just that I hate to see you and Susan like this. Especially after what's happened tonight."

I smile softly and place a friendly arm on my deputy's shoulder. "Thanks, Wayne," I say. I trudge back to my car, thinking about Maggie and my dream. But those thoughts quickly evaporate as my murder theory takes over. Sheryl knew her killer, someone who knew her every move. But if Paddy knew Sheryl was meeting me, would he accompany her? Certainly Sheryl would never consent to the idea.

Which makes Wayne's theory more logical. An angry Paddy followed her here, cut her off, then killed her. That simple. Then why had Paddy lied to protect Sheryl about Hunter's murder, telling me she worked at the bar till closing? Why would he want to save Sheryl only to kill her?

I climb back in my car, my pants soaked from the rain, my body damp and cold. Through the windshield, I give Wayne a quick wave, then start for the exit. I glance in the rearview mirror, my eyes steadying on the illumination from Wayne's flashlight. Then, like the end of a movie, the picture turns black.

23

By the time I reach Salty's, the rain has been reduced to a fine mist. Once inside, my eyes begin to burn as I struggle through the haze of smoke. The bar is engulfed in loud music and loud conversation, with screaming Islanders fans competing for noise control with a group of off-key karaoke singers.

I rub my eyes then glance around. The booth where Hunter and I hung out is occupied by a bunch of guys wearing ball caps backward who look too young to drink. But I'm not here to card anyone; I'm here to find Paddy.

I search the bar, but Paddy isn't serving drinks. Chester Wynn is. Chester's been a weekend bartender for the past five years. Half the time he's off the wagon. But Chester comes cheap, so Paddy keeps him around when the place is hopping. Which is why I'm surprised Paddy isn't pouring drinks alongside him.

"Hey, Chess," I shout over the crowd. "Where's Paddy?"

He stops mixing a drink, shoots a look around, then offers a sloppy grin when he sees me. "Hank, what's doin?" he calls out.

"I need to speak to Paddy," I roar back.

"Paddy?" Chester gazes through the crowd, then shrugs. "He was here a while ago," he yells, then returns to pouring drinks, licking whatever spills on his hand. An employee perk.

I weave through the crowd and make my way over to a waitress. "Judy, you see Paddy?"

Judy sets a tray full of drinks on a table. "Say, Hank. Yeah, he's around somewhere. It's been crazy tonight on account of the game."

"What about before?" I press. "Say around six."

Judy closes her eyes, blocks out the din. "Think so."

I struggle through the crowd and find another waitress who gives me the same "I think so" line. I'm about to ask a few regulars when Paddy emerges from the back and gives Chester a hand. Chester whispers something to Paddy, and I can tell Paddy is not too happy. His eyes narrow as he searches the bar, but he can't find me because I'm standing behind a couple of extra-large athletic types. His intense expression stays as he pulls on his ponytail shaking the excess water from his hand.

I approach him, my eyes steady on his face. He sees me, gives a faint smile, then forms a "what?" with his lips. I point to the back and he follows me.

My ears continue to be stricken by the deafening, buzzing sound as we reach his office.

"For Chrissake, Hank, don't you see how busy we are? Can't this wait?"

There's no easy way. "Sheryl's dead, Paddy. I'm sorry."

At first, he doesn't understand. Maybe the noise is reverberating in his ears, too. "Say what?" he cups an ear.

"Sheryl. She was shot out at the beach."

Paddy freezes like a petrified animal. "What the hell are you talking about?" he says, the timbre in his brogue more pronounced.

"She was supposed to meet me there." That didn't sound right.

"Meet you? What the hell for?" he roars.

"She had some information about Hunter's murder."

Paddy clenches his fist, shakes it at me. "You bastard, Hank. You got her killed!"

I allow Paddy to enter my space. As a law enforcement officer, it's easier to interrogate suspects who live elsewhere. But this is my town, and though Paddy is a suspect, he's also my friend, so I give him time to blow off steam.

He realizes I'm being conciliatory and settles down. "Who the hell would do that, Hank?"

"I was hoping you could tell me," I say my voice neutral.

He cocks his head. "Are you insinuating that I killed her? Because if you are . . ."

I hold up a hand. "Paddy, I'm just trying to find out if someone threatened her lately. You know, a phone call, a letter. Something."

Paddy keeps a critical eye on me. "Yeah, well, I don't like the way you were asking the question. Who else was angry with her?"

"That's my point," I scoff. I'm taking a chance with Paddy. Though he and I are about the same height, Paddy's leaner, faster and hotheaded, so accusing him in tight quarters is chancy. "Where were you around six tonight?" I continue, eyeing him carefully.

"Damn you, Hank! If I were going to kill her, I would have done it when I found out."

"You didn't answer my question," I challenge.

He shakes his head. "C'mon, Hank, I've got a grandstand of people out there. Ask anyone." He stops, realizing why I'm here, and leans against the wall for support. "We were working things out," he whispers to no one in particular.

"I'm sorry for your loss, Paddy. Sheryl was a good friend." When I go to touch his shoulder, he backs off. "You!" he jabs at me. "You killed her. If you hadn't hounded her about your stupid investigation, she'd still be alive."

If this is a ploy, it's working. "I was just doing my job. I never thought—"

"Your job! The whole town is upset with your bullshit

investigation. You should have closed it with Peter Hopkins. Now there's more blood on your hands."

I glare. "I'm tired of being lectured by you and everyone else in this town. I'm going to find the person who killed your wife and Hunter."

"Screw Hunter! You find Sheryl's killer or I will," he rages, then settles down, wipes his eyes. "I want to see her."

I watch Paddy pull on his ponytail again, my eyes following a few drops as they fall to the floor. "Where'd that water come from?" I ask.

He rubs his hands. "What?"

"The water, where were you?"

"For Crissake, Hank, it's raining outside. I needed some fresh air from all that smoke."

The county morgue is forty minutes away. Paddy and I are spending those minutes in silence. I'm wondering how I would be feeling if it were Susan who was killed. Guilty that we hadn't resolved our issues? Angry she hadn't been honest with me? Upset with myself for not taking care of her needs? Susan and I have to come to terms with this Hunter business before it's too late. Only I'm hoping we don't have to resolve our differences between prison bars.

At the morgue, we are taken to a small, sterile room no bigger than a foyer. A sofa facing a window, its blinds shut, acts as a small comfort station for the next of kin.

Over the years as a detective, I'd become immune to death. This is different. Sheryl was my friend, and it's going to be particularly painful seeing her this way.

Paddy is sitting on the sofa, kneading his hands, his eyes glued to the window, waiting for the unveiling. He nods, and I tap lightly on the window. The blind slats lift slowly, and Sheryl, a white sheet draped up to her neck, appears.

125

I motion to the guy manning the blinds, and he turns a spotlight on her. Paddy gets up and trudges over to the window, his nose and hands pressing against the glass. He slides down until his face is even with the metal table. His eyes well up but remain on her. His lips touch the window as though saying goodbye.

I give Paddy enough time to recover, then nod to the young technician. Slowly, the blinds are lowered until Sheryl disappears. I place my hand on Paddy's shoulders. This time he doesn't resist. The powerful bartender has little strength left, so I help him back to the sofa. His unfocused eyes stare through me. "I loved her, Hank. You gotta believe me." His eyes search the floor. "I forgive her," he whispers.

24

I've been sitting in my car for almost an hour, my body tense and clammy from the night's ordeal, and I can't make up my mind whether to venture inside. It's almost midnight, the house is dark, and Susan isn't expecting me. In her delicate condition, I'm afraid to startle her.

My wife should be told about the murder before she sees Sheryl's photograph plastered on the front page of the *Eastpoint Times* and reads the gory details inside, which will say that Sheryl Murphy was shot in the chest at close range. For Susan and the remaining sex maidens, the dots connecting Sheryl's murder to Hunter's will be very unsettling.

My guess is that Sheryl never meant to stop near the rest area. The restrooms were locked this time of year, and Sheryl wouldn't have needed a public phone. She owned a cell phone, which was still inside her purse in the back seat of her car.

I stare out at my house for a few moments longer, then start the ignition, shove the gear in reverse, and tap lightly on the accelerator. Susan will have to learn about Sheryl's murder tomorrow.

Wayne's living room is barely illuminated when I pull up. I use the key he provided and call out as I enter. While my deputy knows I'm staying the night, two murders in one week can be jarring to the average Eastpoint citizen. And Wayne knows how to shoot!

I find him leaning back in his favorite chair, staring blindly at the tube. Four empty Budweisers are strewn on the floor. Two beers remaining from the six-pack along with a bottle of cheap vodka sit on a stack table. The vodka looks as though Wayne made a dent in that, too.

My deputy cocks his head in my direction and greets me with a shot glass filled with the clear liquid. "Say there, Hank. How about joining the party?" He downs the contents, then shakes his head, making a sound like his throat is on fire.

I help myself to a beer and fold my aching body into a casual cushioned chair opposite him. I study Wayne, who is clearly plastered, then take a slug of beer.

"How's Paddy taking it?" he slurs.

"Not great. I took him to the morgue."

He drops the shot glass on the table and wipes his mouth. "Good guy, that Paddy. Good husband, too. She was a slut."

I flinch. "Hey, Wayne, that's no way to talk about Sheryl. Especially now."

He grabs the last can of beer and washes down his vulgarity. "Whatever."

"I know you're upset, but—"

"Upset!" he spits out. "Do I look upset?"

I motion to the stacked table. "Well, for one thing, you generally don't drink, especially when you have to work the next day."

He waves me off. "Yeah, well maybe you don't know me that well, Hank. I drink when I wanna. Tonight, I wanna."

I shrug. "It's your place."

"Damn straight."

Wayne sits quietly for a while, his round, red face looking especially heavy tonight. I ask him with a degree of sympathy whether his drinking has anything to do with Sheryl's murder.

"The slut? Nah."

I lean forward in my chair. "Sounds like you're angry with her."

Wayne remains silent, fidgets with his beer. Then he turns to me, his unfocused eyes struggling to steady on mine like he's about to unload a deep, dark secret. "I knew about them, Hank."

I take another slug of beer, watching Wayne's empty expression come alive. His head begins bobbing about like a mechanical doll. "They belong together, those two," he says scornfully, then makes a thumbs-down gesture.

"That's pretty callous," I say, my voice even. "What did they ever do to you?"

Wayne glares at me like I'm part of the package. "That scumbag was screwing with people's lives."

I wait a few seconds. "Who, Hunter?"

Wayne gives me an it's-about-time look.

"I'm not sure I understand," I say. "Whose lives was Hunter messing with, Wayne?"

He jabs an index finger into his chest. "He fucked with mine."

Wayne's truth serum is confusing me. "You hardly knew the guy," I say truthfully.

"Oh, I knew him all right," he snaps. "Thought he was better than me. Telling me my sex life wasn't worth a shit." Wayne's eyes drop to his drink, and he looks as though he's about to cry. Then he recovers. "That crap he wrote in his column about guys who couldn't get women in small towns. I knew who he was writing about."

Another paranoid victim.

"And all the time," he continues, "the bastard was screwing everyone he could get his hands on." Wayne blinks hard, looks to me for sympathy. "It ain't fair, Hank."

"Fair he could or that you couldn't?"

Wayne scowls. "What the hell is that supposed to mean?"

I shrug. "Nothing. But it's not like he had a normal relationship with these women. They were married." I pause, spread my hands. "Hell, Hunter obviously couldn't find anyone single either."

He ignores my comparison and says, "Yeah, well just the same, he taunted me." Wayne lowers eyes to the floor. "With *her.*"

I remain silent, take another sip of beer, and wonder about Wayne's sudden infatuation with Sheryl Murphy. "You talk to Paddy lately?" I finally ask.

He belches. " 'Bout what?"

"Them. He told you about the affair?"

Wayne almost falls out of his chair. "Shit, no. I told you, I already knew." He leans back in his tattered La-Z-Boy and tries futilely to lift his legs.

"Then how did you find out?"

A puzzled expression crosses his face.

"Sheryl and Hunter. If Paddy didn't tell you, who did?"

That registers, and Wayne helps himself to a mischievous grin. "I'm a cop, remember? I know everything that goes on in this town."

Wayne's hubris makes me uncomfortable. I wonder how many more dark secrets Wayne has been keeping to himself. I let him continue.

"Knew about that slut Jackie Hopkins. Don't care much 'bout that one, though."

I nod. "Everybody knew about Jackie and Hunter after Peter killed himself," I say. "Besides, you're assuming that because you saw her in one of Hunter's paintings."

He gives me an impish grin. "I knew about them before."

"Kept it to yourself, I see."

"Hey, it's my fantasy, Hank. Besides, it ain't no crime."

"Sheryl a fantasy, too?" I push.

He jabs a finger at me. "You leave her out of this!"

"Easy, Wayne," I say defensively. "You just said they were part of your fantasy."

"Not her, dammit! She was clean."

I lean back in the chair, waiting for my deputy to continue his fantasy story, but he tips his head back and closes his eyes.

"You called her a slut before," I say, my voice elevating, trying to keep Wayne awake.

Wayne struggles. "I was just blowing off steam, Hank."

"But you liked her, right?"

"We had fun at the bar, talked a lot. She was always kidding around with me."

Wayne was obviously hooked on Sheryl and misinterpreted her waitress demeanor for something more. It's sad, longing for a relationship and having to create an illusion out of a friendly gesture. But that was Wayne, lonely and desperate. Ironically, in the end, Sheryl was as desperate about Hunter.

"But she wasn't interested in you, Wayne. She was interested in Hunter."

That wakens him. "That prick. He's the reason she's dead," he says, slapping the arm of his chair.

Wayne was probably right. "That's what we need to find out."

"Thought he was a stud, that Hunter. Woulda screwed the whole town if he had the chance."

He did, and still is. "How'd you get the scoop on Hunter?" I probe.

Wayne scratches his head, then extends his hands like a preacher. "Like I told you, Hank. I'm a cop. I got my ways."

Wayne is the type who shouldn't drink. He gets obnoxious and mouths off a lot, bringing out his true feelings. At one office Christmas party, he got plastered and started berating people. The next day, he had no idea what he had said.

Wayne lifts his heavy eyes up at me. "Sometimes I watched them go to his place. They sure weren't going for therapy," he snorts, then makes a circle with one hand and impales it with an index finger.

I let a few moments lapse. I can't let Wayne fall asleep before asking the burning question. "Besides Sheryl and Jackie, who else did you watch go into Hunter's house?"

Wayne's expression changes, becomes more serious. When he doesn't answer, I say, "Wayne, this is an investigation, for Chrissake!"

He rubs his eyes, tries to focus. "Hank, I don't remember."

I leap out of my chair, grab him by the collar, and jerk him out of his seat. "Goddamn it! Who else did you see?"

"Susan, okay?" He tries to free himself, but my grip is too tight. "I didn't want to tell you," he cries.

I let him go, sending his portly body sliding back into his chair.

Wayne reaches for the bottle of vodka and takes a long swallow. "Coulda been innocent," he says, wiping his mouth.

I stare down at my pathetic deputy. It finally all comes together: The painting, the journal, the truth.

"I figured you knew about them on account of you staying here," he tells me.

I wait a few seconds, then take the bottle out of his hand. "You ever see Paddy enter Hunter's house?"

Wayne doesn't respond.

"Well?" I demand. "Do you know something?"

"Thought he could get away with it," he mumbles.

"Paddy?"

Wayne's eyes flutter slightly; his hand smacks the shot glass off the table.

"Wayne, for God's sake, did Paddy kill Hunter?" I grab at his frayed shirt collar, but he doesn't respond. I let go of him, watching his body go limp. Why hadn't Wayne told me about Hunter's escapades before? "It's my fantasy," he told me. Obviously, Wayne wanted to keep those fantasies to himself.

I pace the room like a caged animal. Sometimes when he was sitting around the office, if Wayne wasn't engaged in some girly magazine, he would doodle, usually sketching small pets. But occasionally, I'd catch him sketching something X-rated, though he wasn't as skillful as Hunter. Maybe while Hunter and his women were enjoying the lustful pleasures of life, Wayne was skulking about in his car or hiding behind an oak tree creating his own repertoire. Maybe he included a sketch of Paddy minus the pleasure.

I work my way through the house, tripping over shoes, clothes, and girly magazines, but I don't find any of his doodling. I check Wayne's car, including his trunk, then I go back inside and stand over my friend, who is out cold and snoring like a baby. I'll let him sleep tonight, but tomorrow Wayne has some explaining to do.

25

My eyes, which I'm certain are bloodshot, are gazing up at Wayne's ceiling, which is in dire need of a paint job. My deputy is snoring incessantly in his La-Z-Boy, where I left him last night, filled with angst. Mine, not his.

My body, aching throughout, struggles off the couch. My head is pounding, and I only consumed one beer. Not like my friend here. Wayne would pay for his imbibing later.

I trudge out of the house with a stale cherry Pop-Tart that I found in Wayne's near-empty pantry. I don't have time to make coffee, so if I'm lucky, Susan will have already brewed a pot, though I'm inclined to believe she might pour it over my head.

As I approach my driveway, I realize the paperboy is either unusually late or Susan has already picked up the paper. Considering the kid's impeccable delivery service, I guess that I might not be the first to break Sheryl's murder to Susan.

By now, my wife will be awake, out of the shower, and cranking up the coffeemaker. It's a workday, and as the head teller at Eastpoint Savings and Loan, Susan will arrive ahead of the other tellers.

Standing outside our kitchen door, I feel like a Peeping Tom as I watch my wife sipping her coffee, indulging herself for a few minutes before getting dressed. It's a ritual: shower, coffee with the newspaper. Then Susan prepares her lunch before getting dressed. A few years back, the ritual might have included a morning romp, but that has long been left out of our daily routine. Susan's eyes are fixed on the refrigerator, the news-paper sitting next to her unopened.

It's still my house, but I give a courtesy knock, then enter. Susan doesn't turn her head. I'd give a hundred dollars for her thoughts.

"Morning," I say, starting out with small pleasantries.

Susan ignores me, her eyes burning the refrigerator.

I sit down opposite her, obstructing her view of the white GE refrigerator. She blinks but continues her hollow stare, her face pale and somber. Makeup will certainly be necessary today. My wife's bathrobe is slightly opened, exposing her small but firm breasts. She catches me looking and closes the top as though I'm some slimeball trying to steal a peek. "We gotta talk," I tell her.

Still no reaction.

"It's about Sheryl."

I get the look that begs *not this again,* so I give her a few moments.

"What about her?" she finally asks. "That she was involved with John Hunter? Okay, you win, I already knew. She was in love with him. Satisfied?"

"Sheryl's dead."

She blinks hard. "That's not funny."

"She was shot last night out at the beach. I'm sorry. I know she was your best friend—"

Susan glances over at the paper. "Please tell me you're kidding, Hank."

I slide out of my chair and stand over my wife. "Sheryl was supposed to meet me."

Susan looks up. "What do you mean, meet you? Like for a drink or something?"

"She was going to tell me *everything* she knew about Hunter. About the investigation."

Susan suddenly bolts for the bathroom. In a matter of seconds, primal cries echo throughout the house, then vomiting, then moans.

I rush to my wife's side, find her on her knees.

"Oh, Sheryl!" she cries.

I stroke her forehead and remove some hair from her clammy face.

"Why?" she whispers.

I don't have any concrete answers for her. "Did she mention anything to you? Threats?"

She shakes her head slowly.

"I took Paddy to see her last night. He really loved her."

In a hoarse whisper, she says, "Sheryl didn't love him anymore. She loved—"

"Hunter," I finish. "But he dumped her for someone else. Who do you think that was, Susan?"

My wife stiffens, then pushes me away. "I know what you're suggesting. How could you, at a time like this?"

"I have an eyewitness, for God's sake!"

"You have blood on your hands, Hank. You got my friend killed!" With raw energy, Susan shoves me against the door, my back feeling like it's snapped. "Get out of my life!"

I place my hands up in defeat and back out of the bathroom as though Susan is holding a gun to my head. Glare from her bloodshot eyes suddenly widens as her body trembles violently. She grabs her stomach, screams in pain, then drops to the floor before I have a chance to catch her.

My wife is a bloody mess. The paramedics are strapping an oxygen mask over her face and wheeling her out of the house. I'm numb, but I must say somewhat relieved that Hunter is finally out of Susan's body.

She will never forgive me for her miscarriage, I'm thinking, as my car weaves behind the ambulance. As for my marriage, it's dead.

26

After being assured that Susan is out of danger, I leave the hospital and drive around with no particular place to go. My heart no longer races to find Hunter's killer. He has caused more damage to this town than anyone else I know. Let the investigation die, they told me. They were right.

Sheryl, on the other hand, was a good person. I owe it to her to find her killer. As a cop, I'm obligated to find Hunter's, too. Right now, he will have to wait.

My thoughts are suddenly interrupted by the car radio. "Just heard about Susan. She okay?"

It's Kate. "She's out of danger."

"Thank God. Keep me posted."

"I will."

"Oh, an Olivia Patterson just called you."

I reach in the back of my brain and try to retrieve the name. "Hidden Island?"

"Right. Says she needs to talk to you ASAP."

"What's the rush?"

"You might want to ask her," Kate says, then rattles off the number.

"Thanks. Anything else?"

Kate proceeds to tell me that Wayne showed up late looking like hell and that he must have had a bout with the bottle or something. "Been cranky and drinking a lot of water."

"He say anything?"

"Yeah. He complained there wasn't any coffee left. Guy's got nerve. Who does he think I am, his mother?"

I assure Kate that she is too good-looking to be his mother. Besides, his mother is dead.

"Yeah, well just the same, I can't wait till he makes his rounds and leaves me alone."

"Tell him I need to see him later."

"Will do, boss."

Crossing the narrow drawbridge from the mainland to Hidden Island is a transformation in wealth and time. Affluence drips off the maple trees like golden sap. There are only about thirty houses on the entire island, and each one is worth at least three million dollars. Olivia Patterson's digs probably cost more. A long private driveway leads to a four-car garage that allows my Crown Victoria to squeeze in between a Mercedes and some exotic car, whose name I can't pronounce.

Evidently Olivia has been waiting for me, because the moment I emerge from my car, the front door swings open and a woman in her mid-thirties appears, her lithe body ensconced in a Victoria's Secret negligee that's snapped on at the bottom. I stop. The barefoot goddess smiles, then lifts her chest, revealing perfect silicon breasts and nipples that stand at attention behind Victoria's satin armor. The rich have a strange way of greeting people.

Olivia stands around five-seven in spiked heels and looks as though she's about to participate as Kiki the Maid in a soft porno flick.

"You must be Chief Reed," she says in a voice that must have been trained for seduction.

I'd better be, or Olivia made herself up for the wrong guy, although my identity is pretty apparent from my uniform, minus the hat, and the police car with its yellow and blue Eastpoint insignia sitting in her driveway. "Hi," is about all I can offer.

"I'm Olivia. Please come in."

She turns and disappears inside. I follow, close the door behind me, and marvel at the opulence. I'm thinking that Olivia's husband must be a Gatsby descendent as I pass the living room, its twenty-foot windows providing an expansive view of the bay.

The house is quiet, which doesn't surprise me. Nor does it take my dull brain very long to understand why Olivia invited me over, why the teddy, and why there are two drinks in her hands. One of Hunter's paintings was of a sexy Olivia in some sort of bondage outfit, a nurse's uniform, and holding a whip or some other accessory item, ready to rock on Hunter. I must say Hunter hadn't done her justice with his paint strokes; Olivia Patterson is exceedingly more beautiful in the flesh.

"Is everything all right?" I ask, businesslike.

She appears confused by my question. But then a light bulb must have turned on in her head. "Oh, everything is fine. I mean in the house, anyway. William and I just returned from Europe. Been there a month. Great vacation. Poor William, he had to return sooner. Business."

Right. Poor William.

Olivia giggles, then extends her hand with a glass. "Sherry. Or should I say Jerez. From Spain."

"Thanks, but I'm on duty."

She looks genuinely disappointed and sets the glass down on a Bombay chest. Then, with her glass, she makes a circular motion with her finger, allowing it to whistle. She dips her index finger in her drink, pulls it out slowly, and then suggestively, with the same finger, Olivia points to a Chippendale chair. "Please have a seat." She hesitates. "Do I call you Chief Reed?"

"The town calls me Hank or Sheriff. Your choice." I slide into the chair, check my watch, and give Olivia ten minutes. "May I ask why you asked me out here?"

She sits opposite me, fidgets a bit. "Like I said, I just returned from Europe and thought I'd do some shopping in town."

I glance furtively at my watch. Nine minutes.

"To make a long story short—don't you hate that cliché?—anyway, I heard that John Hunter was murdered."

"Correct," I say, watching her do a cross-the-leg thing, and lose track of time. "About a week ago," I tell her.

"I hear a few things were taken from his house."

I sit up straight. "Taken?"

Olivia wasn't being accusatory, and she must have seen the blank look on my face. "The paintings, Hank."

I settle down. "Right, the paintings."

"That's the rumor, anyway. Must be old by now." Olivia smiles softly, takes a sip of her sherry, then places it on a glass table. I watch her get up, watch her sexy moves, then watch her approach me. She kneels down between my worn leather boots and holds onto my knees for support, staring into my crotch. "I'd like to get mine back," she breathes, in a heavy dose of Jerez that is drifting in my direction.

My body stirs, not so much from the way she says it but rather from the way Olivia's hands are touching me. I swallow hard and forget she's got about eight minutes left. "Evidence," I force out.

Olivia doesn't stop. Her long, painted fingernails work on my thighs. As I attempt to close my legs, she clamps them with her arms. "I'll show you a few things I learned in Paris. Great ideas, those French."

I'm about to throw in all the paintings and the eight-cylinder police car sitting outside, but stop. "Can't do, Olivia," I grunt. "Evidence," I repeat.

Her head drops to my lap and starts foraying into my unprotected area. I extend my arm, wondering if I can get out of here in . . . four minutes. I touch her soft, perfumed hair, which is covering the lower part of my anatomy, then carefully ease her up. "I better go."

Olivia lifts her head, tosses back her head, and moans. "Hank, please. If he finds out about that stupid painting, I'm history."

Right, painting. She should have taken a course in fidelity. I stand up, fix the crease in my pants, and say, "Look, if I don't have to show it, I won't. But I can't promise anything right now."

Olivia nods but apparently has something else in mind. She crosses the room and stops at a hand-painted olive and gold secretary, opens a drawer, and removes a check that was evidently already filled out. "I couldn't get enough cash on such short notice," she says. "But maybe you want to consider this before you say no." She waves the check in my face. All I can see is a bunch of zeros.

I grab her hand. "Olivia," I say firmly. "You don't want to do this. Let's pretend I was never here and you never had that check in your hand. Okay?"

She gives me an anxious glance. "I'm scared, Hank. I don't want to give this place up."

Hell of a time to think about consequences. "You'll work it out, Olivia," I say and start for the door.

"He was a nice guy, John was," she calls out after me. "Too bad about him, huh?"

I could have provided her with a better assortment of adjectives to describe John Hunter. "Nice" wouldn't have been one of them.

27

The stationhouse is generally quiet this time of the day, but when I return from the lovely Olivia Patterson I find Kate, Minnie Taylor, our part-time bookkeeper, and my deputy Charlie engaged in spirited discourse. When they see me, the conversation comes to an abrupt halt. We exchange smiles, but the warm greetings I'm used to are missing.

"Hey, Hank," Charlie says, then checks his watch. "Guess I better do my rounds."

Minnie slides her chair over to her desk and jumps on the computer without saying a word. Kate offers me a benign smile.

"Something wrong?" I ask.

Kate opens her desk drawer, removes an official-looking document, and with an anxious glance says, "Someone slipped it under our door."

I take the document from her and review it with suspicious eyes. It's slightly wrinkled but appears to be an election petition that calls for a change in the "top law enforcement position," a fancy term for my job. "Two murders are enough!" it begins. "Could the chief of police have stopped the murder of our beloved Sheryl Murphy? Petition a change. Demand a new election and make this town crime-free again. A vote of confidence is a vote for Wayne Andrews."

At first, I snicker. That wouldn't be *my* deputy Wayne Andrews, would it? Then I consider the impact of this frivolous indictment and ask, "What the hell's going on?"

Kate offers a shrug. "You better ask Wayne."

I feel my face flush. "I don't understand."

Never at a loss for words, Kate doesn't add anything more than, "I really don't know, Hank."

"He mention anything this morning?"

She shakes her head no.

I crush the paper and throw it in the trash. "That's where it belongs," I say, and storm into my office, slamming the door behind me.

As if the petition isn't bad enough, I glance out the window and see Norman Strong standing outside his candy store handing out copies of the petition like gumdrops. His wife is probably inside sucking down milk shakes. Great loyalty, Norm! I'll never buy another goddamn candy bar from you as long as I live! What the hell is he worried about, anyway? Hunter wasn't into the Rubenesque type.

This petition business isn't about murder. It's about fear. Fear of being associated with John Hunter. And fear that Eastpoint will be regarded as just another Peyton Place. People here don't give two shits that Hunter was killed. But they do care about Sheryl's murder. And one can only speculate about the actions of an enraged husband.

I know this. I feel it. But I can't prove it. Sheryl wasn't raped, there were no signs of a struggle, and nothing was taken from her purse. When I reached the bar the night Sheryl was murdered, Paddy was nowhere in sight. When he showed up from the back of the bar, he told me he'd needed a break from the smoke. What bothers me is that if Paddy's hair was wet, how come his clothes were dry?

According to one witness, Sheryl left the bar around five-thirty and got into her car alone. On a good day, it would have taken her twenty minutes to reach the beach from the bar. The rain would have added another ten, which meant Sheryl and I would have arrived within minutes of each other. That didn't happen.

Kate interrupts my thoughts. "Sorry for the intrusion, Hank. You better read this." She approaches tentatively, waving a copy of the *Eastpoint Times,* and places it in my hands.

I stare at the headlines. More venom. Only this time, Wayne and his henchmen are making accusatory statements, the kind that go beyond political advancement. Wayne wants blood!

I glance up at my secretary, feeling embarrassment. "You don't believe this, I hope."

" 'Course not. But it's damaging."

"It's bullshit!"

"It's still damaging, and you're going to have to address it," she says evenly.

"I'm gonna break Wayne's neck," I huff. "Damn traitor."

"Hank, you don't wanna say things like that right now."

"Where the hell is he?" I demand.

My verbal assault on that good-for-nothing deputy causes Kate to resort to hand motions to slow me down. I must look like I'm about to explode. When she gets my attention, she tells me Wayne took the rest of the day off, that he wasn't feeling well.

I snort. "Right. He's probably out campaigning."

Kate gives me a tender pat on my arm. "You don't have to convince me that what they're writing is crap."

"Yeah, well no one in this town oughta doubt my loyalty. This is the thanks I get."

"People appreciate what you've done for them in the past," Kate assures me. "This is different. They're upset about the you-know-what that's locked up in the closet." She's referring to the paintings, not the journal. That's my secret.

"Don't they realize I'm not trying to hurt anybody? Besides, they should have never found out about those damn paintings in the first place. I bet that was Wayne's doing," I charge. "It's nobody's business. It's police business!"

Kate nods in sympathy, realizes I need to be alone, and leaves. I go back to the newspaper and address all of the allegations in my head. My hands are trembling with anger. I shove it to one side like it's venom, then pick up the phone and call Troy Grayson, the *Times* editor.

"What kind of crap are you printing these days, Troy?"

After a moment of hesitation, Grayson says, "Gee, Hank, you know we only print the truth. I was just stating the facts as I saw them."

I roll my eyes. "What facts? That I'm not doing my job? How would you know? You've got your nose stuck in print all day."

"Hank," he starts in a conciliatory tone, "I wouldn't print anything if it wasn't confirmed. You know that."

"Right. And where did you get your information from?" I demand.

"My sources."

"And of course, you won't reveal Wayne's name."

"Correct."

"So it was Wayne, then?"

"You said it, not me. I protect my sources."

"Your sources. For Chrissake, the only major stories you write about are weddings and funerals!"

"Whatever, Hank. Look, you have every right to debunk any story you can prove false. Any fabrication."

"You bet I will! And then I'm gonna sue your ass." I slam the phone down, open the window, and stick my head out in search of air.

Shit! People are huddling in the middle of the street, copies of that damned petition waving in their hands, and staring up at me, their accused.

I shut the window and charge out of my office. "I gotta get

out of here," I tell Kate, and I start for the back door.

"Hank," Kate calls after me, "I've got Maggie Hunter on the line. She just heard about it in the paper. You wanna say hello."

I wave her off. "Too busy. I have to find Sheryl Murphy's killer."

28

Salty's parking lot is empty. Paddy must have closed on account of the funeral arrangements. Very appropriate.

I pull around the back and park. I start drum-rolling on the steering wheel, deciding whether to get a search warrant.

I stop the drum-roll and step out of the car. Paddy doesn't have an alarm system, so with the help of my nightstick, I smash a basement window. Years ago, I might have been able to slip through an area like this without much trouble. Problem is, I gained a few pounds since I joined the force. Nevertheless, I work my way through the window, gaining access to the basement where the unpleasant mix of humidity and rotten beer greets me.

Stepping over Paddy's stock of liquor, I notice there aren't any cases of Jack Daniel's. I guess there isn't any reason to carry that brand anymore.

I climb the narrow wooden steps that lead to a small private office; an exposed light bulb hangs from the ceiling, and the light is on. I remove a handkerchief from my pocket and open a closet door. That's where I find a half-dozen pair of khakis and a box of white shirts with Salty's brown logo engraved on them. Paddy's wet hair and dry clothes now make sense.

I close the closet door and cross the room to a small wooden desk with two drawers. Inside one, I find a bunch of invoices, Paddy's business checkbook, and some office supplies. The other drawer is stuck, so I give it a yank. When it doesn't give, I get on my knees, grab the handle, and pull as hard as I can. The drawer flies off its rollers and onto the floor.

Great! I'm crawling on the floor retrieving a chewed-up black pen, loose paper clips, and rubber bands. I'm about to dump Paddy's supplies back in the drawer, then I stop. At least a dozen envelopes wrapped in a rubber band are still inside. I trade the supplies for the envelopes, then sit on the floor, slide the top letter out from under the rubber band, and begin reading. "My love, I can't stand being away from you. Your smile makes me sing but I have to wait, wait till I'm finished working at this boring place." It goes on with more love, a little fire, and it's signed "Sheryl." It's not dated. I place the letter back in the envelope and read the next one, then the next.

All of the letters are similar in tone, and all end with "Soon, my love. I'll be with you forever." Paddy must have discovered Sheryl's deepest thoughts. Only they weren't addressed to him.

In some perverse way, I can identify with Paddy. He must have agonized over her love and affection for Hunter. I'm wondering if my wife wrote to Hunter with as much passion as Sheryl.

I open the bottom envelope, which is addressed, "To Whom It May Concern." It doesn't start off like the others. In fact, it isn't a love letter at all; it's a typed suicide note. A joint suicide pact?

I rub my eyes. Hunter and Sheryl? I remember Maggie commenting about the voice on Hunter's answering machine. It sounded desperate, she said. Maggie didn't know it, but that voice belonged to Sheryl. Did Sheryl suddenly get cold feet and try to reach her lover? To tell him they shouldn't go through with it? But if she wanted to save him, why not say, "John, don't drink the bourbon?" Which makes me believe that Hunter wasn't aware of the suicide pact. It was Sheryl's plan for Hunter dumping her.

Oh, Sheryl!

I place the drawer back on its track and attempt to close it, but it doesn't shut. I stick my hand inside and remove a small metal can with an ominous label on it. I drop it to the floor where it lands next to my handkerchief.

Not only are my fingerprints on the evidence, I don't even have a search warrant. And I have no real explanation for being here.

There's another problem. If I wipe my prints from the can, the killer's will disappear along with them.

The phone on Paddy's desk starts ringing. I let his brogue tell the caller to leave a message.

"I need to see you soon." The voice is pleasant, but there's a hint of trepidation. I wonder why *she* is calling Paddy here, on his private line.

29

I storm out the back door, jump in my car, and leave gravel spraying about in the parking lot. I punch a number on my cell phone and pray that Judge Prescott isn't teeing off somewhere.

The judge is an old friend and has lived in Eastpoint for as long as he's been on the bench: thirty-five years. He is one of a handful of judges who handles the criminal court for Suffolk County out of Riverhead. His stark white hair and clear blue eyes add a refinement to an imposing frame. When he's not hearing a case in court, the judge works out of his house, a perk he received a few years ago after being stricken with a heart attack.

His wife of twenty-nine years answers the phone. She is sophisticated without the snobbery, a pleasant and friendly woman and the judge's alter ego when it comes to tough decisions.

"Dorothy, it's Hank Reed. Been a while."

"Hank, how are you?" She sounds warm and sincere. Apparently, she hasn't seen the petition. Dorothy is not connected to the local gossip community. In fact, she devotes most of her time to caring for her exotic orchids.

"Fine, Dorothy."

"And Susan? How is she? Haven't seen her lately."

"She's fine, too," I lie.

"Please give her my regards."

"I will, Dorothy, thanks. I need to speak to the judge. Is he around?"

"He's in the library, Hank. Hold on."

As I'm waiting for the judge, I ease up on the accelerator, realizing I'm doing forty in a twenty-five-mile-an-hour zone down Main Street. Just what I need, more gossip about that crazy police chief ripping up the road like a kid. There are still a few stragglers talking and waving the petition.

I turn in to the stationhouse and park behind the gray, one-story building. It's been a while since I've had to use my secretarial skills, but I need to type the search warrant myself. Too many wagging tongues.

"Hank, my boy. What can I do for you? Is this a social call?"

"Afraid not, Judge. I need a search warrant for Paddy Murphy's place."

There's an uncomfortable silence. The judge knows Paddy. He sponsored Paddy when he needed a green card to work in the States. "The bar or his house?" he asks.

"The bar for now."

"I see. What's up?"

I know he's aware of the murders, but I bring him up to date, leaving out my breaking and entering.

"Sounds more like a gut feeling, Hank. Do you have any hard evidence? Probable cause?"

I'm dying to tell him about the poison, the love letters, and the suicide note, but hold back. "Paddy had a motive, judge. For both murders."

"Of course he had a motive. His wife was sleeping with Hunter. But I need specifics."

"You knew?" I ask, dumbfounded. "How?"

"Paddy confided in me soon after he discovered a pile of love letters she had written Hunter. I'm guessing about three weeks ago. We were at the bar. He'd been drinking pretty heavily, and

I guess he needed someone to talk to. I have a sympathetic ear."

"What did Paddy tell you exactly, Judge?"

"Only that he was quite upset with Sheryl but that they were working things out."

"And soon afterward Hunter turns up dead," I add. I provide the judge a few moments to mull that over.

"I know how it looks, Hank," he finally admits. "But I was with Paddy the night of the murder." The judge whispers into the phone. "Hank, between you and me, Paddy told me she did it."

The judge doesn't mention the accused by name. Damned reverent of him. I'm tempted to mention my wet-hair dry-shirt theory, but I hold off. "And when did Paddy conveniently let this out of the bag?"

"Paddy stopped by this morning. As you can imagine, he was distraught over Sheryl's murder and didn't know what to do. He told me he couldn't believe Sheryl would do such a thing, especially since it was, you know, her lover. She confessed to him, told him how she laced the bourbon then forged Hunter's signature." The judge pauses. "Paddy was afraid she would go to jail.

I chuckle to myself. I have always held Judge Prescott in the highest esteem, but his myopic acceptance of Paddy's bullshit makes me wonder about his objectiveness. I resist the urge to tell him so, and when I don't respond, he continues. "Look, Hank, I wasn't pleased that he hadn't come forward sooner or gone to the authorities, but I'm not going to judge him on that. I might have done the same thing in his situation."

Amen.

The judge then says with textbook authority that he strongly urged Paddy to talk to me.

"Smart call, Judge. Paddy and I can sit down over a few beers and discuss Sheryl's confession."

He ignores my sarcasm. Instead he says, "Look, Hank, under the circumstances, maybe it's best to let it die with her. Who would gain by exposing all this?"

The only thing missing is a red bow for Judge Prescott's neat package. "Honestly, Judge, I find it hard to believe that Sheryl would kill Hunter. She was in love with the guy. And she certainly didn't kill herself."

"According to Paddy, Hunter dumped her. I guess she wouldn't take no for an answer—"

"Did Paddy explain Sheryl's confession in detail?" I ask.

The judge takes a moment. "According to Paddy," he emphasizes, "Sheryl spiked the bourbon with poison, went to Hunter's house, poured him a drink, and . . . Look, Hank, it's hard to understand human nature."

Human nature, my ass! "Don't you find it strange that Paddy came forward at all?"

"I'm sorry?"

"And Sheryl's not around to corroborate his story."

"I know, Hank, it's tragic. I guess he needed to get it off his chest."

"It's bullshit! Did Paddy tell you Sheryl and I were supposed to meet the night she was killed?"

"Yes, he did. And he was upset on account of you putting Sheryl in harm's way, and he thinks your actions contributed to her death. I told him not to hold you responsible, that it was part of your investigation. You couldn't have known—"

"What he didn't tell you," I interrupt, "is that Sheryl swore to me that Paddy killed Hunter. That it was *Paddy* who bought the bourbon from Rusty's the day of the murder, then spiked it. He knew she was still seeing Hunter and waited for the right moment to act. In fact, Paddy was counting on both of them to drink the stuff. He wanted her dead for betraying him, and he had a double suicide note ready for the occasion. Only it backfired when Sheryl returned home that night. You're right about one thing, Judge. Paddy didn't want Sheryl to go to jail: he wanted her dead."

"Jesus!"

"That's right. So Paddy quickly had to draw up another suicide note, this one leaving out his wife's name, then he delivered it himself. By the time he arrived, Hunter was already dead."

"I don't understand how Paddy could have forged Hunter's signature."

He's serious. "Hunter charged most of his bills at the bar. You know that. You joined us occasionally. He liked to pay."

There's a sudden stillness on the phone; like a game of chess, both of us are strategically defending our position. He breaks the silence and says, "We were watching the game till almost eleven, Hank. How could he have planted Hunter's suicide note?"

That stops me cold. "I'm working on that end of it."

"I don't remember Paddy leaving even to go to the john. Isn't it possible Sheryl lied to you to save herself?"

It's possible, since I made the whole thing up. But it makes sense. Oh, Sheryl, please don't make a liar out of me. "I think Paddy killed Sheryl to stop her from telling me the truth. Only Paddy was too late. She told me everything before she died."

More silence, more strategy. "I've known Paddy for years. He's a hard worker, a good husband. I can't believe he would hurt anyone, especially his wife. I think you're going after the wrong guy."

"Then explain how Sheryl's love letters wound up in Paddy's office, along with the double suicide note and the strychnine. That's where Sheryl found them, Judge. You might have been too engrossed in the game to notice that Paddy was missing that night." I'm treading on one of the judge's character flaws. I

155

don't want to allude to his low tolerance for alcohol. He probably had one too many pops to realize where he was that night.

"And as for murdering his wife," I continue, "who else had a motive? She hadn't received threats from anyone . . . except him. And he threatened Hunter."

"You'll need to prove it, Hank."

"I can prove he threatened Hunter, and as for Sheryl's confession, it's good enough for me. I have to find those letters and the other evidence. Then you'll see."

"Can't."

"Why not?"

"He told me he burned them when he found them."

I'm about to tell him that Paddy is full of shit. Instead, I say, "What if I can prove that those letters still exist? I'll throw in the suicide note and the poison." I'm pushing, but I need that warrant.

"But he told me—"

"Trust me on this, Judge."

Judge Prescott hesitates, then says, "Sheryl told you this while she was dying, or are you on some kind of witch hunt?"

I cross my fingers. "Swear, Judge."

The judge's silence gives me hope. "Well, I guess based on her testimony, it does sounds like probable cause. Okay, come over tomorrow afternoon."

Judge Prescott is holding out. "C'mon, Judge, I need to search the bar *before* Paddy gets any ideas."

"Hank, the guy's making funeral arrangements. Have some compassion."

Right, like he had for her.

"He's too busy to be thinking about destroying evidence. Besides, he could have gotten rid of them before if he had wanted to. Tomorrow, Hank, fair enough?"

"It'll have to be," I tell him, not pleased.

Then he hits me in the solar plexus. "And Hank, straighten out the mess in your stationhouse. I know about the petition and newspaper article. The town's gone crazy over these murders. I don't like what I'm reading about you. People think that you are the problem. Prove them wrong, my boy. But don't go fishing on this case, or you'll likely to be hooked yourself. Understand?"

"Perfectly."

"Good. Then let me get back to work. And tell Susan I hope she's feeling better. A shame, what happened."

I hang up, tap the dashboard, and consider my next move. Without a search warrant, I can't go back to the bar, and no one in the town will talk to me. I can always hunt down Wayne, but my depleted energy level is signaling no more confrontations for a while. And that includes Susan. So, instead of paying my wife a visit, I call.

Susan answers the phone after three rings, her voice suggesting she's in a lot of pain. I act civil, ask her if she needs anything. She replies with suppressed anger. "Right now, I need a painkiller and life without you, in that order."

At least I'm not a priority. When I ask when she's going home, she says: in a few days and by then, she expects more closet space. Until then, I'm free to stay in her house.

"Anything else?" I ask sarcastically.

"Say a prayer for Sheryl's soul at the funeral tomorrow. Tell Paddy I'm sorry I couldn't be there. He'll understand."

After a few uncomfortable moments of silence, Susan tells me she's going back to sleep and hangs up.

30

Funeral services for Sheryl are being held at Calverton Cemetery, which is now a bit more crowded since Hunter was put to rest. Like Hunter's, Sheryl's funeral is simple. Unlike Hunter's weeping women standing alone, most here are represented by couples. The busy Father O'Brady is comforting the bereaved husband.

Susan is absent from the affair, though I hate using her name in that context. As for my clothes, they are neatly folded inside a dresser drawer at the Country Inn, a modest home-away-from-home lodge. Wayne's hospitality has come to an abrupt end, although he doesn't know it yet. In fact, I haven't spoken to him since his drunken tirade.

The steady drizzle causes my body to shiver. I'm standing under an oak tree, whose bright red and orange autumn leaves are hanging by a prayer. The leaves don't shield me completely from the rain, as my fresh gray jacket and spiffed-up boots and hat attest to. I can't wait to get back in the car and turn on the heater.

If that sounds callous on such an occasion, it shouldn't. I've already paid my respects to Sheryl several times since she was murdered. I think of her constantly and am guilt-ridden. It's already gotten around town that I was the last to see her alive. I can just imagine Wayne adding an addendum to the petition. " 'Do you want *your* police chief to put your life in danger?' "

Suddenly, the rain stops hitting my hat, the sound of which

was driving me crazy. I look up and realize I'm standing under a black umbrella.

"Thought this might help," Maggie says with a quick smile.

It's the first smile I've received in a while, and I smile back. "Thanks. Left mine back at the office."

She glances around. "Surely one of these nice folks would have offered you shelter if you asked."

I'm not about to tell her my new name is Chief Pariah. "Glad to see you," I whisper, as though concerned someone might misconstrue my innocent remark.

"Who would do such a thing?" Maggie says sadly, motioning to the casket.

My head jerks slightly toward Paddy, who is standing motionless over his wife's coffin. It's bad manners to point, so I tell Maggie we have a person of interest and leave it at that. After a few moments, I glance up at the sky and sigh. "Funerals always seem to be filled with rain."

"That's part of death, Hank," Maggie adds. "But then the sun follows, then flowers. It's part of life's cycle. At least, that's what my shrink tells me."

I nod. "Makes sense."

Maggie waits a few minutes before asking, "I never met your wife. Is she attending the service?"

I shake my head slowly. "She's having a . . . procedure done at the hospital. Nothing serious. She'll be out tomorrow." Then, as an afterthought, I say, "I moved out for good."

She touches my elbow. "I'm sorry. I didn't mean to pry." Then she says lightly, "I guess your deputy has a permanent roommate."

"I moved out on him, too," I say, staring straight ahead.

Maggie chuckles quietly. "You must be a tough guy to live with, Chief Reed."

I'm about to answer when Wayne shows up, standing twenty

feet from us. He's not wearing his regulation hat or raincoat, and he looks as though he's had another bout with the bottle. I check my watch. He's also twenty minutes late.

Wayne glances in my direction, nods quickly, then turns to the casket, which is being lowered into the ground. From my vantage point, I see him wiping his eyes, but I'm not sure if it's from the rain or tears.

"Where are you staying?" Maggie asks, breaking my thought.

"The Country Inn. Just outside town, but I'd rather no one knew about it just yet." My eyes drift toward Wayne. "Though I'm sure they'll find out soon enough."

"Could get expensive," Maggie tells me, like a concerned parent.

I smile to myself, change the subject, and let Maggie know the town appreciates her attending the funeral.

She glances sideways. "Well, your town was very kind to me with John's funeral." Maggie pauses. "Although, I must admit, I had an ulterior motive."

I raise an eyebrow. "Oh?"

She nods. "I'm thinking of putting the house up for sale. John's attorney told me I was the beneficiary. I guess John wanted to lighten his guilt for that period in our lives." She stops, notices my face deflate, and says, "Of course, I could have done that over the phone." She gives me a teasing elbow in the ribs and smiles.

It's a relief to see her recover from the incident with the photos. I ask whether she plans to stay in town a while.

"Unfortunately, I need to get back to the city. I'll catch a train after I finish with the realtor."

"You have a long wait," I say. "The next one doesn't leave Eastpoint until six-o-five tonight."

"Oh. Well I guess I'll just have to do some shopping."

I smile.

"But if you don't mind, Hank, I could use a lift to town."

"Glad to."

As Sheryl disappears into the ground, Judge and Dorothy Prescott turn to Paddy and comfort him. Wayne leaves abruptly, without relating his respects, which doesn't surprise me, given his sudden contempt for Paddy. The others walk slowly past Sheryl's coffin, gently tossing flowers, most teary-eyed, and give Paddy hugs. He appears to be caught up in the moment.

"You go," Maggie says, motioning me to the gravesite.

"Be back in a minute." The rain has turned into a slight drizzle as I follow the other mourners to Paddy, wondering how my presence will be received. His eyes stray from the well-wishers and catch me approaching. Paddy's face contorts.

Then it's just us, face to face, accused and accuser, the body resting below. He glimpses the coffin, then back to me.

"She was a good friend," I say. "I'll miss her."

He grabs me, draws me in, and whispers, "You're wrong about me, Hank. You'll see."

I free myself from his grip, my eyes settling on Sheryl's coffin. "I hope so." I turn to leave, feeling Paddy's stare on my back.

As Maggie and I step over a few puddles on our way back to the car, it dawns on me that people must be talking about *us*.

"You okay?" she asks.

"Yeah," I say, but I'm not. We drive back to town in silence, my mind preoccupied with the search warrant. Upon reaching Jackson's Realty, I turn to Maggie. "Good luck," I say, my voice flat.

She must sense my indifference. "Thanks," Maggie says, touching my hand lightly.

I stop off at the stationhouse to pick up the warrant, which is ready for the judge's signature. Kate's in. Wayne's not. She feeds me a rumor that the town is pushing for a quick election.

I ask her if she knows who's really behind the petition, knowing that Wayne isn't the brightest guy around.

"I really don't know, Hank."

"Well, someone must have approached Wayne on this."

She shrugs. "I'll try to find out."

"Please, Kate. Nobody will talk to me."

My secretary's eyes search the floor. "There's another rumor, Hank. I'm not prying, mind you, but are you and Susan calling it quits?"

Fucking small towns! Her eyes meet mine. "It's okay, really," I assure her. "I'm sure Susan and I will remain friends."

She nods sadly. "Where will you be staying?"

"At the Country Inn, but no one knows it, so I'd appreciate your secrecy."

"Of course."

"It's only temporary," I tell her. "I'll be looking for a place in town soon."

I walk back to my office, pick the warrant off my desk, and study it for third time. Kate stops at the door, her face grim.

"What?"

"There's more."

There's always more. "Go ahead."

"They're saying it's because of the miscarriage."

I close my eyes. More fodder for the petition. "Chief leaves wife after she loses baby." Insensitive bastard! "It had nothing to do with that," I defend.

"A shame, Hank. You guys were trying so long."

"We've been having problems for a while, Kate. Maybe it was just as well . . ." I stop. "That's not what I meant."

" 'Course not."

"I still love Susan." After a few dead moments, I say, "Kate, tell Wayne we need to talk. Sometime today."

"Will do, Hank."

I start for the door.

"Everything turns out for the best," she calls out.

31

Judge Prescott is removing his tan raincoat when Dorothy opens the door for me. From his frosty expression, I can tell he isn't pleased to see me. He doesn't understand my urgency; Paddy isn't going anywhere, he assures me. The judge thinks I'm completely insensitive to add *this* to Paddy's grief right now.

"The cemetery workers haven't even covered her casket, Hank."

"Judge, Paddy doesn't need to grieve. He needs to be arrested. He can grieve while he's doing time."

Judge Prescott frowns, hands Dorothy his raincoat, and motions me into his study. He turns to me, sees my hand extending with the warrant. The judge grabs the warrant from me. He studies my request and shakes his head, then removes a Mont Blanc from his pocket and scribbles his signature across the bottom of the warrant, his hand trembling. Then he thrusts it back at me as though it were a death sentence.

I thank him and charge for the door.

"You tell Paddy I didn't want to do this," he calls out after me.

The warrant is barely dry from the judge's pen when I reach Salty's. At least Paddy had the decency to honor his wife's death by not opening the bar, though I'm told the difference between an Irish funeral and wedding is one less person. Perhaps Paddy hadn't heard that one.

In any event, the bar is dark but the door is open, so I slip inside and find my favorite bartender holding a Guinness in his hand. Paddy hoists the bottle as I approach him. "To Sheryl." He then removes a cold one from behind the bar and watches me as he removes the cap. "It's safe," he says, setting it down.

I don't drink on the job, but I make an exception this time, take the bottle, and lift it in his direction. "To Sheryl. Maybe she's in a better place."

He blinks hard, takes a slug. "Anywhere is better than here, Hank."

"You got that right, Paddy."

"You've got your own demons, I'm sure," he says. His eyes weigh heavily on mine, waiting for my reaction. He doesn't get one.

"Hunter ruined this town. You, me, Sheryl, Susan."

He's taunting me, but I don't take the hook.

"I thought Hunter was screwing only my wife," he says with a sense of calmness. "Guess I was wrong. To Susan," he says without malice. "But I guess you already knew that."

I still don't fly into his web.

"Am I talking out of turn?" he asks. "Or are you and Susan separating 'cause of political differences?" He takes a quick gulp, wipes his mouth with his hand.

"You tell me. You seem to know more about my life than I do."

He offers a tight smile. "Fact is, Hunter and Susan were going at it after he had his fill of Sheryl."

I stiffen. No matter how many times I hear it, my reaction is the same.

"Guess you didn't know," he says. "That Hunter was quite a guy."

"Who told you this?" I demand.

"About Susan? Hell, Hunter was doing half the town. Women, that is." He smirks.

"Then how come that rumor never circulated around the stationhouse?"

Paddy downs his beer, places it on the bar. "Easy. Hunter was discreet. At least I'll give him that much. Otherwise, he would have had a bunch of angry husbands after his ass."

"Like you?"

"Or you, Hank." He opens another Guinness, takes a long belt. "It certainly wasn't Peter Hopkins," Paddy says, deadpan. "My guess is that Hunter killed himself before any of us had a chance."

I snort. "You'd like me to believe that, wouldn't you?"

He hunches his shoulders. "Hey, it's your investigation. You wanna waste everyone's time, go ahead." He pauses, shows some teeth. "Although I'm told they're thinking about holding elections for your job. You might want to hurry up and find your killer."

I point the long neck bottle in Paddy's direction. "I already have."

His eyes lock on mine. "Prove it!"

"I intend to. And if you think once Wayne takes over my job, the investigation is dead, you're wrong. I've got connections with the county. I worked homicide, remember? All I have to do is pick up the phone and tell a sympathetic ear the investigation is being stymied." I wink. "You'll have detectives living in your pants."

Paddy doesn't reply. He's probably wondering if I'm blowing smoke up his ass. "To the investigation," I say and treat myself to the rest of the Guinness.

"Yeah, well they might just go after you as well. You're as much a cuckold as I am."

My calm expression belies the anger inside me. "Since you seem to know what went on, why don't you tell me about Susan and Hunter?"

Paddy stares down at his beer. "I found some love letters in Sheryl's closet." He glances over at me. "They belonged to Susan. When I confronted Sheryl about them, she told me that Hunter and Susan were having an affair. She begged me not to tell you." Paddy shrugs. "I would have kept the promise if you hadn't pressed me."

My eyes hold steady on Paddy.

"You look like you can use another drink."

I nod as Paddy scoops another beer from the ice chest under the bar. He removes the cap and hands the beer to me. "You see, Hank, either of us could have killed the bastard. We both had motive."

"Like I said, I didn't know about it at the time."

Paddy shrugs. "That's what you say now."

I don't believe for a moment that Sheryl told Paddy anything. Yet Paddy knows about Hunter and Susan.

He picks up on my silence. "I think about it all the time, too, Hank. Makes me crazy."

"Enough to kill her," I accuse.

"You're wrong, and you'll never prove it."

I take one long gulp from my Guinness, remove the warrant from my jacket pocket, slap it on the bar, then place my half-empty bottle on top. "Let's find out."

Paddy tugs at the warrant, knocking over the bottle and sending beer streaming down the bar. "You fuck! You couldn't wait."

I point a finger at him. "The sooner I get you, the better."

"Go ahead, search the bar! You're not gonna find anything. I promise."

Paddy's remark makes me uneasy. "I'll start inside." I leave Paddy, storm into his office, and flip on the light. This, too, is unsettling, since the light was on when I rifled through his desk yesterday. I hadn't turned it off.

Rather than waste anyone's time, I go directly to his desk,

remove a pair of latex gloves from my jacket pocket, and fit them over my hands. I force the drawer open like I had yesterday and find the envelopes where I left them. I then help myself to a slight grin.

I search for the can of strychnine, but it's missing. I get on my hands and knees and reach inside the drawer, but the poison is gone.

The letters will have to do. I slide myself into a chair, open the top letter, and begin reading. I stop, drop the first letter on the desk, and search the next one. These aren't the love letters I found yesterday. These are typed. And they don't belong to Sheryl. And the joint suicide note is missing!

"Is that what you were after, Hank?"

My head shoots up. Paddy is leaning against the door, beer in hand. He's savoring a big smile, the grieving husband.

"You bastard!" I leap over the desk and fall short of him, pick myself up, and grab him by the throat, swearing, threatening. Paddy's face is turning blue, his hands are on mine but my grip is too powerful. He's trying to say something, but my hands are clamped around his neck and squeezing. Every part of me is burning inside; my head is pounding. I want to kill someone for the hell I've been through, and Paddy is gonna be the one.

Someone is shouting behind me, but I can't stop; I'm blinded by rage. My hands won't let go of the killer.

"Murderer!" I scream.

Wayne's arms are locked in mine as he pulls me off Paddy, who drops to the floor like a sack of potatoes. He's gasping for air, then vomits on his leg.

"You're crazy, Hank!" Paddy forces out. "He tried to kill me, like he did the others."

I'm sitting on the floor next to Paddy, my head spinning. My world is coming to an end. I feel the butt of my .38 inside my jacket and for a split second, I'm thinking of blowing everyone away.

Wayne is attending to Paddy, helping him off the floor.

"Crazy," Paddy growls, holding his throat. "It's a good thing I called the stationhouse."

I gaze over at my deputy, then back to Paddy.

"He already threatened me once." Paddy shoots a look over at Wayne for approval.

Wayne dismisses Paddy's comments and turns to me. "What happened, Hank?"

How do I explain what I've been feeling these past few weeks?

"I oughta sue you for this. I just buried my wife," Paddy moans, holding his throat. "You got what you wanted. Now leave me alone."

"What's he talking about, Hank?"

I ignore Wayne. "I'm gonna get you, with or without the evidence you destroyed."

"Yeah, well maybe you oughta check with your office. I had a break-in yesterday, or didn't you know? That's the guy you need to go after."

I wipe Paddy's sweat and grime on my pants, then pull myself off the floor. The bastard knows I've already been here.

32

Wayne and I are sitting in my patrol car after leaving Paddy in his own vomit. "I'll be back to fry your ass," I told Paddy with a bit of Schwarzenegger bravado. He didn't appear shaken by my threat; Paddy knows the hard evidence against him is burned, buried, or moved to a new location. My thoughts stay on him until Wayne taps me on the shoulder. "Are you listening to me, Hank?"

I turn, still fuming.

"What were you thinking back there? You almost killed him."

I let Wayne continue his admonishment, knowing it has nothing to do with my actions. He couldn't care less if I strangled Paddy for what he did to Sheryl; it has to do with this impending rigged election.

"He deserved it," I charge.

"You're a cop, Hank! I don't think you can be objective anymore."

He's right. I'm too personally involved. Perhaps that's why Wayne strongly urges me to step aside. Or, quite possibly, my deputy has a hidden agenda.

Wayne's expression suggests he is asking for my blessing. Fat chance. Wayne is no homicide detective; he's better off investigating missing farm animals. "You're right. I'm gonna get the county involved."

Wayne's jaw drops. "We have enough deputies *here* to handle it."

He's serious. "Nothing personal, Wayne, but I was a homicide detective for eight years, and if I'm having a hard time solving the murders, you and the rest of the guys—"

"That's exactly what I'm talking about," he interrupts. "You're trying to solve the case yourself." Then he mumbles, "You should have stayed with the county."

Underneath that cherub face and easy demeanor lurks an angry soul. Every once in a while, it surfaces. Wayne believes he should have been elected police chief after my father died in office—not that he died while performing his official duties. Will Reed died of a heart attack attempting to bring in a big white off Orient Point. Maybe it wasn't that big.

Anyway, a few years before he considered retirement, my father talked me into leaving the Suffolk County Homicide Department and joining Eastpoint's Finest. His motive was clear: he wanted to perpetuate his namesake as chief of police. The town loved ol' Will, and he promised they would love me, too. He offered me a cut in pay, but promised it would be offset handsomely by the prestige of being top honcho. Wayne never forgave my father for overlooking him and felt betrayed. And since I was guilty by association, Wayne never forgave me, either. And so, if the devil inside Wayne emerges through quick, caustic remarks, I understand.

"This is not the time for past differences," I tell him evenly.

"It's never time," he complains.

There really isn't anything further to discuss, but I say, "I never wanted to hurt you, Wayne. I never realized how badly you wanted the job." I'm pacifying him, but in reality he wouldn't have won if Kate ran against him. Don't get me wrong, she's a great secretary, but I think you get my point. Wayne isn't the brightest bulb in the box.

"What was Paddy talking about back there?"

"Just some bullshit."

He thumbs the back seat. "That it?"

I nod.

He stretches for the letters, and I grab his arm. "I just want you to know the stuff in there isn't true. But it could be evidence, so use a handkerchief."

Wayne nods, then digs deep into his pocket and pulls one out that looks like it's been through a few colds.

"Believe me, there's no truth in them," I emphasize.

Wayne ponders my remark. "Could be Paddy was protecting Sheryl."

Maybe Wayne isn't as dense as I thought, except he's got the wrong scribe. "Look, I found some letters yesterday. Not the ones you're holding. Sheryl's love letters to Hunter."

He gives me a puzzled look. "I thought you got the warrant today."

I give him a look back, and he gets it.

"You're the one who broke in?"

I nod sheepishly.

"Shit, Hank, that's exactly what I'm talking about. You can't run this investigation anymore."

"I told you that in confidence. Besides, the letters I found yesterday are gone. Someone tipped Paddy off. Was it you?"

"Are you fucking crazy? I hate the bastard. I know he killed his wife."

I nod. "Those letters you're looking at have to do with *Hunter's* murder, not Sheryl's."

Wayne blinks.

"Right now, we need to let Hunter's murder ride out for a while or the town is gonna hang both of us."

Wayne thinks a moment. "You're sure the original letters were destroyed?"

"They weren't where I found them yesterday, so I have to believe Paddy got rid of them."

He waves the letters in my face. "And you're sure these aren't them?"

"Right."

Wayne sits quietly for a moment, then says, "We can't destroy them, Hank. Not unless we can prove they're fake."

I remain silent.

"You understand?"

Maybe he would make a good detective. "Whatever you say. But before you make a decision one way or the other, have an open mind and understand what Paddy is capable of doing."

My deputy is about to read the top letter when I ask, "Who talked you into the election? I know it wasn't you, even though you'd kill for my job."

He peers out the window and shrugs. "I don't know, Hank, I swear. The petition was already prepared. It made sense at the time. Still does. I guess some citizens got together—"

"Like the signers of Declaration of Independence," I quip.

He scowls. "Go ahead, make fun, but they're right. You're gonna make a circus out of this town if those paintings go public."

I lock my eyes on Wayne. "And who leaked their existence in the first place? I checked with the other deputies and Kate. They swear it didn't come from them. Are you gonna swear to me, too?"

Wayne doesn't respond.

I study my deputy, who is immersed in the first letter. Would Wayne let Susan fry? Or would he grant her freedom to elevate his career? Police Chief Wayne Andrews!

"Paddy told me he found those letters in Sheryl's closet," I tell my deputy. "He figures Sheryl and Susan were good friends and didn't keep secrets from each other. Not even when it came to Hunter. Paddy wants me to believe the revolving door to Hunter's place was girlfriend friendly and that Susan, who recently started an affair with Hunter, was already thinking of killing him. Does that make any sense to you?"

Wayne mutters something but doesn't hear a word I'm saying. He and his dirty handkerchief are miles away in romance heaven. When he finishes the last letter, he looks up. "These are damaging."

No kidding! You don't have to be a homicide detective to come to that conclusion. But I let it go; let him have his day.

"I really should follow up on this, Hank. I mean, I know it's Susan but . . ." He stops, scratches his head. "Then again, the town wouldn't appreciate me expanding Hunter's investigation, would they?"

Wayne hadn't used the *we* word about following up. Obviously, I'm not about to interrogate my own wife, though I had before. But that was off the record.

"That's why I think *we* need to concentrate on Sheryl's murder instead."

Wayne considers my proposal. He must be thinking if we stop Hunter's investigation, there won't be a need for an election. "How about this, Hank?" he starts. "If I can prove who killed Sheryl before you, you'll step aside." He doesn't wait for an answer. "Who knows, maybe we won't have to pursue Hunter's killer after all."

A tough bargainer, that Wayne. Though my deputy has me in a tight spot, I gaze out the window as if I'm pondering his idea. As for finding Sheryl's killer first, it might be a draw. I turn to Wayne and nod. "Deal."

He's about to shake my hand and realizes how foolish it looks. Instead, he says, "I'm going back to the bar and search for Paddy's gun. Maybe he hasn't disposed of it yet."

"Good idea. I'll take the letters to the lab and have them dusted."

He stops me. "I'll hold onto them for a while," he says

without hesitation. "Just in case."

I smell blackmail. Maybe Wayne isn't as dumb as I thought.

33

Wayne and I go our separate ways. We're working independently for a while, which suits me just fine. I pull out from Salty's and catch Wayne through my rearview mirror. He appears to be hesitating, but finally ducks back into the bar as though he's on a secret mission. That's my detective.

The crime lab is located in Hauppauge, attached to the medical examiner's office. I call ahead and speak to Jerry Stone, a forensic guy. He tells me I must have been reading his mind because he was about to call me.

I assume Jerry's interest in me has to do with Sheryl's murder. "Have you found the spent shell?" I venture.

"Not yet, Hank. The rain probably washed it away or it's buried somewhere in the sand." He pauses. "There's something else. We recovered photographs from the victim's car. They were under the floor mat on the driver's side. I figure maybe the victim put them there when she sensed danger."

"What sort of photos?" I ask, my heart beating faster.

"The sexy kind. I thought they might have something to do with the murder."

I regard Jerry's remark. "Is Sheryl, the victim, in any of them?"

"No, some other woman and a guy. They posed for all of them. The babe's got big tits."

"Can you describe her for me, outside of the tits, I mean?"

Jerry laughs. "Hold on, let me check." He comes back to the phone a few moments later. "Oh, yeah, this one is better. She's got dark sexy eyes and long black hair. Think you might know her?"

"Could be."

"Well, hurry up and bring some protection. There's a lot of heat coming out of these."

I smile to myself. "I should be there in less than a half hour if the traffic holds up."

Jerry Stone is sitting behind his desk reading some technical magazine when I pop my head in. He is wearing latex gloves and chuckling to himself. I must be in the wrong profession.

I knock. "Am I interrupting anything?"

He glances up still chuckling. "Hank." He stands and approaches me, his arms open.

"Been a while," I say, meeting him halfway.

"Damn, you look terrible. You get into a fight or something?" he says, squeezing my aching body.

He should only know. "It's these cases. They're driving me crazy. How about you? Heard you got married."

He lets go of me and smiles. "I finally found true love."

You have to understand, Jerry is a lady's man. True love for him can only last so long. "You told me that last time," I say. "And the time before that."

He grins. "That was before Jeanie entered the picture."

We both laugh.

"It's been years, Hank," Jerry says. "How many murders did we solve together?"

"I stopped counting."

He smiles. "And Susan, how is she?"

My eyes shift to the floor. "I moved out recently."

"You're kidding? I thought you guys were solid."

I shrug. "The marriage thawed out."

"Gee, that's too bad."

"So tell me about the photos," I say, changing the subject. "Is there anything written on the backs?"

"No. And no explanation needed, either," he cracks. "They're standard Polaroids in living color with lots of smiles and body parts." Jerry returns to his desk, opens a drawer, and removes an envelope, then he lays out the glossies like he's dealing a deck of cards.

I look down, somewhat embarrassed, since I know the parties, and examine them from a distance. The happy infidels. "Whose prints did you find on them?" I ask.

"Only the victim's."

I'm wondering how Sheryl had them in her possession. Could she have been the photographer?

"I gather you know these folks," Jerry says, interrupting my thoughts.

I nod. "He's the victim's husband and she was the wife of another victim, Peter Hopkins. He killed himself." I point to one of the photographs. "She was also doing Hunter."

Jerry meets my eyes and smiles. "The woman gets around. Wouldn't mind living in her town."

I shake my head.

"What?"

"I thought you said you were happily married."

He smiles, displaying a chipped front tooth. "Did I say that?" Then Jerry noses the photographs. "They still a couple?"

I shrug my shoulders. "Beats me. I didn't know they were involved in the first place."

"Well, if they are, it could have been big tits who did the shooting." Jerry offers a wily grin. "Just a hunch. I heard the husband had an alibi."

"I'm still exploring that end of it," I say thoughtfully.

"Let's assume it sticks," he continues. "Bartenders I know generally carry big pieces. It helps them keep rowdy patrons in line." He stops, waits for my reaction.

"Go on."

"The victim and girlfriend knew each other, right?"

I nod.

"I'm thinking the girlfriend might have set the wife up, asked the victim for a ride, then used a small-caliber revolver on her. She could have easily fit it in a purse. And since your victim probably took a hit with a .22 or .25 . . ." he stops, looks for my reaction.

"I'll give it some thought," I say, not too enthusiastic with his theory.

Jerry starts assembling the photos when I ask, "Could I check the bottle of Jack Daniel's you guys found at Hunter's place?"

Jerry stops. "Sure, why?"

"Just a hunch."

Jerry manages a grin. "Are you holding back on your old buddy?"

"Let's just say I'm nosy."

He studies me a moment, then motions inside. "It's in the lab."

I follow Jerry. We pass a few forensic types playing with microscopes and approach another room, a sign on the door reading "Evidence." Once inside, he ushers me over to a small cubicle, reaches for a box labeled "John Hunter," and sets it on a table. He finds a pair of sterile gloves for me and watches me snap them on.

I open the box and pull out the infamous Jack Daniel's bottle, turn it, then twist off its black cap and place my nose to the opening, sniffing traces of quinine.

"What are you thinking, Detective?"

I'm thinking about Paddy and the bottle of Guinness he opened for me back at the bar. He told me the cap wasn't tampered with. Not like this one.

"Hello. Earth to Hank Reed."

I glance up. "You took fingerprints, right?"

"Clean, outside of Hunter's."

"Did you dust behind the seal?" I ask.

"Behind it?"

"Right."

Jerry blinks quizzically. "What are you getting at, old boy?"

I bring the bottle closer to Jerry. "See these perforated edges at the bottom? A black plastic seal is used to cover the cap. In order to get to the cap, you have to pull down on the tab like a zipper, remove the seal and throw it away. It's customer friendly. I'm hoping your guys found the seal somewhere in Hunter's house."

Jerry searches my face. "Behind the seal."

"I'm thinking the killer didn't want the bottle to look like it had been opened, so he must have previously removed the seal, unscrewed the cap, added the poison, and somehow glued it back on."

Jerry takes the murder weapon out of my hands and examines it for a long moment. "Hold this," he says, handing me the bottle, then searches the evidence box and removes the perforated seal. He waves it at me. "Got it." He brings it up to a light. "I don't see any traces of paste or glue inside the seal."

"Nothing?"

"Looks clean to me."

"Did your guys check the seal for prints before?"

Jerry smiles. "You looking for a job?"

"Yeah, yours if you don't find any prints. How about we do it now?"

"Pushy, aren't we? Okay, let's find out."

Jerry gives the seal a quick dust-over, then places it under a microscope. "Sorry."

My thumb glides over the ridged neck of the bottle, feeling

the bottom part of the seal, below the perforation marks. How did you do it, Paddy?

"Maybe the seal was off all along," Jerry tells me.

"Maybe," I say, not convinced.

My thumb keeps returning to a slight bur on one side of the seal. "Jerry, do you have a sharp blade?"

"Sure. What's going through your head now, Detective?"

"I want you to remove the remaining part of the seal around the neck of the bottle."

"What are you suggesting?"

"Anything is possible," I say desperately.

Jerry opens a desk drawer and pulls out a blade. "This sharp enough?" he asks, not waiting for an answer, taking the bottle out of my hands. He makes a slit down the center and pulls back on the seal. "Let's see where this takes us."

I watch Jerry cover the inside of the seal with fine black powder, then gingerly dust the surface and place it under a microscope.

"I'll be damned . . ."

"You found something," I say with excitement.

"It's not a full print, but enough for identification." He rubs his eye, turns to me. "Homicide could use you again."

"Could happen if I don't solve these murders soon."

Jerry leans over the microscope again. "If we can match this, I think you'll have your killer." He straightens up, turns to me, then asks, "How soon can you get me a set of prints to compare this to?"

I help myself to a grin, then, from my back pocket, I remove one of the letters I found in Paddy's drawer, the one that didn't stay with Wayne. "You might find a couple of prints on this one, mine included. I didn't have time to be careful."

"Another story, huh, Hank?"

I smile.

After Jerry works some magic, he turns, and says, "Hank, I think you might have your man."

"Man," I emphasize.

"Or some lady with a big paw, but I don't think so."

"Paddy," I breathe.

"Looks that way. They were a busy couple. You did say she was schtupping Hunter, too, didn't you?"

"Right."

"Hell of a town you got there, Hank." He laughs.

I don't.

34

I'm in the middle of rush hour traffic and haven't even reached the Long Island Expressway. My patience is wearing as I pound the horn at the slow driver in front of me. They're all slow! I attempt the shoulder, my lights flashing, but there is a car broken down up ahead.

All those accusations against my friends and loved ones are now behind me. Sheryl, Susan, even Wayne. Done, finished, *kaput.* I'm especially relieved about Susan. Divorce is one thing; but I would hate to visit her in jail.

As I pass the Wading River exit, Kate calls. "Judge Prescott wants to talk to you. He's upset, started using some legal language about Paddy Murphy. Never noticed that accent before."

"That's his brogue," I tell her. "He's been working to Americanize his accent for years. It comes out when he's upset."

"He's upset, all right."

I hang up, put my thoughts in order, then dial the judge's number. Dorothy answers, the ever-friendly soul. "It's Hank, Dorothy. The judge around?" Like he might be at the Tanger Outlet Mall shopping for a new three-iron.

"He's expecting you, Hank." Ever so gracious.

There's a slight delay, then another phone is lifted off the cradle, and I hear the judge tell his wife to hang up. Definitely, not a good sign.

"Have you lost your mind?" he scolds, skipping the pleasantries. "Do you realize you could be removed from the force or, at a minimum, sued?"

Sued maybe. I'm not about to fire myself. "He taunted me, Judge."

"What did you expect? He just buried his wife. I told you to wait. I trusted you, but you misguided me with your zealousness."

"If you're going to admonish me about choking him, I accept. I was wrong. But Paddy destroyed evidence. For God's sake, Judge, he typed up some phony love letters that Susan supposedly wrote to Hunter."

"Paddy told me he found those letters with Sheryl's personal effects."

"He's lying!"

"Let me finish," the judge snaps, his brogue giving away to his displeasure. "Paddy wasn't going to produce them until he realized *someone* set him up with the suicide note and rat poison. He would never have come forward with Susan's letters otherwise. Then you beat the hell out of him."

I resist the urge to laugh. "Paddy wanted to get back at me because he knew I was closing in on him."

The judge breathes heavily into the phone. "You'll get nothing but grief out of this, Hank. Maybe more. The town is looking to take away your shield."

I attempt to put the judge on the defensive, by asking him why everyone seems to know every little detail of the investigation.

"That's a question you ought to address at your next staff meeting," he says, coming back at me.

"Maybe Paddy's poisoning the town, trying to get me to stop the investigation or else."

"Leave Paddy out of this," he demands. "You better hope he doesn't sue you and the town. Hell, we'll all wind up bankrupt!"

I'm finally off the L.I.E., and I jam on my brakes to avoid an accident. "Shit!"

"There's no need for profanity, Hank. Apologize to Paddy, and maybe he won't sue us. And I'm sorry you had to find out about Susan."

I roll my eyes. "I'm going to arrest Paddy Murphy for the murder of John Hunter."

There is a sigh on the other end.

"Forensics found Paddy's fingerprints inside the Jack Daniel's seal."

"I don't doubt his fingerprints were on the bottle. It was probably taken from his bar."

"You're not listening, Judge. I said *inside the seal.* And if we go with your theory, Paddy's prints would have been all over the bottle. They weren't."

"You'll just have to ask him. Scratch that. Don't go near Paddy until you're ready to apologize."

"Did you hear me, Judge? Paddy's prints were found on the inside. It's not that easy to do. They use a machine to slap on the seal to eliminate tampering. So how did Paddy's prints get there?"

There is no repartee this time.

"Well?"

"I can't answer that, but there must be an explanation."

"When you find one, call me. In the meantime, I'm arresting Paddy and no one is going to stop me."

Judge Prescott lets a few seconds lapse before he speaks, his imperious voice returning. "True, you are Eastpoint's top law enforcement official. But the case still has to be tried."

"That sounds like a threat, Judge."

"Where are you, Hank?" he asks, changing the subject.

"On fifty-eight. The damn traffic is worse than ever."

"A good reason to work in your own back yard," he quips.

Then says, "Well, I hope you know what you're doing, Hank," and hangs up, leaving me with an uneasy feeling. It's not until I reach Sound Avenue that it dawns on me: Judge Prescott is about to broach my impending arrest. I let him checkmate me.

I track down Wayne, who is on his way home. "Arrest Paddy."

"What for?"

Two murders in Eastpoint, and he has to ask.

"He killed Hunter."

"Hank, I thought we agreed to hold off on Hunter's investigation," he protests.

"Fuck the deal! Listen to me. Forensics found Paddy's prints inside the seal of the bourbon bottle."

Wayne remains silent, and I'm wondering if he is grasping my order.

"Wayne, just go to the bar and arrest him. I'm twenty minutes away, and I'm afraid he's been tipped off."

"I'm on my way, Hank."

"Call me if he's not at the bar. And have Charlie meet you there." It's tough finding competent people these days.

When Wayne doesn't call back, I aim my patrol car toward Salty's. It's dusk by the time I arrive, and except for a light behind the bar, the place is dark and quiet. Damn that Wayne! I'm about to start for Paddy's house when I hear the frenzied sound of an ambulance siren. I wait a few moments and realize it's getting closer.

I gaze over at Salty's and swear, then dash inside the bar, my gun drawn, hoping Wayne didn't get carried away. I'm thinking this until I see my deputy on the floor, his hat off and his gray uniform dotted in red.

"Wayne?"

He looks up, dazed.

"Did Paddy do this?"

He nods.

That fucking judge! "Where's Charlie?"

He tries to shrug.

"I didn't see your car."

"Back." He points with his good arm.

I wait for the medics to charge through the door. They greet me quickly, then attend to Wayne, one helping him off the floor and onto the gurney.

"You'll be okay," he tells my deputy. "Looks like a flesh wound."

I approach Bill Kolowski, a six-foot paramedic with a heavy red beard, and ask, "How did you find out about the incident? I mean, there's no one around."

He thinks a moment. "Someone must have called it in, Hank."

I nod absently, then follow the team as it wheels Wayne outside. "You're gonna make it, Deputy," I call out as they slide him inside the ambulance. I say that for myself, as well.

35

I'm not going to waste precious time driving to Paddy's house. Instead, I take a shortcut to Judge Prescott's place, bypassing the downtown area then shooting up Eastpoint Path.

On the way, I radio in to June Winters and ask her to put out an APB. Paddy is probably driving his black Pathfinder, I tell her.

My fists pound on Judge Prescott's front door, but Dorothy doesn't answer. As gracious as she is, this is not a time for informal friendliness. The judge opens the door and glares at me as though I'm the one who shot Wayne.

My eyes lock on his. "You're as guilty as he is," I charge. "I'll see you on the unemployment line. Now where is he?" Normally, I would have to be crazy to defy the judge with such indignities.

"You instigated this," he chides, waving his fist at me.

I take a step back. "How can you call yourself a judge by your actions? You were the only one I told about arresting Paddy. You warned him."

"That's bullshit!"

That's a first from his lips. "Then why do I have a wounded deputy?"

He stops, throws me a confused look. "What are you talking about?"

I nod rapidly. "Right. Paddy must have left out a few details, like he shot his way out of the bar just as Wayne was about to arrest him."

Judge Prescott stiffens; his molten eyes soften. He steps back and leans against the door for support. "My God! I had no idea, Hank."

"Loved ones are the last to know."

He gives me a fleeting glance.

"Which is it, Judge? A nephew or the son of a friend you knew back in Ireland?"

The judge shoots a look over his shoulder, then motions me outside. He turns on the outdoor lights, and I follow him down a soft slope leading to the Long Island Sound. It's too dark to see the water or the judge's thirty-foot Bayliner.

He stops at a black oak, waits a few moments before turning to me. "It was an indiscretion."

"Paddy's your son?"

He doesn't answer.

"Christ, Judge!"

"What was I supposed to do, Hank?" he says in a conciliatory tone. "He swore he didn't have anything to do with the murders." He stops, gazes past me, and says, "Look, I'm truly sorry about your deputy. Paddy must have panicked. I'm certain he just wanted to escape."

"If he was innocent, Judge, why did he run?"

The judge bows his head. "It has nothing to do with this." He wipes his mouth with his hand. "He's here because he can't go back to Ireland."

I lift an eyebrow. "Don't tell me he killed a British cop."

Judge Prescott raises his head proudly. "He infiltrated a terrorist group, and they found out. They killed Paddy's informant and were about to capture him when he escaped. Narrowly, I might add. Of course, I got him here as quickly as I could."

"A cop?"

"RUC . . . Royal Ulster Constables."

I scratch my head. "I thought they were a British outfit."

He nods. "They are, predominantly. Paddy was tired of all the killings and—"

"Not good," I interrupt.

The judge's face registers concern. "You have to believe me, Hank, Paddy would never kill a civilian or a police officer. He's been living in anonymity ever since he left Ireland. He's a marked man."

I let a few moments pass, trying to process Paddy's predicament. "It was you who set me up with that phony petition, wasn't it? A threat if I didn't accept Hunter's death as suicide."

"The town was afraid," he says softly, averting his eyes. "Our town, Hank."

"Don't lie to me, Judge!" I say, my voice echoing over the calm evening. "You wanted to protect your son at any cost, including obstructing a murder investigation. You're supposed to uphold the law for Chrissake! Remember the vow you took as a judge?"

"Your sarcasm isn't helping things," he protests.

I glare. "And neither is your betrayal."

The judge bows his head and remains quiet a moment. When he returns to me, he says, "Hank, you know how I feel about you. You're like family. You father and I were best friends. I tried to resuscitate him on my boat." He pauses. "What would you have done in my case, Hank?"

Hunter's painting of Susan flashes in front of me, and I swallow hard. "Did my father know about Paddy?"

He nods. "He was the only one I told. We trusted each other like brothers."

"Why the big secret?" I ask innocently. "I mean, why couldn't you have told people that Paddy was your son from another marriage?"

The judge sighs. "Believe me, Hank, I wanted to. I'm proud

of Paddy." He motions to the house. "It was Dorothy. She forbade it. She's so . . . proper, and would never consent. I had to honor her wishes."

I remain silent.

"I love Paddy more than anyone outside of Dorothy and could never betray her. Not again." He pauses. "I loved Sheryl like a daughter, even after I found out about her affair. Paddy would never have killed her over it. Or Hunter. He would have only drawn attention to himself."

The judge leans against the tree for support. "Look, maybe Paddy wasn't the best husband. He wanted to be a successful saloonkeeper, and he worked seven days a week trying to prove himself." He stops, gazes over my shoulder. "In the process, he forgot about Sheryl's needs. She started going to Hunter for counseling, though I don't recall him having a practice in town. Maybe that should have alerted Paddy, but he was too busy with the bar." The judge's eyes settle on mine. "I blame Hunter for not upholding his ethical and moral responsibilities."

"Like *you*, Judge?" I say sarcastically.

"Touché, Hank."

We fall silent, which provides a temporary calmness between us. "Paddy could have killed you this afternoon if he had wanted to," the judge says without malice, breaking the silence. "But he restrained himself."

I laugh. "How did he expect me to act, taunting me with those bullshit love letters?"

"Paddy says you planted the first ones on him, along with the poison, because you needed to make an arrest. He wanted to let you know he was on to you." The judge wipes his brow and sighs. "There's no excuse, of course, except survival. He knows a lot about that."

"And Dorothy, how much does she know?"

The judge's eyes stray, stopping at the house. "Only what she hears from me, which is very little. She's upset about Sheryl, of course. She loves Paddy as much as she would her own child, especially since she had problems conceiving."

I nod. "Why isn't Paddy in some kind of witness protection program?"

The judge shakes his head in defeat. "Paddy's stubborn and figured he was safe with me in the States. At least, he consented to a new name." The judge smiles wistfully. "I would have been proud had he used mine."

I offer the judge a tender moment, but soon his expression changes, becomes serious. "Paddy's name might have changed, but his face is very much alive over there. You have to do something, Hank."

"Dammit, Judge! He should have thought about that before messing up."

The judge begins to respond, but then stops himself.

"Are you going to tell me where Paddy is, or do I have to get the county involved?"

"I really don't know, Hank," Judge Prescott says, the imperious voice of the court, succumbing to a whimper. "All I can tell you is that Paddy phoned me as soon as it happened. He never mentioned the shooting but asked me to call nine-one-one, which I did. He said he would contact me soon, when things settled down. He's got to think this through, especially now that he had the altercation with your deputy."

Altercation? Try attempted murder. Not to mention the other two murders. I glance over my shoulder toward the house, focus on a light coming from a bedroom window. "Can I check the house?"

"You may, of course, but I'm not lying to you, Hank." Then he says, "I'm afraid he's armed. And as a former member of the force, he has the ability to evade."

I'm not sure if Daddy is proud of his little boy or just warning me. "I put out an APB, Judge. I had no choice."

He nods. "I understand."

"And since he shot a police officer . . ."

Through patches of light emitting from the moon, I can see dread in the judge's face. "Please bring him in alive, Hank. For past friendship's sake."

For a man of pomposity, Judge Prescott is suddenly humble.

"I can't promise," I tell him and turn to leave. About ten feet from the judge, I stop. "If you want to guarantee Paddy's safety, tell him to give himself up," I say into the air, then continue up the path without waiting for a response.

36

As a police officer, I find it painful going after a fellow crime fighter. Deep inside, there's hope that a viable explanation for his misdeeds will surface. And though I'm too close to this investigation and have overwhelming evidence against Paddy, I let the word out to the other departments about Paddy's past and his valor. That ought to earn him a few points.

I drive over to the county hospital and ask the receptionist for Wayne's room number.

She smiles warmly and points. "He's down the hall in recovery."

I enter Wayne's room and find him sitting up, staring out the window. I knock, break his concentration, and wave. He gives me a tired smile and waves back with his good hand. Then he holds up the other one and grimaces.

"How are you doing?"

"Just a flesh wound," he slurs.

He's obviously doped up on painkillers, so I don't expect too much from him. "What happened back there?"

Wayne's expression turns cold, and he shakes his good arm. "The bastard tried to kill me!"

I nod sympathetically. "Did you notice where he took his gun from? Behind the bar?"

Wayne takes a moment, shuts his eyes, then shakes his head. "It happened too fast."

I pull up a chair. "I'm sorry, Wayne. I didn't realize Paddy would react that violently toward you. Me, maybe, but not you."

He nods absently.

Wayne's eyes are unfocused, so I decide against telling him about Paddy's background for the time being. Instead, I lean forward in my chair and say pointedly, "Paddy killed Hunter, Wayne. I have proof."

Wayne's glazed look informs me I'm wasting my time. He mumbles, "They want me here a while."

"Makes sense." I check my watch, then get up to leave. I place a hand on his shoulder and say, "I'll stop by later and see how you're doing, okay?"

"Okay." Then he motions me closer. "Where do you think he went?"

I shrug. "Could be anywhere, but I doubt if he's still in Eastpoint."

Wayne's eyelids flutter, and he attempts to nod.

"Get some rest, Detective."

I could use a hot shower and decide to freshen up and change my uniform.

The Country Inn is about ten minutes outside of Eastpoint. It's more of a B&B: the charm without the price. Extended stays are cheaper, so I settled on a week-to-week deal. Soon enough I hope I'll find someone in town willing to rent out a room, though I might have to pay double.

I think of my father and the devotion the town had for him. Those same people who embraced him as their respected leader now feel betrayed by his namesake. Good old Dad. He was the politician in the family. I wish he were still around.

The innkeeper is a woman whose last name I can't pronounce, but I know it's Polish. Her first name is Lucy.

"Evening, Chief Reed." She provides a cheery smile.

Lucy is a formal gal.

"Evening, Lucy," I say, too weary to return the smile.

"A friend of yours is staying in Room 102." She points to the room next to mine.

I draw my gun.

"Oh, God!" she cries and ducks under the counter.

"Male or female?" I whisper.

Her head surfaces over the counter. "A lady."

I frown. "Lady?"

She nods rapidly. "Something about missing her train."

"Maggie Hunter?"

She continues her nod.

I walk over to Maggie's door and knock, then turn to Lucy and wink. "Police officer," I call out with authority.

Lucy is still recovering from the shock of my behavior, but she offers a thin smile and watches as the door opens, then steps out of range, just in case.

Maggie emerges with a smile. She's wearing a thin blue cotton nightshirt and a towel wrapped around her head.

"What are you doing here?" I ask, my eyes fighting to stay on Maggie's face.

Her expression registers disappointment. "You don't seem happy to see me, Hank."

I shoot a look at Lucy, who is busying herself at the counter. "It's not that," I say quietly. "I'm just surprised to see you."

She twists her mouth. "I got caught up with shopping and, well, you know women." She points to three bags sitting on the chair. "Is it a problem that I'm here?"

"No, of course not," I assure her. "Just surprised," I repeat, then sneak in a quick smile.

She smiles back and shrugs. "It's just that I don't know too many people in town and—" She stops. "Who am I kidding? I thought maybe we could have dinner or something."

"Dinner or something?" I say, sneaking a peek below her neckline.

Maggie catches my glance and suppresses a laugh. "Dinner is what I had in mind, Detective." She thumbs behind her and laughs. "I do have my own room, so you're safe."

I shoot an anxious look back at Lucy, who is nowhere in sight, then turn awkwardly back to Maggie.

"Look at you, Hank. You're turning red." Maggie grabs my arm and pulls me into her room. "Relax. She can't hear us."

Without warning, she reaches up and draws my head toward hers, planting her lips on mine. "That's for driving me back to the city the other night."

I offer her little more than a flat kiss. "It was nothing," I say, wishing Maggie had given me more notice. After a few moments of impure thoughts, it dawns on me why I returned to the inn. I inform Maggie about Wayne.

Her eyes register concern. "Oh, Hank, I'm really sorry. Will he be okay?"

I nod. "I just came from the hospital."

Maggie sits at the edge of the bed. "You were there at the time?"

"Afterward."

"Good. I mean it might have been you, too." Then she asks, "Do you know who shot your deputy?"

"Paddy Murphy."

"The husband?"

I nod.

"That's so tragic," Maggie says softly. "He appeared so bereft at the funeral."

"Probably from guilt," I offer. "We think he killed her because he found out about her affair with Hunter."

Maggie stiffens. "It always boils down to that, doesn't it, Hank?"

I know where Maggie is coming from, but I remain silent.

"Infidelity," she breathes.

"It's certainly not worth killing over," I defend.

Her eyes meet mine. "No, of course not."

There is an uncomfortable silence between us, then Maggie says, "Anyway, I'm sorry about before. The kiss, I mean. It was inappropriate of me, considering you're still technically married. And in light of what's been happening . . ." She trails off.

I sit beside her on the bed and touch her hand. "It's okay, Maggie. My marriage has been dying—"

She places a finger over my mouth.

"I was even going to send your wife flowers, but I got tied up with the realtor and shopping and forgot. And . . . what was I thinking?"

My smile comes through her finger. "It was a nice gesture anyway." I kiss her forehead, inhaling her perfumed hair, and wonder what it would be like to stay the night. But my romantic notion is broken when Maggie says, "Since John's house is empty, Hank, you're more than welcome to stay there until you find something more permanent."

I hold Maggie's chin lightly. "Hey, I appreciate the thought. Let me think it over, okay?"

She smiles softly. "Sure."

I don't want to leave, but my weary brain cautions me. It's that law enforcement mentality that beckons me back to the investigation. But my feelings for Maggie, which have intensified since we met, are fighting me. Maggie's beauty and radiance are intoxicating. It would be so easy to take her in my arms and forget about the outside world.

Maggie must be sensing the same feelings and offers an alluring smile, giving me the go-ahead. I'm about to move in with a more passionate kiss when she places a hand in front of us. "Maybe I better let you get back to your investigation."

"When are you leaving?"

"Tomorrow morning." She places her hand on mine, plays

with my knuckles. "Though I could stay longer."

My eyes light up.

"I really do love it out here," she starts. "I'm wondering if I'm acting too hastily about selling the house."

"You could hold off a bit," I say too quickly.

"I suppose I could tell the broker to wait until spring," she says, almost to herself.

"I'd really like to take you to dinner sometime, Maggie Hunter."

She smiles wistfully. "Maybe breakfast, if you're around."

I place my hand over hers. "I'm really glad you missed your train."

37

After a few hours of dead leads, I drift back to my room, kick off my shoes, fling my socks in a corner, and splash my face with cold refreshing water. I could spend the rest of the night cleansing my body.

There is a light tap at my door. I wipe my eyes with my hand, look in the mirror, then tiptoe over to the door and find Maggie smiling at the peephole. I'm debating if I should let her in, but she must sense my presence and waves. Caught! I open the door.

"Too early for breakfast?" she asks.

I gaze at my watch. It's after midnight, so technically it's not too early.

Maggie is wearing the same outfit as before, minus the towel. Her perfumed hair glistens.

"I couldn't sleep," she says. "I heard you enter your room and thought maybe you could use some company."

I smile wearily.

She pushes past me into the room, turns, and says, "You look like you could use a shower, Hank."

"I was just about to . . ."

Maggie closes the door, grabs my hand, and pulls me into the bathroom like a dog. She shuts off the sink faucet, pulls back the shower curtains, and turns on the water. She waits a few moments, tests it. "Perfect." She proceeds to remove her nightshirt, hops inside, and closes the curtains, then she pokes her head out, her face dripping. "Well?"

I hesitate.

"Are you coming?" she says teasingly.

I have been faithful to Susan from the beginning, so it's been years since I've stripped in front of a woman. I start with my shirt and have difficulty with the buttons.

"For heaven's sake, Hank, get over here."

I approach Maggie like a schoolboy. She pulls me inside, the water bouncing off my clothes. She unbuttons my shirt, rips it off, and tosses it outside the shower. "We'll worry about the pants later." She reaches for me. This time, I don't hold back. I taste Maggie's soft lips, and she reacts strongly to my kiss.

She explores my mouth with her tongue and moans softly. I react with my hand on her breasts. I'm not a fancy lover; Susan hasn't cared in years. But Maggie wants to be touched and reacts with heavy primal moans, causing me to react harder. I move my head down and taste her hard nipples.

Maggie rubs against me, feels my hardness. I want to rip off my heavy, soaking pants, but I can't stop kissing her.

"Slow down, Hank. We have plenty of time."

I stop for a moment. God, it's been so long!

She peers up and smiles. "You can continue, Chief Reed."

I brush back Maggie's hair, kiss her neck, her ear.

"That's better, Detective."

Our kisses are in sync, wild, lasting.

Suddenly, the shower is shut off and Maggie starts for my belt, peels off my wet pants, and motions me to the bed. We're wet, but we dash for the bed, soaking, laughing.

Maggie immediately climbs on top, something I'm not used to. She fits me inside her, then gyrates her body slowly, smiling at the ceiling. I feel like I'm ready to explode.

My eyes close.

"You okay?" she breathes.

I don't answer, but Maggie can tell I'm in total ecstasy.

Her supple body works its way on me. She kisses my lips and whispers, "You're mine tonight, Hank." Then Maggie goes back to her position and works harder, faster, moans louder. I'm wondering whether Lucy the Polish proprietor and everyone else in the inn are listening, but I don't care about them or anyone else right now.

I'm rushing, which Maggie senses, so she slows her rhythm down a notch. But I can't stop, and I explode inside her. Maggie lasts a while longer, calls out something unintelligible, and then drops beside me.

Maggie's legs are still locked in mine when my cell phone goes off. My eyes open, and for a brief moment, I forget where I am. Daylight has already entered the room. I check my watch, which, luckily, is waterproof. That lovemaking session wore me out.

Kate is on the other end of the phone, and she informs me that Wayne left the hospital sometime during the night. She called his house and cell phone, but he doesn't answer.

I gingerly undo Maggie's legs. "When did he leave the hospital?" I ask, sitting up.

"Nobody seems to know. The hospital never checked him out. And his patrol car is still at the stationhouse."

Kate is a mother hen when it comes to her deputies, even Wayne. "He probably called a cab and is sleeping off the painkillers," I tell her. "He was pretty out of it when I last saw him."

"Maybe," she says unconvinced.

I feel Maggie's finger rub playfully on my back. "Tell you what, Kate. I still have a key to Wayne's house, so I'll drive over and see what's up. I gotta get up anyway."

"Up as in still sleeping?" she questions.

I glance over my shoulder. Maggie has a mischievous look on her face. "Something like that. I'll call you later."

"Thanks."

I hang up and start for the bathroom.

"Hey, Sheriff, where are you going?"

I turn around and find Maggie's finger motioning me back to bed.

"Gotta go. Something's come up."

"I was hoping for that," she says with a breathy laugh.

My eyes drift down at my flaccid manhood. I approach Maggie and place a kiss on her forehead. "How about later?"

She draws me to her. "Promise?"

I offer her the Boy Scout salute. "Promise."

"I'll be waiting," Maggie says, yawning.

By the time I return from the shower, my lover is fast asleep.

38

I pull up to Wayne's house, hoping he hasn't OD'd on painkillers. His white Wrangler isn't in the driveway, but I enter the house anyway and search around. The bed is still made, so I'm guessing my deputy didn't spend the night here.

On my way downtown, I place a call to Norman, who tells me that Wayne called for car service shortly before midnight. He told Norman he felt better and wanted to go home. Something about a more comfortable pillow. So where is he?

Main Street is quiet this hour of the day, and I notice one of my squad cars sitting idly at the end of the block. I pull alongside and find Brent Holland inside munching on a corn muffin, his other hand clutching a cup of coffee. Brent is my newest deputy and the only one still in his twenties.

I roll down my window. "Morning, Deputy. You haven't seen Wayne by any chance, have you?"

Brent washes down his muffin and greets me. He thinks a moment, then says, "Not since last night, Hank."

I nod. "You visit him at the hospital?"

"Around eleven," Brent says, his teeth sinking into the muffin.

"Wayne say he wanted to go home?"

"Never mentioned it to me," he says, spraying a few crumbs. "He was upset, though. Told me he was gonna get Paddy."

I scowl. "What did he mean, gonna get him?"

Brent takes another sip from his coffee, clears his throat, then says, "He wasn't very verbose. I guess he was using colloquial-ism."

The kid's a college grad. "Yeah, but did it sound like he meant it personally or through procedures?"

Brent gives me a puzzled look. "Gee, Hank, I assumed Wayne was just blowing off steam. Anyway, it was hard to tell on account of the drugs."

I shake my head. This kid has to go back to basic training. "I think Wayne is going after Paddy alone."

"You think so? He certainly didn't look like he was in any condition to arrest anybody."

Maybe I should have told Wayne that Paddy wasn't a pushover. Trying to impress me might get him killed. "Keep an eye out, Brent. And if you find him, call me."

"Sure will, Hank."

I make a U-turn and pass the deli, then the stationery store, and stop in front of the closed pharmacy. Peter must be turning over in his grave. He always opened the shop at eight A.M. sharp. Evidently, Jackie is less customer-friendly; she opens up whenever her fog lifts. I decide to go directly to her house.

I aim the Ford south, past the stationhouse and down a narrow road, which is beautifully lined with red and orange leaves spiraling down from the trees like snowflakes. It's like driving on my own private runner, the carpet leading me to my destination. I think of Maggie. Actually, I've been thinking about her ever since I woke up. There is no depression, coldness, or frigidity in that woman. I have no idea where this relationship is heading, but for now, I just want to hang on and cherish last night.

Jackie's Lexus is sitting in her driveway. I knock on the front door, wait a few minutes, then knock again. I walk around the side, cup my hands against the back door window, and peer inside. I tap on the glass, wait a moment or two, then turn the doorknob and enter.

"Jackie, it's Hank," I call out.

The kitchen smells like old food, and by appearances, it hasn't been cleaned in a while.

"Jackie," I call out again, then climb the stairs. There is stirring coming from one of the rooms, and I follow it to Jackie's bedroom.

I pop my head inside. "You okay?"

"Hank," she says, struggling to lift her head off the pillow.

Jackie is fully clothed except for her shoes. Her eyes barely show through the slits, which makes sense, considering the three vials of something or other sitting on her night table.

I cross the room and sit on the bed, shaking her. "Where's Paddy?" I demand.

The lids of her eyes work hard to open, blinking in the process.

"Paddy. Where is he?" I persist.

She glances around, her eyes glassy and vacant.

"He was here, wasn't he?"

Jackie moves her head from side to side. I'm not sure if she's trying to answer the question or shaking off her drugs.

I whip out the photos from the ME's office and shove them under her nose.

Jackie stabs at the pictures, rubs her eyes. "Where did you get these?" she mumbles.

"It's not important. Are you going to tell me or do I have to take you downtown?"

"Hank, I don't feel so good."

I stick the photos back in my pocket and hold her chin tightly, forcing her to look at me. "You always say that when I ask you tough questions, Jackie. I've got a missing deputy who's flying on painkillers somewhere and will probably get himself killed if I don't find him soon."

"Paddy wasn't here," she forces out.

I keep my eyes fixed on Jackie. "What was the plan? That you and Paddy would run off after Sheryl's murder?"

She pulls away from me. "No, of course not! Paddy and I are just friends."

"Really? These photos tell me another story."

Jackie sweeps back her hair. "I didn't kill anyone, Hank. I swear."

The lovely couple. I find it hard to believe that Paddy would get mixed up with this pill popper unless he had an ulterior motive. He needed a link to Hunter, and Jackie obviously served that purpose. Only I believe the pharmacist's wife was merely his pawn. She might have contributed to Hunter's murder, but as an unwitting partner. While I'm okay with that theory, I'm falling short of the other link. How did Paddy know about Jackie and Hunter in the first place? Right now, Jackie doesn't have the mental wherewithal to provide an answer. So instead, I say, "I was wrong about you being Peter's errand girl that night. You were Paddy's."

She pulls the sheets over her head. "Go away and leave me alone."

"Your lover almost killed Wayne last night."

Jackie remains silent for a moment, then lowers the sheets. "That's not true."

I nod. "Seems Paddy is in a murdering mood."

Jackie reaches for her pills, but I backhand them off the table. She lets out a wail, then scrambles to the floor. I pull her up by her armpits and toss her back on the bed, then whip out my handcuffs. "Goddammit, Jackie, I'm taking you in for murder unless you cooperate. Now, where the hell is Paddy?"

She throws up her hands. "I don't want anyone to get hurt."

"It might be too late for that."

I give her a few minutes to calm down. "He could be in Wading River," she throws out to me.

"Wading River?"

"A cabin maybe."

I think a moment. "You don't mean that old log cabin the judge owns?"

She shrugs. "Could be."

I take the photos out of my pocket and study them, this time paying more attention to the background. "This is the place, isn't it?"

Jackie avoids my eyes. "Paddy told me he always felt safe there."

"Oh, it's safe all right," I tell her. "It's in the middle of nowhere." I rub my chin. "Did Paddy take these with a self-timer?"

She gives me a blank stare.

"These pictures," I point. "Who was the photographer?"

Jackie seems to be wrestling with the question. "Sheryl?"

"Freshen up. We're going for a ride."

39

We've been driving west on Sound Avenue for the last ten minutes, my foot heavy on the accelerator. You'd think Jackie would be sitting in a crash position. Instead, she's dozing off, her Styrofoam coffee cup listing to one side.

I keep one eye on the road while shaking her shoulder, spilling the coffee.

"Ouch!"

"You gotta stay alert," I tell her as we flash by the Butler farm stand, where some members of the Butler clan are preparing for the day. I can't make out which family member is pushing the wagon. There's no time to wave. There's no time for anything but finding Judge Prescott's cabin. And hopefully, Paddy and Wayne still alive.

With the last farm on Sound Avenue behind us, private homes come into view. The road will eventually dump into Route 25A. If I had time, I could follow it all the way to the Big Apple.

Instead, I bear right and take North Country Road.

"Are you and Paddy still lovers?" I ask, pointedly.

Jackie doesn't answer.

"I was at Salty's the day of Sheryl's funeral. You were trying to reach him on his private line."

"I told you we're friends," she defends.

"Right."

She takes a sip of her coffee, wags a finger at me, and says,

"You're a self-righteous shit, you know that, Hank? Just because you're able to live in a dead marriage."

I keep my eyes on the road. "I'm not judging—"

"The hell you're not," she says, cutting me short.

I resist the urge to lecture her about marrying old guys for money. Instead I say, "You make the best of it or get out."

"Well, it's not always that easy."

"That's bullshit!"

"Let's not discuss it," she begs.

"Fine."

I remove the photos from my jacket pocket and wave them at Jackie. "Why do I think there's more to this story than what you're telling me?"

She rolls her eyes, pushes the glossies away from her face. "Here we go again."

"You weren't surprised when I showed them to you. You've seen them before. Sheryl showed you, didn't she?"

"Wrong."

"And when she confronted you, you blew her away?"

Jackie shakes her head and turns to the passenger window.

"We found them under Sheryl's floor mat. She was going to meet me that night and tell me everything she knew about Hunter's murder." I pause, staring hard at one of the glossies. "I'm pretty sure it had to do with these photos, only I don't see the connection to Hunter," I say, almost to myself.

Jackie shrugs.

"Unless Sheryl showed them to Peter." I let a few moments pass. "Is that it, Jackie? Peter's final humiliation? First Hunter, then Paddy. He wanted to kill someone and probably thought he had a better shot with Hunter."

"You leave Peter out of this, Hank! He had nothing to do with it."

I hit a nerve. "Why the sudden loyalty to your dead husband,

Jackie? How come you're not trying to save your lover's ass and blame Peter?"

"Because it's not true, okay?"

I edge toward her. "Doesn't sound too convincing, especially since Peter already admitted killing Hunter."

Jackie's hand snaps the Styrofoam cup, spilling coffee on her jeans. "Because Wayne took those pictures!"

I swerve the car to the shoulder, jamming on my brakes and creating a dust storm behind me. "What did you say?"

"It's true," she says glaring at me. "Wayne threatened to tell Peter."

My brain conjures images of Wayne snapping his camera at the fornicating couple. God knows what else he was doing!

"Wayne," she breathes with contempt, "was blackmailing me."

"Blackmail?" I say, puzzled.

"I had no choice, Hank . . ."

"For pills?" I ask innocently.

"Christ, Hank, for sex!"

I close my eyes tight. My fucking deputy was doing Jackie while she was popping pills and doing Paddy. No wonder she was always spaced out. "Did Paddy find out about this?"

She shakes her head slowly. "That was the deal. Wayne promised not to tell anyone, especially Peter." She pauses, composes herself, then says calmly, "Had Paddy found out, he probably would have killed Wayne."

My same sentiments, which is why I have to find them. In Wayne's state of mind, he might just brag to Paddy about his photography skills.

I ask Jackie how Wayne found out about the affair.

She lets out a snort. "Knowing Wayne, he must have followed us to the cabin."

"Just like that?" I snap my fingers. "For no apparent reason?"

"Christ, Hank, you are so naive. Wayne follows people around. For fun."

Wayne, the lonely deputy, blackmailing for sex. The stalker-doodler turned photographer of the infidels. At least he never complained about being bored. Wayne must have given the photos to Sheryl, I tell Jackie.

"He promised he wouldn't," she assures me.

"That was before Peter killed himself. So much for deals."

I let her digest Wayne's broken promise. She glances out the window and breaks the silence. "After Peter died I told Wayne I didn't want him touching me anymore. But he wouldn't stop. Said he had enough dirt on me and could do as he pleased."

Now I can add blackmail and sexual assault to an already bruised town. And of all people, my deputy! Not being with a woman in years, Wayne had gone beyond temptation, beyond the glossy magazines, and sadly, lost his way. I place my hand on her shoulder. "Hey," I say, "for what it's worth, I'm sorry."

Jackie doesn't respond, so I wait a few moments and ask her if Wayne had been blackmailing Sheryl as well.

Jackie waves me off. "He would never do that. Wayne was in love with her. If anything, he handed her the photos just to get back at Paddy." She pauses, looks grimly at me. "Wayne is certain Paddy killed Sheryl."

I nod in agreement.

"Can you imagine what was going on in Wayne's head? He must have thought he'd have a chance with Sheryl once she found out about Paddy and me. He was delusional." She faces me. "Wayne had about as much chance getting her as you . . ."

"Thanks."

"You know what I mean."

"Wayne obviously didn't think so. And now he's going after the guy who killed the only woman he ever loved."

I pull out of the shoulder, leaving more dust. "Is that why

Wayne stopped by your place? He wanted you to help him find Paddy? Or was he looking for one last fling before war?"

"That's not funny, Hank. He thought I knew where Paddy was hiding."

"What did you tell him?"

"The truth. I don't know where he went. Before he left, Wayne threatened me if I told anyone that he was at my house looking for Paddy."

Jackie hasn't been honest with me from the start, but her story makes sense. "I suppose Wayne is still following my orders to arrest him," I say evenly.

She glares. "I hope Paddy kills him for what he did to me."

I'm sympathetic, of course, but keep my thoughts to myself. Instead, I ask how long Wayne's been blackmailing her.

"A few months," she forces out.

I'm curious to ask her more, but I don't believe Jackie wants to share Wayne's sexual preferences. I can only guess.

Jackie leans toward the windshield. "I think it's coming up soon, Hank."

I nod, taking note of the heavy clouds forming overhead.

"That's it," she says, pointing to an old sign partially hidden behind a vine wrapped around it.

I make a hard right and follow the narrow road until it reaches a fork, then I stop.

"Well?"

Jackie cranes her neck. "I'm not sure which way to go, Hank."

"Great!"

"I wasn't paying attention, okay? Paddy drove."

The dirt roads are identical, no houses on either side. I strain my eyes futilely through the dense forest. "Try, Jackie."

"It's around here somewhere," she says, her eyes darting about.

"That's encouraging."

"I'm doing the best I can, Hank. I remember seeing a sign that said 'Wildwood Cabins' or something like that."

"Wildwood Village?"

"That's it. You know the place?"

"Over there," I say, pointing at a small sign nailed to a tree. I hit the accelerator and follow the road, traversing in a northern direction.

"Shouldn't be too far. I remember the road ends at the sound."

"Give me a quick description of the place."

"There are a bunch of cabins with a community pool in the middle, barbecue pits—"

"Just the important stuff, Jackie! How far off the road is the judge's cabin?"

"It's the last one on the right just before the bluff."

As I approach a cluster of cabins, I ease my foot off the pedal. Wayne's Jeep is parked behind the first cabin. I angle my car behind his, blocking the road.

"You stay here," I demand. "If you see anyone coming in from the road, tell them to turn back. Police business."

"Who the heck is going to be driving down here this time of the year?"

"You and Paddy did."

"That was different."

"Just the same, be on the lookout."

She nods.

"And if Paddy or Wayne come back this way, tell him I coerced you out here."

She glances around nervously.

I climb out of the car and turn back to Jackie. "If I'm not back in fifteen minutes, call Kate on the car radio and tell her what's going on. Have her contact the county police."

She nods repeatedly. "Take care, Hank."

"Make sure she tells the county I'm in pursuit of Paddy Murphy for the murder of Sheryl Murphy. You got that?"

"Think so," she says nervously.

I shut the door, then remove my gun from its holster.

"And John Hunter?" she asks through the window.

"He's dead," I say, moving from the car.

"I mean . . ."

I know what she means, but I'm too busy running toward the cabins.

40

Of all times, my cell phone goes off. I duck behind one of the cabins. "Reed," I whisper.

"Hank, did I catch you at a bad time?"

"Jerry? You could say that. I'm in pursuit."

A short pause, then, "I don't think this can wait. We made a mistake back at the lab."

My eyes dart about for signs of life. "What kind of a mistake?"

Jerry goes into extended detail about how the crime lab sends out prints for identification to confirm his findings.

"Jerry," I charge impatiently. "I'm in pursuit!"

"Sorry, Hank." He comes back with a shorter version, and as my brain comprehends the screw-up, my vision strays back to the patrol car.

I enter the summer community, picking up my pace, my boots crunching on the pine needles that carpet the forest floor. Between the denseness from the trees and the dark sky, the place has an eerie feel about it. After passing several cabins, I spot a late-model white Lincoln Town Car about twenty yards ahead. If I'm right, the vanity license plate will read *Judge*.

Judge Prescott's cabin is a small, boxy structure, sitting on cinderblocks, probably built in the thirties. I work my way over to a window and peek inside, squeezing my eyes to get a better look, but it's too dark to notice any movement.

I walk around to the front door and place my ear against it, but there's no sign of life. Crouching down in position, I hope the door isn't locked. I turn the knob, and the door opens easily. I'm greeted by a dank smell. At least it wasn't a gun.

I wait for my eyes to adjust to the darkness, then call out, "Wayne. Paddy. It's Hank."

When no one answers, I enter the living room, which is decorated with rattan furniture. It doesn't look as though it's been disturbed, but the kitchen tells me another story. I find a few bags of groceries sitting on the counter. I'm about to check the refrigerator when I hear a muffled sound coming from one of the rooms. It's more like a groan. I follow it, pushing a door open with my gun barrel. That's where I find the judge lying on a bed, staring over at me, duct tape slapped against his mouth, his hands bound from behind.

I place my gun back in the holster and rip the tape off, maybe a little too quickly. Judge Prescott is not on my best friend list right now.

He lets out a burst of air. "Thank God!"

"Where are they?" I demand.

The judge rolls over on his stomach and makes a feeble attempt to remove the tape around his wrists. Frustrated, he turns his head toward me. "Wayne did this to me. Your deputy."

"I know who Wayne is. Where did they go?"

The judge must be waiting for me to undo the tape, but I resist. "Goddammit, Hank, they probably took off for the beach. Now will you remove this thing? It's killing my circulation."

Before I have an opportunity to free him, the judge starts ranting about how Wayne kept brandishing his weapon and threatening him for harboring a fugitive. "He can't threaten me, Hank!"

"Sounds like he already did, Judge."

The judge scowls. "I'm going to make a formal complaint."

I free his hands. "Great. Does that mean you're not going to vote for Wayne in the next election?"

"I don't think it's very funny, Hank," he says, sitting up and shaking his hands back to life. He doesn't look up at me.

"What the hell are *you* doing here, Judge?"

"I—"

"Forget it," I say, brushing him off, "I already know. Did Paddy have a gun with him?"

He meets my eyes. "Yes, for protection."

"Well he's certainly going to need it."

The judge's expression turns grave, and he scrambles to another bedroom, me charging after him. He opens a chest drawer and swears to himself. "Paddy didn't have time."

I glance inside. "Which one is his, Judge?"

He rakes his hair. "The thirty-eight. The other belongs to me. Paddy ran out as soon as he heard a car engine."

I remove a handkerchief from my jacket pocket, two-finger the judge's revolver, and study it. "Sheryl might have been killed with this caliber," I tell him.

"Well, I certainly didn't kill her," he says.

I shove the gun in my jacket pocket. "I'm not accusing you. Yet. Any objections if I hold onto it?"

"As you wish," he says. "Just stop Wayne before he does something we'll all regret."

I inform the judge that Wayne is the police officer, not Paddy, and if anyone needs a weapon, it's Wayne. I tell him that, knowing damned well that it's Wayne who is out of control. But I'm not about to side with the enemy just yet.

"What are you waiting for, Hank? Hurry!"

I glare. "If you had listened to me yesterday—"

"That's why I drove out here this morning. To try and convince Paddy to give himself up."

I jab at his chest. "Then how do you explain a week's worth

of groceries in the kitchen? What is this, some kind of welcome wagon?"

The judge has a defeated look on his face. "I didn't know what Paddy would say."

"No, but you made it easy for him."

"Hank, please. Let's not argue over this now."

I nod. "Fair enough. Did Wayne see Paddy duck out of here?"

"No, but your crazy deputy forced me to admit that he was here. Then he taped me up and bolted for the door."

I ask the judge why the beach, already knowing the answer.

"My . . . boat."

I regard his remark. "That's how Paddy got here, isn't it?"

He nods sheepishly.

I shake my head. "Not good, Judge."

Judge Prescott, aging rapidly from these past few stressful weeks, says he doesn't care what happens to him. Just help Paddy.

I point to the door. "I want you to get into your car and drive the hell out of here. And before you ram into my police car, have Jackie Hopkins back it up so you can get out. I don't want to have to put through a claim to the insurance company."

"Okay."

"Tell Jackie to block the road again."

"I will."

"And tell her I'll need another half-hour. She'll understand."

He nods.

"Now leave and forget you were here today."

"Thanks, Hank. I owe you."

"You already paid me by being a good friend to my father."

He offers a quick smile, takes a quick look around, then scurries out the door to his car.

I take off in the opposite direction. The wind has picked up speed, and the clouds are getting bigger and more ominous.

This is not going to be fun.

I meet the bluffs and glance out at the expanse of Long Island Sound, my eyes searching eastward. Other than a few seagulls foraging for food, the beach is empty.

My vision shifts west and follows the water's edge until it bends in toward the main road. I'm guessing that's where the judge's boat is tied up.

I charge down the bluffs, not paying attention to the large "Please Keep off the Bluffs" sign. I don't feel environmentally sensitive right now. The bend is about a hundred feet away, but it feels like miles. My heart is pounding in my chest. I should have joined a health club years ago.

The waves are smacking against the rocks near shore, and I'm wondering if Paddy is going to make a run for it by boat. That thought pushes me harder, but the wet sand is slowing me down. Just before the bend, I hear a deafening explosion. Then another.

I pick up speed and reach the bend in time to see my one-armed deputy standing behind a rock wide enough to cover his girth. I'm assuming he's been taking target practice at Paddy, who must be holed up in one of the boats tied up to the dock. The judge's boat is next to a few smaller crafts and a houseboat. Although the weather is deteriorating, I can see the top of Paddy's head; he's on the houseboat.

Before my deputy fires another round, I call out. "Wayne, behind you."

The echo confuses him, because his head jerks about, but he doesn't turn in my direction.

"Behind you," I call out again.

He shifts from his position and sees me waving at him. "I can handle it alone, Hank," he yells at the top of his lungs, pointing to the dock.

I take a tentative step toward him. "I'm coming anyway."

He motions with his gun in protest. "Don't, Hank. Paddy's got a gun."

I'm not about to tell Wayne that Paddy is unarmed. Instead, I call out, "Paddy, stay where you are."

"Don't do that!" Wayne roars. "Go to the car and call for backup."

I pull out my cell phone. "I already did," I lie.

"Why did you do that?" he screams. "I can handle it alone, Hank. Go back and wait for them."

I take another step toward Wayne. "I can't do that, Wayne. I have to arrest you for murder."

"C'mon, Hank. This is serious."

"For the murder of John Hunter," I continue, my voice lingering in the air.

"This is not a good time for jokes," he says, keeping one eye on the boat.

"I'm not joking, Wayne," I say, advancing through the sand.

"Stay, dammit!" he demands, wheeling his gun in my direction.

I place my hands in the air. "Slow down, Wayne. Let's talk this through." In the corner of my eye, I see Paddy crawling out of the boathouse and inching his way toward us. I have two killers in my range, and one is pointing his revolver at me. I try to keep Wayne distracted.

"It's over, Wayne," I say, lowering my hands slowly. "And you can forget about the election."

His eyes search the sand for answers. "You told me Paddy's prints were on the inside of the seal."

With effort, I drag my boots through the sand, closing in on Wayne. "I never thought your fingerprints were on Susan's letter to Hunter. I assumed they belonged to Paddy."

He shakes his head and says almost to himself, "Can't be."

"It's true. The lab matched the prints on one of Susan's letters with those inside the Jack Daniel's label. At some point, you must have touched the letter without your handkerchief. You screwed up, Wayne."

After my deputy processes his mistake, he brings his gaze back to me. "Hank, don't come any closer."

My gun is at my side, but I'm afraid to move it. "Sorry, Wayne. I gotta arrest you."

"Forget about Hunter," he begs. "It's Paddy we want. He killed Sheryl. He killed his own wife, for Chrissake!"

Wayne isn't about to give up on Paddy, so I calmly tell him that I might have found the murder weapon that was used to kill Sheryl inside the judge's cabin. "If it is, Paddy's history," I say encouragingly, taking two steps forward.

Wayne backpedals. "Hank, don't make me use this."

His gun is pointed at my head. "How about we discuss it back at the stationhouse? Just you and me."

He shakes his head defiantly. "Can't do, Hank. Not until Paddy pays for killing Sheryl."

"That's not how we operate, Wayne. You know that."

Wayne wipes his mouth with his sleeve. "It's too late for jail."

"Maybe you had a reason for killing Hunter," I offer, softening.

He glares. "He had it coming!" Wayne storms. "He humiliated me and took her away . . ."

I glance out at the sound, then back to Wayne. "But Sheryl was never yours, Wayne. She was married to Paddy. If you give me your gun now, we'll talk to the DA, maybe make a deal."

He snorts. "I'm not an idiot, Hank!"

"I didn't say that . . ." I place my hands in the air slowly, my gun dangling from my thumb.

"Shut up and get out of here, or you'll be next!" he sneers.

My eyes fix on Wayne's angry ones. I know his limit and

don't want to die a hero. I drop my revolver in the sand and inch toward Wayne. "Can we at least talk this over?"

He fires a round over my head.

I freeze, feel my heart pumping against the judge's revolver.

"You know I'm a good shot, Hank. Don't test me."

I'm taking a calculated risk, but Paddy realizes what I'm up to and has been using the time to crawl off the dock and is within twenty feet of Wayne.

"Paddy isn't worth it, Wayne. Don't end it this way."

He shakes his head sadly. "Don't you see, Hank? I need to do this for Sheryl. It's her justice."

My arm motions toward the bluffs. "Don't let Paddy get away!"

As Wayne jerks his good arm and aims, I charge for him, kicking up sand in every direction. When he realizes I'm bluffing, he snaps back at me in bewilderment. He's gotta think I'm crazy, which I must be.

My eyes stay on Wayne as he takes aim, but then Paddy's voice echoes in the air, and Wayne turns quickly to see Paddy charging him as well. It's not hard to figure whose body Wayne's .38 is going for, and within seconds, he gets off two rounds. I'm screaming at the top of my lungs, watching Wayne follow Paddy's fall. Then he dashes past his victim toward freedom.

I run over to Paddy, his hand stretching out to me. "I swear, Hank, I didn't kill her."

Some people lie to the end. "Hang in there, Paddy. I'll call for help." Then I leave him lying in red sand and scurry after Wayne, punching 911 into my phone. When connected, I identify myself and ask for an ambulance.

My legs cut through the wet sand, but I can't keep up with my deputy's pace. I desperately call out to him before he disappears.

By the time I reach the top of the bluffs, Wayne is within

twenty yards of his car. He slips on a cluster of pine needles, picks himself up, and continues. That's when he notices my car blocking the road, and he stops in his tracks.

He turns back to see where I am, makes a quick decision, and races toward my patrol car. That's when I realize Jackie's in the car! But then Jackie emerges from the passenger side. My one-armed deputy's gun is still clutched in his good hand, so I scream out to Jackie to run, but it's too late. One shot rings out, then another, then one more.

41

I approach the crime scene out of breath. Jackie is standing over Wayne, gun in hand, extended from her limp arm. She doesn't move; she looks mesmerized. I gently remove the gun from Jackie's hand, then I kneel beside my deputy, whose vacant eyes are staring into space. I hold my friend, comfort him as best I can. But I know Wayne is gone. He painstakingly attempts to form a word. I make out "sorry." At least, that's the word I'll keep with me. Then Wayne closes his eyes and goes to sleep. I say a short prayer for his soul and ask myself, how did it get this crazy?

I glance up at Jackie, who is oblivious to the distant, now familiar frenzied sound of sirens crackling the air. At this point, my only concern is Paddy.

I help Jackie inside my car, but she's still in shock. I try comforting her, but there is no response. When the paramedics arrive, I point to the beach and inform them that a white male is down with at least one gunshot wound. Then I tell them my deputy shot him and that I believe he's dead. That's enough information for now.

One medic, a young athletic type, grabs the stretcher and lifesaving gear and dashes off to the beach. His partner, short and wiry, examines Wayne, checking for vital signs, but his grim expression confirms my assessment. He glances over and shakes his head. "Sorry." Then he stands and follows his partner.

I keep my eyes on Wayne for a long moment. There's nothing

I can do for him, and I wonder why I hadn't seen it coming.

The commotion from the responders doesn't seem to disturb Jackie, who is leaning against the headrest, eyes shut. When the paramedics are in sight, I run to meet them, but their grim faces tell me the bartender, ex-cop, is in bad shape.

I watch the paramedics transfer Paddy to a gurney inside the ambulance. Because this once-tranquil place is now a crime scene, Wayne's body remains on the ground and will wait for the investigators to arrive. I watch the ambulance fade into the trees, taking with it the clamor of death, then close my eyes and breathe in the fresh scent of pine. With the exception of Jackie, who is now weeping softly inside the car, the area is still.

I sit beside Jackie, place my arm around her shoulders, and draw her close to me. She shoves her head against my chest and sobs. I let her cry, stroke her hair.

"It just happened, Hank. Wayne had a gun." She stops, meets my eyes. "He had that look in his eyes. I've seen it before," she says, her body trembling. "I didn't know if he was going to shoot me."

I nod. "You found the gun in my glove compartment?"

"I was scared to be alone. I wasn't going to use it . . ."

"I know," I say sympathetically.

Jackie wipes her eyes and tells me it was Wayne who killed Hunter. "He knew Hunter drank bourbon at home and made me bring a new bottle that night." Jackie stops, waits for my reaction. I motion for her to continue.

"Wayne promised it would only make Hunter sick," she says, her voice trembling. "After seeing Susan's painting I wanted to leave, but John persuaded me to have a drink with him." She stops. "I couldn't, of course. So John drank alone, smiling, telling me he still cared about me, that there really wasn't anyone else. I was so tempted to grab the drink out of his hands." She pauses. "But then it happened. Oh, God, Hank, it was terrible."

"The convulsions?" I say.

"I never saw anything like it before. John was fighting for his life, and all I could do was break his fall. When it was over I dragged him back over to the sofa. Oh, John, I'm so sorry," Jackie laments, meeting my eyes. "I did everything I could to help him, Hank. I swear."

"I believe you, Jackie," I say, taking it in. "It was you who made the call."

She nods. "I didn't know what else to do."

"You did the right thing," I say, softening the pain. Then I tell Jackie that everything will be okay. But I know that it won't.

I hold off a few moments before asking more about Wayne. Her eyes harden. "I panicked afterward and called him, but he wasn't concerned. He said it would look like Paddy did it. He said he planned everything and waited for the right time."

"How?" I ask, wondering how Wayne pulled it off.

"Wayne told me he swiped the last bottle from Salty's, knowing Paddy would need to order one for the weekend. He figured you would check with Rusty's to see who had purchased a Jack Daniel's recently."

"He was right," I add. "Good timing for Wayne, bad for Paddy. And the rat poison?" I ask. "How did he manage to sneak it into Paddy's office?"

Jackie frowns. "He was in the bar waiting for Paddy to go out for a smoke break." Jackie stops, gives me a thin smile. "He said he almost got caught when Paddy decided to cut his break short."

"I can only imagine Wayne stammering his way out of that one," I say, knowing Wayne doesn't generally think things through. But apparently, he planned and executed Hunter's demise without a hitch. All in the name of love.

In light of Jackie's history of holding back on me, I play into her emotional condition and ask if she has anything else I should know about. I'm hoping she'll explain how Sheryl and Susan's paintings were snatched from the house or how Paddy planned Sheryl's murder. But her silence disappoints me. Instead, she offers a look of contrition and says, "I'm willing to pay for my sins, Hank. But you have to believe me. I never meant to hurt John."

I nod, wondering if I can finally believe Jackie Hopkins.

42

While Wayne is laid out at Wollinsky's Funeral Home, I'm at my desk leaning back in my chair observing a group of townsfolk anxiously milling around on Main Street. The town has been the subject of much talk lately. Vultures from major newspapers and prime time television have converged on Eastpoint with impunity and without decency, trying to get a glimpse of the freaks. Imagine if they knew about Hunter's infamous artwork! At this point, I see no reason to display the paintings. John Hunter's killer is dead, so what's the point in further humiliating an already devastated town?

I'm trying hard to believe Jackie's story. Maybe Wayne naively thought the rat poison wouldn't kill Hunter. Or if he knew, he never got around to telling Jackie. Either way, by making Jackie his accomplice, Wayne added fuel to the blackmail equation. As for Jackie killing Wayne, I can't read her mind. I'm not sure she can, either.

My eyes shift to the neon lights blinking from Rusty's Spirits, and I think about Paddy, who is alive and fighting for his life. The judge and Dorothy have been by his side ever since the paramedics delivered him to Riverhead General yesterday. A cop and a fighter, that Paddy.

My private line lights up, so I figure it must be the hospital. It turns out to be a detective from the First Precinct in Manhattan. A guy by the name of Greco tells me he thinks they found Carol Warner, a.k.a. Carol Hunter. She's alive but out of it. And scared. Right. Scared ever since she clubbed me over the head in Hunter's boudoir.

"They found her clutching papers and a few photographs," Greco tells me. "After piecing things together, we discovered that there was an APB out on her. Your name was associated with it."

"Thanks." Although my investigation is pretty much over, with the surfacing of the judge's .25-caliber revolver, which is now being tested, I figure since Greco was nice enough to call, I'd listen. I ask him if they found paintings. Greco claims Warner wasn't carrying any at the time, but he's quick to point out that she might have been walking around with paintings at some point. After all, Carol Warner was picked up in New York City. He laughs, then asks, "They worth anything?"

"Probably not."

"She appeared homeless," he says. "A patrol car stopped her near Battery Park. She was having a helluva conversation with herself." Greco laughs again. A happy-go-lucky guy, this Greco. "We haven't been able to get through to her and don't know where she lives or if she has any relatives."

"No identification?"

"None, except for the papers she was holding. Her name was on some of them."

"Can I interrogate her?"

Greco regales me with more laughter. "You'll get about as much out of her as you would a moth, but if you want to make an ID, be my guest. You'll probably want to read the stuff she had on her, anyway."

"Where is she now?" I ask.

"Bellevue. She's undergoing a battery of tests as we speak."

"I can be there in a few hours."

"Believe me, she's not going anywhere. Ask for me at the front desk."

I hang up, lock my office door, and tell Kate I'm driving to the Big Apple. I ask her to say an extra prayer for Wayne. I've already said goodbye, but an extra prayer won't hurt. Then I duck out the back door, eluding the press vultures.

I enter the Midtown Tunnel and think of Maggie. She's just outside Eastpoint, waiting for me and I'm in her neighborhood getting ready to ID her phony sister-in-law.

I arrive at Bellevue Hospital and ask the receptionist where I can find Detective Greco.

A young African-American woman smiles and tells me J.R. is in Room 212.

J.R., not Detective Greco. He must be a regular.

There's only one guy in Room 212, and he's sitting on a metal chair reading the *New York Times* financial section. "Greco?"

He glances up from the paper. "That's me. You Hank Reed?"

"Hi."

He tosses the paper aside, then stands up and extends his hand. Greco's got a good grip; he shakes my hand with exuberance. "Have a seat."

"Thanks, but I'd rather stand for a while. I've been sitting in my car for over two hours."

Greco and I share a few pleasantries and some detective stories. We're about the same height, but that's where the similarity ends. Greco is broad-shouldered, with a goatee and a crisp military crew cut. He's casually dressed in a pair of Dockers and a heavy sweatshirt that reads "Sex Academy." I asked him if he attended.

"Head of my class," he smiles.

The sparse gray room has a long steel desk and three chairs and appears to be an interview area. I'm wondering if Carol Warner was brought in here.

"Warner is pretty fucked up. Incoherent," Greco says, his tone neutral. "I don't have a clue when you'll be able to interrogate her, but at least you can make an ID."

"Yeah, I'd like to. I'm very interested in the stuff she was carrying around with her."

"Sure. It's in the desk," he says, motioning to the drawer on my side.

I stretch my arms in the air, then bend my body, attempting to touch my boots, which I haven't done in years. I fold myself in a chair, open the drawer, and remove a part of Hunter's past, which includes a few old pictures of my favorite shrink. He looked much younger back then. And alive. I sift through the rest of the pile and come across a few love letters that Warner had written to Hunter. The same sick verbiage is found in every letter. I suspect Hunter hid them somewhere in his bookcase. These could have been what Sheryl was referring to. Something I might want to find before anyone else does, she told me.

I shake my head, wondering why Hunter would keep these sick letters around. Unless he thought Warner might track him down in Eastpoint, where he would threaten to go to the authorities again. They must have been the mementos she was eager to find.

"Interesting reading?" Greco asks.

I nod without glancing up. "Carol Warner was certainly delusional. Thought she and Hunter would find happiness together. Too bad she got mixed up with a guy with such a lustful appetite and empty promises."

"I gather she and Hunter were a couple."

I glance over at him. "At one time. Though in her mind, she still believed he was still interested."

"She needed a shrink," Greco says.

I laugh quietly. "He was her shrink."

Greco chuckles.

"Hunter seduced her and paid dearly for it. He wound up losing his license. I guess he didn't realize what he was getting himself into." I pause. "Funny, don't you think?"

"What's that?"

"As her shrink, he should have known how delicate and sick she was from their sessions."

He shrugs. "That's the seduction. He was probably on the edge himself."

I raise an eyebrow. "You study this stuff?"

Greco points to his shirt and smiles. "Told you I was the head of my class."

I match his smile. "Apparently, Warner wouldn't take no for an answer until she received the restraining order, but my guess is Hunter feared she would never stop stalking him. That's when he moved out of the city and disappeared into the Eastpoint landscape." I shrug. "She obviously found him."

"She kill him?"

"No, my deputy did."

Greco screws up his face. "Hunter was dipping into your deputy's wife?"

"Nothing like that," I assure him. "My deputy was delusional, too. It's a long story."

"Hunter was gay?"

I laugh. "If he was, we wouldn't be having this conversation. It was more like a love triangle, once removed, since my deputy really wasn't a part of it—the love part, that is."

He shakes his head. "Helluva town you live in."

"Yeah, I've been told that before. It was great before Hunter moved in. Did I mention he was from New York City?"

Greco smiles. "You sound protective of your little town."

"I've lived there my whole life, know just about everyone. The deputy and I were good friends."

He nods sympathetically. "You're lucky. I don't know any of

my neighbors, and I've been living in the same Manhattan apartment for the past five years."

I shake my head. "Too bad."

"Nah, I like it that way. Nobody knows my business, and I don't know theirs. It's a matter of what you're used to. I wouldn't know if a serial killer lived next door to me."

I smile thinly. "Sometimes I think living anonymously might not be so bad."

"Try it."

I think of Maggie living alone in the city. "Maybe I'll hang out a while. See if I fit in."

"You do that, Hank. You might never go back east."

I like Greco. He has an easy demeanor, doesn't take life too seriously. "I guess I better finish reading these love letters."

"You go ahead," he says, snatching the newspaper. "I was just trying to figure out where the market was heading when you arrived. You follow it?"

"Only my grocer's produce prices."

"You're smart. I'm losing my ass," he says and disappears behind the paper.

I pick up a black, leather-bound book and start reading. It was Hunter's daybook, his professional diary. I hadn't seen this one at his house.

Greco must be reading my face in between stock quotes. "Find something?"

"Plenty."

"You look like you can use some coffee."

I meet his eyes. "You read my mind."

After Greco leaves, I place the journal down and rub my eyes. Unlike *Hunter's World,* this diary was used for Hunter's therapy sessions. He'd scribble sound bites, memory joggers. I search for interesting sessions and stop when Susan's name crosses the page. Hunter wrote about *us,* our predicament, which Susan must have discussed with him. He mentions her overwhelming desire to have a child, the depression, and me. She wanted my baby, and her clock was about to stop, which only intensified her depression.

I glimpse the bare walls. He really was her shrink. Though Hunter lost his license back in New York City, he must have decided to help Susan as a friend to me. He was trying to get Susan off the antidepressants and suggested I get involved in their therapy sessions, which she refused. Apparently, Susan felt I wouldn't be receptive, especially since I was the problem. Ouch!

Hunter then suggested I join them in a session. A family thing. But Susan refused again, suggesting that since Hunter and I were friends, he wouldn't be objective. He then recommended another therapist, but Susan decided against that, too.

It appears they had a number of sessions, some productive. At the end of one, Hunter scribbled a footnote. It was a general comment, nothing specific to Susan's issues. He seemed to be directing his own foibles in a positive way. These therapy sessions felt good, pure, and he didn't want to spoil the moment. Not like the past. I assume he meant his disastrous experience with Carol Warner. He wrote, "I am *no longer* going to compromise my position as a healer and facilitator of this process. While Susan Reed is a beautiful woman, very desirable, and vulnerable, she is also sacrosanct. Hank is a good friend. I'll leave my desires to my writings, paintings and . . ."

The *and* probably referred to his other Eastpoint women.

I close the journal, place it on the table, and close my eyes. I was wrong about Hunter. And Susan. My wife was pregnant with *my* child. All those accusations: the affair, the pregnancy, the murder. Then I think of Maggie. She must be told of this . . . mistake.

I open the journal again and flip through a few pages, searching for Hunter's comments from Susan's last session, stopping when my eyes come across a rather strange notation. It was written a few days before his murder, soon after Susan's session. His handwriting was quick, nervous. "She wants to come and see me, will drive out for the day. She still doesn't get it after all these years. Poor sick woman. I should have realized it during therapy."

Carol Warner had finally found Hunter and was driving out to him. Had she seen Hunter with Jackie, Sheryl, or Susan? That would have enraged her. I slow down, catch my thoughts. Can't be. Wayne killed Hunter.

Greco returns with my coffee and asks how I'm doing.

"If you were going to rent a car in the city, where would you go?"

Greco thinks a minute. "Hell, there's gotta be dozens of car rental agencies. Why?"

"I'm trying to tie up some loose ends. Can you help me cut through some red tape?"

He smiles. "You'll owe me big-time for it."

"You like apples?"

"Sure."

"How about I bring you a bushel next time I come into the Big Apple?"

"Funny. How about inviting me out during apple picking next season?" Greco beams.

"You're on. I'll throw in some peaches and strawberries."

"Deal. What do you want me to check out?"

I tell Greco what I found out about Carol Warner.

"*No problemo.* I'll start with the major car companies." Greco moves to leave.

"Wait. She might have rented it under the name Carol Hunter, using a phony driver's license."

"I'll check both."

I glance at my watch. "How soon can you get back to me?"

He gives me a look. "I thought you said you wanted a touchy-feely of the city."

I hold up Hunter's journal. "That was before I read this."

"Okay, but if you should change your mind, there's always the academy. I got connections." He smiles.

"I hope I don't have to," I tell him. "In the meantime, I'll ID Warner, if that's okay."

He laughs. "Sure. She could use the company."

43

Detective Jose Greco comes through in fifty-five minutes, thirty-two seconds. He tells me that the Avis on Seventy-sixth Street rented a car to a Hunter three times over the past month. Only they didn't rent it to Carol Warner or Hunter. Avis' records showed that a Margaret Hunter, residing on Amsterdam Avenue, rented a silver metallic Pontiac G6, the first time, the day of Hunter's murder. Records show that Maggie drove approximately two hundred miles for the first two trips, enough to get to Eastpoint and back with a few miles to spare. Greco informs me that Maggie rented a car a few days ago and hasn't returned it yet.

Maggie lied to me. She told me she didn't drive. She drives, all right. And possesses a New York State license. I'm wondering what else she possesses.

In Greco's unmarked car, I'm thinking about the journal Carol Warner was clutching when the cops picked her up. John Hunter wrote that *she* wanted to see him. "She still doesn't get it after all these years. Poor sick woman. I should have realized it during her therapy." Could Hunter have been referring to Maggie? Was she his patient before they were married?

Greco's car is struggling through snarled traffic.

"How can anyone get around this city with all those cabs blanketing the streets?" I complain.

"Hey, they're just trying to earn a living," Greco defends.

"And all those people. I can see how Carol Warner got lost

here. Anyone can."

Greco laughs. "I guess the city is not in your blood, Hank."

"Sorry. I'm just anxious to get there."

Greco removes a siren from under his seat and sticks it on the roof of the car. It wails, and we start moving. "That better?" he asks as a sea of yellow taxis part in the street in front of us.

"Thanks. And thanks for getting a judge to sign the warrant on such short notice."

"I expect you'll throw in a vegetable stand when I retire from the force," he says, chortling.

I try to share in his levity, but my laugh is flat.

Maggie's apartment building is a prewar brick-and-mortar vintage. The lobby is adorned with two leather sofas, imported marble floors, an antique chandelier, and a sleek wooden desk, behind which a guy old enough to have retired three times is sitting and entertaining himself with a crossword puzzle.

"Morning."

The guy recoils and is about to challenge us when Greco whips out his shield.

"What can I do for you, Detective?" He squints.

"You the doorman?"

"I do everything around here," he says, lifting himself out of the chair. He strains to study the yellow and blue insignia on my jacket sleeve. "Where's Eastpoint?"

I tell him it's next to heaven. Then I tell him I need to get into Maggie Hunter's apartment.

He eyes my sleeve again and says, "You're not NYPD."

The guy can read. "I still need to get into her apartment."

"You gotta see the super. I'm not the super."

I look around. "Where is he?"

He shrugs. "Probably in the basement. You want me to page him?"

Now he's getting the idea. "If it's not too much trouble," I say with a hint of sarcasm.

He glares through his thick glasses, picks up the phone, and punches in a number. "I just paged him," he says, then returns to his puzzle and shields it as though he's afraid I might find him cheating.

Greco excuses himself and steps outside. A few minutes later, the black phone on the doorman's desk rings. The guy extends his arm and tells the caller he's wanted. Then he hangs up and says without looking up, "He'll be here in a minute."

I pace the floor, lifting my arm every so often to keep an eye on the time. After about five minutes I stop by my friend, who is oblivious to his surroundings. "Where is he?" I ask impatiently.

"He'll be here," the guy grumbles, seemingly stuck on a four-letter word for an annoyingly stupid person.

I glimpse his puzzle and say, "Jerk," helping him along.

The guy drops his pencil and swears.

Greco is on his cell phone, probably talking to someone from the academy, because he's giggling like school kid. Not that I'm jealous, mind you. He catches my stare and gives me a thumbs-up.

A few minutes later, a short, middle-aged man with a full head of brown curly hair and a cheap cigar stuffed in his mouth approaches. He checks my uniform and asks, "There a problem, Officer?"

I go through the same routine about Maggie's apartment.

"You got a search warrant?"

Not that it's any of his business, but I point to Greco.

The guy shrugs. "Follow me."

I get Greco's attention, then catch him throwing a kiss into the phone. We follow the super to the elevator and take it to the fifth floor. After he opens Maggie's apartment, I bid the super goodbye.

"Just close the door on the way out, okay?"

"Sure," I say, wondering if the guy's cigar is pasted to his upper lip.

Greco and I step inside Maggie's apartment and survey the living room.

"Hasn't changed much."

I turn. The super hadn't left. "How's that?"

"The place is pretty much the same as when they were married. I'm told she took the shrink to the cleaners." He snickers.

"She invite you in here a lot?" I ask.

The super smiles through his cigar. "Only to fix things. Nice lady. Good tipper, too. She do something wrong?" he asks, ashes building on his cigar.

"I don't think the *lady* would appreciate you smoking in her apartment," Greco says.

The super gives him a look then removes the cigar from his mouth, ashes spiraling downward and landing on the carpet. "I'll be in my office if you need me."

I nod.

"You'd think she would have wiped out the past by now." This is coming from Greco.

"I was thinking the same thing," I tell him. "Unless she was still in love with him."

"Obsessed is more like it. Same as the other babe."

I nod in agreement, then snap on a pair of latex gloves and enter Maggie's bedroom. Looking around, I can't help but realize just how emotionally hooked she was on Hunter. Photographs of happier days are perched on her night table like a shrine.

I shake my head and open the closet door. That's when I find the missing painting of Hunter and Sheryl. Greco whistles.

I had forgotten about him.

"That isn't her, I gather."

"The murder victim."

"That would explain the missing head."

I nod, staring at Hunter straddling a headless Sheryl.

"I'll check the other bedroom," Greco says.

I sit at the edge of the bed, staring out the window through the hole in the painting. It was Maggie who told Hunter she was coming out to see him. Not Carol Warner. And when she arrived, Hunter was already dead. She must have found his suicide note, and in her own sick mind, thought she was responsible. That is, until she discovered that Hunter was murdered. That's when Maggie Hunter decided to avenge her *man's* murder.

I lean the painting against the wall to search the rest of the room. I get on my knees and lift up the dust ruffle, sticking my hand under the bed and feeling around, my fingers gliding along a coarse piece of cloth. I drag it out and discover it's a blank canvas with a hole in the center. When I turn it over, my eyes become glued to the black X painted on it. Only this time Susan's head is missing.

I drop the painting and rifle through Maggie's dresser drawers, then her desk. I find nothing but bills and legal papers. Just as I'm about to close a drawer, I notice a piece of paper folded up, looking like it was headed for the wastebasket. I unwrap it, smooth it out. It's a gun permit for a .25-caliber Browning automatic pistol.

I search the room again, but the gun is nowhere to be found. I call out to Greco and ask him if he's seen one, but he tells me he hasn't. Then I realize Maggie has the murder weapon with her.

I grab my cell phone and call the inn. Fortunately, Maggie is still there. I tell her I'd love to see her as soon as I get back to Eastpoint.

"Hank, I've been wondering when you were coming back," she says, her voice seductive. "Where are you?"

"Bellevue," I lie. "I found Carol Warner. I need to finish interrogating her. I'm pretty sure she killed Hunter."

When Maggie doesn't answer, I ask, "You there?"

"I'm here, Hank. I don't know what to say. I'm relieved, of course."

"Anyway, I'm dying to see you." Poor choice of words.

"Gee, that sounds romantic."

"Yes, romantic. How about waiting until I return? I'll bring a bottle of champagne."

"Can't wait."

I hang up and call Kate. "You need to get whoever is on duty over to the Country Inn and detain Maggie Hunter until I get there." I pause. "On second thought, she's probably armed, so send two deputies over and bring her in."

"Hunter's Maggie Hunter?"

"That one. She killed Sheryl."

"But I thought Paddy—"

"I'll explain later. How's he doing?"

"He's fighting hard, but they think he has a good chance."

"Thank God!" I hang up, motion Greco, and charge out the door.

44

The Midtown Tunnel traffic is flowing at a good pace, but by the time I reach the Queens-Nassau border, the expressway is like a parking lot. It's half-past three, and I'm hoping to arrive in Riverhead in just over an hour. Then another half-hour to reach the stationhouse, where Maggie Hunter better be locked up and waiting for me to interrogate her.

Maggie Hunter, the woman I made love to last night. The woman now responsible for Sheryl's murder. You'd think that after Hunter cheated and humiliated her, Maggie would have been glad to rid herself of him.

Instead, she loved him to the day he died. When she discovered he'd been killed, it fractured her already fragile mind. Someone killed *her* man. And that someone was going to pay. But Sheryl hadn't killed Hunter. Her conclusion was speculation without foundation.

My thoughts are interrupted by a surge of brake lights. I flip on my overhead lights, aim for the shoulder, and am about a hundred feet from an accident, when, out of the corner of my eye, I see a car veering toward me. The driver of a BMW M Series, phone in ear, cigar in mouth, jerks forward upon impact, his head snapping in my direction, causing the cell phone to fly into the back seat. I'm cursing at the guy for being an asshole and leap out of my car.

The thirty-something driver in a business suit steps out of his car, dazed, and looks at the damage. "Shit!"

"What the hell were you thinking, asshole?" I blast.

"I just leased this car" is his response. He becomes sullen and attempts to rub my chrome off the side of his black fender.

"Well, you should have been paying more attention to the road instead of playing with the phone. It's against the law anyway. You can get a fucking ticket!"

He glances over at me. "It was business," he says, his tone suddenly filled with arrogance.

"Yeah, well, you just blew the deal."

He gives me an "up yours" look and swears to himself.

I point to a white and blue highway patrol car approaching. "I'm gonna leave you with him."

After identifying myself and giving the officer the short version, I leave the driver in the hands of the HPB and pull out, leaving gravel in the guy's face.

Exiting at Great Neck Road, I take the auxiliary road, which isn't much better than the expressway. Traffic lights and construction trucks are slowing me down.

Kate's voice comes alive on the radio.

"Maggie's gone."

"What do you mean gone?" I say in a panic.

"The innkeeper told Charlie that Maggie hadn't checked out yet, only that she was going shopping and wouldn't return until later. But when the maid went in to clean her room, it was empty."

"Shit!"

"Seems Maggie left in a private taxi about twenty minutes ago."

"The driver must have dropped her off near her car," I say, thinking aloud. *Where did you park your car, Maggie?*

"You there, Hank?"

"Listen, Kate, you need to find out where the driver dropped her off. She's driving a red Pontiac G6. Hold on." I take a piece

of paper out of my pocket and spit out the license number.
"Call the county and tell them to keep an eye out."

"Right."

Where are you going, Maggie?

"That it, Hank?"

"For now. Keep me informed."

The light ahead is turning yellow, but I step on the accelerator, missing an oncoming car by inches. At Glen Cove Road, I jump back onto the L.I.E. Damned parking lot. The road finally opens up at exit 63, and I keep the pedal floored until exiting at the end of the expressway.

Why were you returning to Eastpoint after you killed Sheryl? Was it for me, Maggie?

Then it dawns on me. I get on the radio and tell Kate to check with the innkeeper. "Find out if Maggie made any calls from her room today." I hang up and call the hospital.

"Transfer me to Susan Reed's room, please."

I'm waiting to the sound of Kenny G, his horn irritating me. "Where the hell are you?" I yell into the phone.

Then a real voice comes on. "She was released a short while ago."

"How short?" I ask impatiently.

"I'm not sure. Is it important, sir?"

"Gravely important. I'm her husband."

"One second, please."

Kenny G again.

When she returns, the woman tells me Susan checked out about a half hour ago.

"Someone must have picked her up. Can you find out who?"

A sigh. "I'll check."

"Just don't put me on—"

Kenny G finishing up.

"The nurse who wheeled your wife out front is on a break.

Can you call—?"

I hang up and punch in the house phone. Susan's voice comes alive. Damned machine. "Susan, this is Hank. You gotta get out of there and drive directly to the stationhouse. I'll explain later."

I call Kate back.

"I was just going to call you. Maggie made one call."

"Eastpoint Medical," I blurt.

"How did you know?"

I ignore her question. "Maggie is going after Susan!"

"I don't understand."

"We gotta find Susan before Maggie does," I say gravely. "Did you find out about the cab?"

Kate informs me the driver dropped Maggie off at Legion's Park.

Of course. It's walking distance to the train station.

"Did the driver notice which direction she was going?"

"Nope, but he did say she was acting strange. Kept talking to herself. He thought it was weird, her taking an overnight bag with her to the park."

"Listen, Kate. Maggie's got Sheryl's murder weapon with her. Get someone over to my house as fast as you can."

I reach Route 58, the farms now in view. I'm watching out for Maggie's car, but I doubt she's heading my way. Not yet, anyway.

"Hank, Susan's car is in the driveway but no one answers."

It's Charlie.

"Any other cars around?"

"Just hers."

"Try the doors. Break in if you have to."

A few minutes later I hear the smashing of pane glass. Then silence. Hurry up, Charlie.

"There's no one in here, Hank."

"You sure?"

"Hank, I looked everywhere."

"Okay, drive to the beach. Check every road in town!"

"We'll find her, Hank."

"Alive," I beg.

The "Welcome to Eastpoint" sign is just ahead. As I pass Victory Lane, I slam on my brakes, back up, and take a hard left. Hunter's driveway is empty, and I'm about to turn around when I remember the night of the stolen painting.

I shove the car into park and scramble across the lawn, the yellow tape now strewn on the ground. The late afternoon sun is not quite setting, but I notice a light on in Hunter's secret room. The same light that was off the last time I was here.

45

The front door is locked, so I dash around to the back. No luck. I don't want to break glass and make noise, so I force open the basement window and enter. I'm getting used to this.

I find the stairs, climb quietly, and enter the kitchen. I listen for voices, but all I hear is the sound of my own heavy breathing. I draw my gun and search the first level. The place is eerily calm.

I tiptoe to the second landing, enter the room below Hunter's boudoir, and hear Maggie's voice cascading from above. As I climb the ladder, her voice becomes louder, threatening. She's admonishing someone, and I can only imagine that it's Susan. At least my wife is alive.

My chin reaches the opening, but Maggie must have turned off the lights; the shades are drawn over the window, so my eyes are struggling to find Maggie's location. Her imperious voice is echoing from the other side of the room, possibly near the sex bed. Susan is answering Maggie in a soft yet unwavering voice. "I swear to you, I've never slept with John. He was my therapist."

Maggie laughs. "Right. John never told you he lost his license for screwing a patient? And that his therapy sessions include screwing the patient."

"We never! I swear to you."

"Don't swear, or it'll cost you."

Susan pleads, tells Maggie she doesn't understand what she wants.

"Oh, I think you do. You took my husband, now I'm taking yours."

"Hank?"

"John and I were getting back together. He never told you that?"

A pause. "Why would he tell *me?*"

"Never mentioned it while he was doing you?"

"I told you—"

"Shut up, you whore! I'm tired of your lies. He told your friend."

Another, longer pause. "My friend?"

"That blond slut. But neither of you would leave John alone. He was mine!" Maggie's anger resonates throughout.

"You killed Sheryl?" Susan whimpers.

"I'm asking the questions, sister!"

I can't tell if Maggie is holding a weapon, so I wait.

"If she hadn't taken him away . . ." Her voice drifts.

"Oh, God!" Susan starts to break down. "Why?" she sobs.

"I just told you. Are you stupid or something? She wanted my John. I waited so long for him to come back to me. That slut and *you* tried to take him away. You killed him!" she rages.

"That's not true," Susan cries. "I wouldn't kill John. He was my friend."

"Yeah, right. And Hank and I are just friends." Maggie's laugh drips with sarcasm. "Or didn't you know we're lovers. He's mine, little girl, and once I'm finished with you, I won't have to share him with anyone. We're gonna live in the city, none of this country shit."

Thanks for being a kiss and tell.

"You can have Hank," Susan says, her voice flat.

"Well, thank you very much. But I already have him, hon. And he's great in the shower. You probably don't do stuff like that, do you?"

"We haven't made love in a while," she says sadly.

" 'Course not, you've been fucking my John."

"That's not true. Hank and I haven't been . . . in love for a while."

I'm wondering if she's answering for both of us.

Then Susan says coolly, "I don't care what you two do. In fact, I hope you leave town and take Hank with you."

"Tst tst, tst. You sound hurt," Maggie says with a degree of satisfaction. "As soon as you're out of the picture, we will. You're the last piece of the puzzle. Or should I say painting?" Maggie chortles.

"What painting?"

Maggie takes a step toward Susan. "Don't act cute with me, you whore."

Susan must be weighing her options, decides not to antagonize Maggie, and remains silent.

Maggie's voice is directed in my direction, and I freeze. "I thought you might want to confess before you die. And none of this stuff that Hank's deputy did it, either." She turns back to Susan. "Don't you want to tell me the truth before I use this on you?"

Susan moans.

"No? Too bad. You're going to hell for your sins. Adultery is a mortal sin, you know. I was going to absolve you of it, but now I can't."

"Please don't do this." Susan sniffles.

"You're right. You should see my face when I shoot you. Just like your friend. She should have never picked me up that night, the Good Samaritan," Maggie cackles. "At least she admitted to having an affair with my John."

When Susan doesn't answer, Maggie says, "Your friend didn't know I had the paintings. Disgusting positions, you two." She stops, then giggles. "Hank almost caught me."

Susan doesn't share Maggie's levity.

The night table light goes on.

"Hey, I'm talking to you!"

Susan is sitting on the bed, her hands taped together in front of her. Maggie doesn't see me, so I attempt to inch up another step, but my leg must have fallen asleep and I slip. I grab hold of the ladder, but it's too late. Maggie turns quickly, brandishing her gun.

"It's me, Maggie. Hank."

Maggie's rage changes to confusion as her gun is pointed at me. "Hank, what are you doing here?" she demands, starting toward me.

"I've been looking all over for you, Maggie. C'mon, we don't need her."

My eyes stay on Maggie's gun. It doesn't budge.

"She needs to be taught a lesson, Hank."

"I don't love her, Maggie. I love you. She and I haven't been together in years." *Touché.*

Maggie gives me a crooked smile. "You're mine."

I nod furiously. "Let's leave her here, go back to the inn."

Maggie shakes her head. "She's bad, Hank. She was doing John while she was married to you. That's infidelity. I can't tolerate that. *He* did that to me."

I shake my leg, lifting my foot up a step.

"Don't, Hank. I can handle this alone." Then she says, "At least *you* were separated when we made love."

Technically that's true. "I should be upset with her, but I'm not." I glance over at Susan, her head angled in my direction. I provide a hopeful smile, a small reassurance, but her grim expression doesn't change.

"I'm doing it for us," Maggie says.

"Forget her, Maggie. Leave with me now. We'll move to Manhattan, your apartment. It's beautiful—"

She scowls. "You saw my apartment?"

"No, I—"

"Don't lie to me, Hank! You were spying on me." She inches closer, waves her gun. "I can't trust you anymore. You're like John."

"That's not true," I protest. "I would never cheat on you."

The corner of her mouth curls. "Don't you see, Hank? You invaded my privacy." Maggie aims her weapon at me. "Get down and leave, or I'll be forced to use this on you, too."

"I can't, Maggie. My leg fell asleep."

Maggie moves closer, stands over me. My left hand is holding on to the ladder, my right on my gun. I drop the gun and leap for Maggie's leg, grabbing her ankle, and pulling her toward me. I'm hanging flat against the ladder, my foot searching for a rung, Maggie's leg with me.

"You bastard!" she screams, kicking wildly with her free leg. "I'm doing this for us," she roars.

Maggie kicks me in the face, sending me flying down the ladder, my face smacking the rungs on the way down.

I gaze up. Maggie is attempting to shut the hatch, but when she realizes the ladder is in the way, she swears and turns back to the room, ranting, "Where the hell are you, bitch?"

I pick myself up off the floor, holding on to the ladder for support. Catching my breath, I search around for my gun, scoop it up, then steady myself before starting up the ladder, only to hear Maggie screaming. She's out of control.

I take a few steps, then wipe the blood that's dripping off my chin with my jacket sleeve. About halfway up, I hear a sliding sound screeching against the floor above me. I duck. Maggie has pushed Hunter's king-size bed over the opening. I shove the gun in my holster, continue as far as I can, then push, but the bed won't budge. My right shoulder heaves upward, but it's no use.

I leap off the ladder, take the stairs two at a time, and run outside to the garage. Maggie's swearing is reverberating outside.

I find an aluminum ladder hooked to the inside of the garage wall, rip it off, and charge to the side of the house. I pull on the rope for extending the ladder, lean it against the house, and start climbing. It's not until I pass the first level that I notice Susan on the roof. She must have opened the window and crawled outside on the windowsill, then boosted herself onto the lower part of the roof along the gutters. Her hands are still bound, and I'm wondering how adept she'll be at climbing to the chimney.

"Susan," I call out.

She stops momentarily but doesn't turn.

Maggie pokes her head out the window, follows my eyes, and realizes what is happening. She turns back to me, our eyes locking in on each other. Then with a sardonic smile, she waves her gun.

"Maggie, don't!"

Maggie points her weapon at Susan and releases a shot, hitting the chimney just above my wife's head. She swears, steps out on the roof, and with one foot attempts to push the ladder away from the house. My weight frustrates her, so she decides to go after Susan.

Daylight is disappearing from the top of the chimney, but Maggie is resolved on killing Susan at any cost. She gets off another shot, but Susan is now behind the chimney. I'm at the windowsill; Maggie is halfway between Susan and me.

"Maggie, stop or I'll shoot," I threaten, my gun aiming at her hand.

She swings around and fires wildly, nicking my wrist and knocking the gun out of my hand. With dusk engulfing us, I'm certain my gun is lost somewhere in Hunter's bushes.

I turn back to Maggie, but all I see is the extension of her hand. One round goes off, then three more. Finally, the sound of something sliding off the roof.

I climb down the ladder, get on my knees, and feel around for my gun.

"Why?"

I stop. The voice in pain behind me sounds like Maggie's.

"I love you, Hank," she whispers. "You should have believed me."

I crawl over to her. "I'm sorry it happened this way, Maggie," I say without malice.

I hear movement on the ladder and call out, "Susan, are you okay?"

"I'm here, Hank," she says, struggling for breath.

I turn back and realize it was Susan who had fallen off the roof. I charge for the ladder, knocking Maggie into Hunter's hibiscus bush. I can't see the expression on her face, but I feel her hot breath on me, and the cold metal in her hand. We struggle for the gun, but Maggie is flying on adrenaline. No longer is she ranting; all her strength is being used to loosen my grip and finish me off like she did Sheryl. We continue to fight for control until a shot rings out, and for a brief moment I don't know which one of us is hit.

EPILOGUE

John Hunter was Eastpoint's biggest celebrity, though not the kind you'd want as a neighbor. Especially if you had an attractive wife.

Hunter ruined more lives in this town after his death than when he was alive. Counting the number of funerals I've attended these past few months, I realize Eastpoint will never be the same. The last funeral took place over a month ago. Like the others, it was simple, only this time it was held in a small cemetery outside New York City. Not many people attended Maggie Hunter's funeral, and I was the only one representing Eastpoint.

I needed to attend, put some closure between us. Maggie and I were lovers, albeit for only one night. At the time, I was certain our relationship would blossom in light of my seemingly doomed marriage. Her death has left a void in me, a reminder of what she represented during that painful period. A safety net. I'm sure the circumstances drew me to Maggie, but I also know I fell in love with her, and she is still very much alive inside me. It was her spirit, not the confused, delusional woman, I allowed into my heart.

In the end, her mental state unraveled; Maggie thought she was retrieving John Hunter as a partner, her lover, whom she believed would be committed to her this time. Her apartment was evidence that Maggie could not take rejection well, and she kept his past as it was before the breakup. Somehow, in her own sick way, Maggie misplaced me for Hunter. And I was vulner-able.

John Hunter left many women in his wake. Carol Warner, the patient-turned-stalker, is doing time in a mental facility, not able to shake her unwavering love for him. Carol was a fragile woman in therapy with Hunter, and he placed her in a defense-less situation; she may never recover.

The women of Eastpoint, the ones whose paintings are now destroyed, can breathe easier. At least the women who lived can—women like Olivia Patterson, who still lives on Hidden Island with her husband. There was never any reason to release the paintings once Hunter's killer was dead.

Jackie Hopkins, who killed Wayne and helped contribute to Peter's suicide, entered rehab, purged herself of drugs, and is in the process of selling the store. She was never charged in Wayne's murder. A grand jury investigation resulted in a dismissal due to a self-defense plea. I stood up for her. I saw Wayne aim his gun at her. At least, that's what I told the jury.

Sheryl Murphy was the saddest of all Hunter's victims. Searching for love, Sheryl thought she'd found it in Hunter, only Hunter, as in the past, was reckless. Perhaps if Paddy had demonstrated a stronger commitment to her than to his bar, there would have been little reason for Sheryl to stray.

Judge Prescott retired from the bench. He owed me and was willing to have someone backdate a search warrant to Maggie's apartment if I needed him to. I didn't, thanks to "first in his class" Greco. The judge takes his boat out on the sound oc-casionally, thinks about his life and what it amounted to over the past few months. His resolve to save his son compromised every oath he ever took, though he was right on all counts. Paddy was innocent of all charges. That's what I have to deal with, since it was I who pursued him with such vengeance.

As for the paintings I found in Maggie's apartment, they too have been destroyed. Perhaps if I had been faster in getting to Hunter's house that infamous evening, there would have been little reason for Maggie to go after Sheryl or Susan, and the outcome might have been different.

The town was grateful that I solved the murders, and of course they postponed the election indefinitely. The pariah I had become in those painful weeks was recast as a hero, and I got smiles and support as though nothing had happened. But something did happen. I stepped down as chief of police, over cries and remorse to no avail.

I'm back with Suffolk County as a homicide detective. I'd been doing that job ever since John Hunter was killed anyway. I finally realized that the tranquil life of a town sheriff was too dull for me. Charlie took over and became the first black chief of Eastpoint.

I'm inside Salty's, sitting at my regular table. These musings have been with me ever since Maggie was killed behind Hunter's hibiscus bush. I say *was killed,* not that I killed her. The gun went off . . .

"More coffee, Detective?"

I glance up. "Thanks."

"It's you I should thank, Hank. You saved me. From him."

Jackie hasn't used Wayne's name since the incident. I touch her hand and offer a wistful smile.

She smiles faintly, fills my cup, then heads off to another table. Jackie looks great cleaned up. I hadn't seen her eyes sparkle in a long time. She works for Paddy now; he hired her a few weeks ago. Both have been in a lot of pain. Who knows where the job might lead?

"Mind if I sit?"

I glance up. "It's your bar."

Paddy searches my face, then pulls up a chair. "We haven't said too much to each other since it happened."

I nod. "I guess we've been trying to sort things out."

"I know you were convinced I killed them," he starts. "As an ex-cop, I would have thought the same thing. Motive, means. All that stuff."

I nod. "It looked that way," I say without malice.

Paddy forces a smile. "Yeah, it did, didn't it? I'm sorry about those letters I wrote about Susan and Hunter. I was angry at you for accusing me." He stops. "I really did think Susan was having an affair with the guy, you know."

"Me, too," I say.

"I never realized she was just seeing him as a patient. I guess my warped mind over Sheryl led me astray." Paddy stops, searches my eyes with regret. "I'm sorry, Hank. You had every right to go after me."

I wait a few moments before asking, "Susan told you she was in therapy?"

He motions to the bar. "Recently. She told me everything. Why Sheryl got involved with Hunter." His chest heaves. "Sheryl was trying to save our marriage, only Hunter must have charmed her and . . . I guess some shrinks can do that."

"Especially the charismatic ones with strong sex drives," I add in jest.

He smiles thinly. "Anyway, for whatever it's worth, I don't hold any ill will toward you. And thanks for going easy on my father."

Paddy stands, extends his hand. I take it and place my other on his. "He was just protecting his son. I would have done the same."

Paddy sighs. "I better get back to the bar. Come around one night after you get off from work. We'll have a drink together." His hand slips out of mine as he turns to leave.

"Paddy."

He looks back.

"I'm glad it wasn't you."

He nods.

I go back to my sandwich, start playing with the bread.

"Not hungry?"

My head jerks up. "Hey." I begin to rise, but Susan raises a hand. "Don't get up. I was just passing when I saw your car out front. Thought I'd say hello."

"Please, sit with me for a while."

Susan hesitates, then slides in a seat across from me.

"You look great," I say, meaning it.

"Thanks. The new job seems to agree with you," she says, her eyes staying on mine.

"I guess I'm back in my element. Shootings, stabbings . . ." I stop. "Sorry."

She grimaces. "That's okay."

"That was a hell of a fall," I say.

Susan nods slowly. "The doctors tell me I'll mend in time. Mentally, too. I'm seeing a real shrink."

I lower my eyes. "I'm sorry I doubted you, Susan. I'm sorry about a lot of things."

She touches my hand lightly. "It's okay, Hank. I guess I should have told you I was seeing Hunter. I mean, in therapy."

I sigh, search her eyes. "Is the pain bad?" I ask, changing the subject.

"Only when I laugh." She smiles warmly. "I'm trying to laugh, though."

"That's great. I mean about the laughing."

She starts to laugh, grimaces, but continues. "Remember when we used to laugh, Hank?"

Susan is still wearing her wedding band. I smile to myself. "Yeah. We did that a lot, didn't we?"

"What happened to us?" she asks, holding my hand tightly.

I shake my head slowly. "I don't know."

Then she asks, "Are you over her yet?"

I regard her remark and take a few moments before answering. "It was never like that. I never wanted to hurt you," I add quickly.

She wipes her eyes. "I hadn't been much of a wife the past few years," she says and pauses. Then she continues and tells me that she is no longer on antidepressants.

"That's great." I smile.

She smiles back. "Therapy has put me in a better place, Hank."

"I can see that. I'm really happy for you, Susan."

She asks if I'm still staying at the Inn.

I shake my head. "It was too expensive on a week-to-week. I found a small apartment in Wading River. It's a quiet place, just what I need right now."

"Maybe I could see it sometime," she says.

My expression changes to confusion. "My apartment?"

"It sounds nice. Quiet and all."

"Sure, but I don't have much furniture."

"What about a bed, Hank? You must have a bed." Susan gives me that old Susan look and smiles radiantly.

"Yeah, but it's not as good as the one we had."

"Maybe we could test it sometime," she teases.

"I'd like that," I say warmly.

"What time do you get off work, Hank?"

I check my watch. "Hell, I'm off right now."

"This minute?"

I nod and ask her if she needs permission from her doctor to see the apartment.

"Which one? My shrink or orthopedic?"

I smile. "Both."

"They'd tell me that time heals all pain. I'm ready to heal if you are."

"I've missed you, Susan. I want to heal, too."

ABOUT THE AUTHOR

Fred Lichtenberg is a native New Yorker who currently lives with his wife in Jupiter, Florida. He has one son. This is his first novel. He is now working on his next novel.

Visit him online at www.fredlichtenberg.com.